MW01711280

…E OF GOD

Dear Brad

Best wishes

Jyo

The Angel of God

Jyothi Menon

Published by

Cedar books

Distributed by

Pustak Mahal®, Delhi

J-3/16 , Daryaganj, New Delhi-110002
☎ 23276539, 23272783, 23272784 • *Fax:* 011-23260518
E-mail: info@pustakmahal.com • *Website:* www.pustakmahal.com

London Office

51, Severn Crescents, Slough, Berkshire, SL 38 UU, England
E-mail: pustakmahaluk@pustakmahal.com

Sales Centre

10-B, Netaji Subhash Marg, Daryaganj, New Delhi-110002
☎ 23268292, 23268293, 23279900 • *Fax:* 011-23280567
E-mail: rapidexdelhi@indiatimes.com

Branch Offices

Bangalore: ☎ 22234025
E-mail: pmblr@sancharnet.in • pustak@sancharnet.in
Mumbai: ☎ 22010941
E-mail: rapidex@bom5.vsnl.net.in
Patna: ☎ 3294193 • *Telefax:* 0612-2302719
E-mail: rapidexptn@rediffmail.com
Hyderabad: *Telefax:* 040-24737290
E-mail: pustakmahalhyd@yahoo.co.in

© Copyright : *Author*

ISBN 978-81-223-1041-2
Edition : 2009

All rights reserved. No part of this publications may be reproduced, stored in a retrieval system or transmitted, in any form or by any means, electronic, mechanical, photocopying, recording or otherwise, without the prior permission in writing from the author/publisher.

Printed at : Param Offsetters, Okhla, New Delhi-110020

For Pooja, my daughter
Born Fighter
Amazing is your potential
Conquer the world
There's nothing to fear
I am here
For you.

And

For Bobby, my husband
Who inspires me
To become
That which I chose to be
In this journey
That is Life…

Acknowledgements

Thank you Cedar Books for believing in this work – I'd like to particularly thank the Director, Mr. Rohit Gupta, the Editor, Neha Gupta, and the team of Cedar Books, who are simply amazing.

Thank you Rathish Babu, CEO Access Atlantech (www.accessatlantech.com), and his wonderful team, their guidance helped us through many rough seas.

Thank you Ap. Shreethar and Nirmala Shreethar – the countless design hours you gave us. This world is going to sing paeans about Ap. Shreethar's beautiful paintings.

Thanks a lot to the many people who don't want to be named but helped immensely by their contribution of stories that made this book possible.

Contents

Preface

We live in a world that is seemingly driven by perception. We perceive, we make judgements and we make decisions based on our perceptions. We are dangerously living in a time when perceptions *are* the reality.

As someone who has spent considerable time in Human Resources (read Relations), I have increasingly seen at close quarters how we go about making decisions based on our perceptions. This has caused animosity and breakages in relationships; and it has also caused irreparable damage.

And what is increasingly happening is that because we do live in such a world, more and more people are perception-driven. It seems that there is no longer any space for human warmth, for caring to evolve into humanness and no longer is there any patience for kindness to come to fruition in a relationship. In an ever-increasing younger population that seems to thrive on fast games, fast food and fast everything – the old world of genteel good culture and the old world goodness are becoming rare to the point of extinction.

So I began to look around and found that our perceptions could be wrong. Some of us are doctors, engineers, accountants, scientists, carpenters, plumbers, software professionals, unemployed dreamers, homemakers and so on, as much as we are father, brother, wife, sister, son, daughter, friend. A hard-working doctor is a couch potato at home. Yet he is a caring father or mother. So how many masks do we wear? What are the perceptional values that we are judged by and from which perspective are we seen?

I took some examples – almost like a photographer taking many shots of a good scenario. Mine was of a criminal. As I began to look closer, there emerged another figure. Of a hero! Of course – he was a hero in a society that would not accept you or me as worthy of being considered for such worship. That society is a different world. In fact – it's called 'The Underworld'. Their rules are different. Their ethos, if there does exist such a word in their dictionary, is, well, different. And as I began to look deeper and deeper what emerged as the perception faded into a dim background. In fact, it no longer was a perception. That was just a label that 'society' pinned on a citizen of this 'underworld'.

What a paradox of a difference? From one perspective a hero, and from another level, another society – the scum of the earth.

It was indeed surprising for me to find loyalty in such a world. I found that the word 'attracting talent' was not half as difficult as I had found when I was a young recruiter trying to send programmers to United States of America. Attrition, another dreaded word for me as an HR manager and a word which had no consonance with either loyalty or commitment kept appearing as the total antithesis of its meaning in the New Economy companies. I found that high wages, great work environment, stock options and other such dollops did not get people into these dark organisations as much as the lack of it prevented them from leaving.

In this fascinating world, I found stories of valour, of human greatness, of abject poverty and such terrible dastardly acts that should they happen to us 'normal people' we'd probably die merely from their visitation upon us.

Just like the many tales that some of us have seen of corporate gamesmanship in action, in this 'other world' too were stories of cut-throat treachery, back-stabbing and such masterly deceit that it'd make the games of the White Collar Knights look merely like child's play.

This is neither about judgement nor about morality. It's a story.

It made me aware that behind each and every one of us is another person. And more often than not – we are *that* person not the mask we wear for whatever reasons that we choose to don these masks.

Then there is this thing about Transformation that has attracted me always. Each of us is changing constantly. In fact, change is the only thing that is constant in our lives. We are born a baby, within a few years we become a young boy or girl, and then we come into our adolescence, then our young adulthood onto become parents and so on does life swiftly go by. Till the end we are metamorphosed into something that can no longer walk to its grave, but has to be carried there for time to paint its eulogy and for the kindness of others to keep us alive in their memories.

My protagonists in this book are transformers. They not only transform themselves, but those around them. I believe passionately that we have the power to transform, if only we believe. If only we accept the infinity of transformation, such is our power and such is our ability to transform. But, we have to care to do so. I believe that both individuals and corporate (whether that is private, government or otherwise) have the power to transform and should they act upon it in a cohesive manner, the results could be mind-bogglingly amazing.

This book then is also about the power that comes from caring. As someone who has spent considerable time in good organisations, I have often wondered how profitability can be achieved for all concerned. I passionately believe that good governance is about sharing. I believe that good leadership is about showing the way to others lesser blessed than ourselves to 'make it' in this world of ours.

I believe that it is the duty of those who have to be compassionate to those who do not have to.

Just as much as I believe that within each and every human being is a mine full of fabulous potential. And I believe that Leadership Excellence is about showing the way to tap into that potential, show ordinary human beings to become extraordinary and brilliant.

I believe that each of us is created by the same hand of God.

Except that some of us are **The Angels of God**. Regardless of our circumstances, our environments, our social status – when that realisation dawns upon us, the transformation from ordinary to extraordinary happens within a flash.

It has happened in the past. As much as it can happen again. And again...

—*Author*

1

Jeddah, Saudi Arabia

Dawn. The city is still sleeping. A few cars are out; headlights from oncoming trucks pierce the fading darkness. From its silken and warm embrace, only a few stir outside.

The sky is gradually shedding its inky blackness. It seems that the earth, pregnant with the sun's imminent rise over this Middle Eastern city, is showing off its reddish hues, almost like some surreal artist with a masterpiece of a canvas.

Suddenly as if on cue, the quiet, or rather solitude of the atmosphere, is shattered by the cacophony of loudspeakers turned to maximum volume. The *muezzins* are calling the Muslim faithful to the first of their five prayers in the day.

And just as suddenly, cloaked figures, some in the traditional head garb of the Arabs, some with just the *kuffiyeh*, and some without, emerge from darkened doorways, making their way to the mosques closest their homes. Most carry the prayer beads, fingers hurrying over them, as if in a frantic race with some unseen Force to recite as many *suras* as is humanly possible.

Inside the mosques, they come together… men of all races, white, black, brown… rich and poor alike, all in awe and in utter reverence of the One and Only… the God that Was, the God that Is, God of Abraham, God of Moses, the one who sent

Muhammad, the last Prophet, Peace Be Upon Him. Their Worship is one, their Prayer Complete. In total surrender, they bend, their foreheads touching the earth that He created, You are the Master – Do what you will with us – We are yours.

Not far away, quite close to the heart of Jeddah, a single window is illuminated in the rather staid but very modern-looking Emir Faisal Building overlooking Emir Abdullah Road. No, it was no mistake that someone made, not turning off the light before they left for the day. Security and the Facilities Administration in the building was second to none and a glance at the parking bay would reveal a lone dark blue Porsche occupying the now desolate parking yard that it was parked in.

And a look inside the office of that single window would also reveal a study in controlled chaos. Papers were everywhere, although the temperature inside the room would be several degrees lower than the weather outside, the man at the huge, imposing table (a glutton for space actually) was perspiring. The tiny beads that appeared on his broad forehead was wiped away impatiently by an elegant hand, clutching at once a wet handkerchief and a cigarette that was half smoked.

On the floor, a couple of full ashtrays would weep if they could, choking on the innumerable cigarettes that were crushed into them. Coffee cups were also overflowing with cigarettes stubbed hurriedly into the dredges. Musty would not be a bad description of the awful smell that enveloped the upholstery and the papers. It hung in the very air. It seemed impossible that one would have to breathe from this atmosphere if one were an occupant of the room.

The phones that were on display were multi-coloured and many. There were a few cellular phones thrown in for added benefit. This man it seemed, if he needed to be reached, had to be available, somehow. In one corner of the table was a sleek laptop that begged attention amid this confusion of equipment and documents.

There was a lot to be done, but the priority was a man called Hamza and his attention was riveted to one phone – third from his left.

With carefully manicured fingers, he picked up the receiver. Dialling long distance, he placed a call to Kozhikode, on the West Coast of India. When it was answered, there was no venom, no anger – just another thing that needed to be done.

"Take care of Hamza, tomorrow. Don't fail me."

Then with great care, he put the receiver back into its cradle.

Perhaps, for the first time that night, the man smiled. No one would walk away and live to claim that he or she had taken this man for a ride. It would never happen.

Glancing at the sleek Cartier Pasha on his wrist, he remembered suddenly that he had promised that he would be home for dinner, at least today.

"It's almost time for breakfast," he muttered to himself, pulling shut the door to the office, behind him.

2

Kallai, Kozhikode, The West Coast of India

The Kallai fish market is one of the oldest on the Malabar Coast. From here, traders had sold fish from ages ago to far-flung markets all over Kerala and as far as the Persian Gulf and as some said even to faraway Cairo too. The market is busy, small and very very loud. You never get to see a dull moment in this fish market. Most other markets that you have seen probably have a dozen other things apart from a staple commodity. Not here! Here all you get is just fish, fish and more fish, and of course, no fish market in Kerala is complete without the Mathi and Aagoli. You also get squid, cuttlefish, lobster, prawns, shark.... And why! The other day one of the traders had on display, a rather serious-looking dolphin that had somehow managed to stray into a fisherman's cast nets. If there is a kind of seafood that can be consumed by humans, it ought to be available in Kallai, and if it isn't, it's not worth eating.

There are no preposterous hoardings announcing the market to a stranger, not even a sign. There isn't a bay of reefer trucks that might announce, even if inadvertently, the presence of a market. But what it lacks in advertising and announcements, it makes up in smell. Boy, you needn't tell anyone that you've been to Kallai fish market if you've been there. The smell permeates your clothes; your fingers would smell of the flavour of all those fishes that swam that day or perhaps a day before in the waters of the Arabian Sea. And more than anything else, if you ask someone to smell your hair, it smells of the breeze of the sea.

They say that this is one smell that ain't a stink, it ain't a bad smell or anything close to that, it's just the perfume of the sea, the essence of Kallai and stories abound of the fishermen who made this market a centre to reckon with. And there was honour here. No one would sell you rotten fish. They prided in selling fish… just plain good fish. And it was clean, all placed on banana leaves and always a man sprinkling water on them, or shooing the flies away. The colours were brilliant. And somewhere amongst the heap, you would see the green of the banana leaf.

Tales of yore are spun of the ordinary men who became Muthalalis. Of boatloads of fish going out in Arabian *Dhows* to far-off Dubai and coming back laden with biscuits of gold and silver…. And so to this day, the stories remain of men and fairy tales. Each interwoven into the other so intricately and so realistically that it would not be easy to separate fact from fiction, even if one tried….

Just behind the market, there are a few rooms. In the old days, these used to be the rooms in which men bargained over fish deals. And no outsider would understand the deal, too. A handkerchief would be placed on two pairs of hands, and then in sign language, the price would be decided between the seller and the buyer. If a deal was clinched, it was just a handshake under the handkerchief, and if it was not – one palm slapped the other away. No one other than the buyer and the seller would know of the details. Not even if one stood in the very room where the deal was conducted in. In the old days, they also used these rooms for tired fishermen who had not slept for days, who would be given a bottle of the best available Military rum and a corner to sleep off its effect.

Not anymore! Two offices were locked, in both senses, physical (you ought to be blind not to see the huge padlock) and legal. Some bygone tenant sued the landlord refusing to leave on a plea to vacate, and now the matter was sub judice, being fought in a distant court… all that energy being wasted over a long forgotten piece of a leaking, run down room. Two egos fighting over who was right…. But the other three were occupied. Although the rusted board over on office said 'Bismillah, Wholesale Fish Dealers', there was neither fish nor anything else that resembled a fish dealer.

Instead, there was a desk, a creaking ceiling fan that was black or was it just covered in the dust and the grime?

The other two offices were just small rooms, nondescript and one of the walls had a picture of the Kaaba, from some old calendar, which said 'Ahmadiya Hotel and Restaurant, Mecca, Saudi Arabia'. But you could not miss the long benches, worn smooth by the backsides of many a visitor sliding across its wooden surface. It was not difficult to imagine that these two rooms were the waiting rooms to the other 'office'.

The only piece of modern equipment in this office room was a very powerful cordless telephone. At this minute, it was ringing… and very loudly. Footsteps hurried across the narrow corridor that separated this part of the market from the fish and the crowds.

A large man, with a huge moustache, came almost on a trot. His presence was unmistakable. He was fully dressed in spotless white that was somehow totally out of place in the market, the white *dhoti*, worn to the left and very clean too.

He muttered under his breath, "*Varunu, Varunu*, I am coming!"

He eased behind the desk and lifted the receiver. When he heard his name being called over the line, his whole countenance changed; his face became softer and he almost skipped a breath for a minute.

"Ha, Bhai, tell me, what can I do for you?" He said with the least bit of annoyance at having to run that short distance to answer the call. It was as simple as a vassal accepting an order from a higher authority.

He listened intently over the phone for a couple of seconds, picked a pen from the stand on his right… an old-fashioned pen that one would have to constantly dip into an inkwell and then write, dipped it into the inkwell, and then wrote one name on the back of an old newspaper. Hamza.

3

Beypore, Kozhikode, A Long Time Ago

In Beypore, a small village off Kozhikode, the chief trade from past so many centuries was *Dhow* making. Some families would make the sails; some would make the wheel. Almost every family contributed in one way or another. Others would concentrate on fishing. Most of the men were sailors, if not ship-makers or fishermen. Some of these sailed with the finished *Dhows* to hand them over to their Arab owners.

And when a *Dhow* left from Beypore, it would hold not just fish, but supplies that would be sold in souks of Dubai, Bahrain and many more places around the Gulf. It carried pepper from the highlands over Cochin and cashew, fruit and vegetables – Oh! Just so many things! Sometimes these same boats came back laden with gold and silver biscuits and goods, some of which were contraband, which would fetch handsome profits. These boats evaded the sparse Coast Guard boats effectively. Not that they took great pains to hide themselves; the authorities were taken care of and well. They too knew that when these boats came in, they would have to look the other way. No searches, no heroics here. They just did what was safe – Let them pass.

But these were not just run-of-the-mill cases. These were controlled activity; the men on these runs would know whom they owed their allegiance to. They, their families and their loved ones knew that one word to the authorities, one betrayal – then that day the ever hungry fish in Beypore harbour would not be that desperate for food. These demi-gods were called Muthalalis or Bosses. They had fantastic wealth, had great connections and more than anything else, they had a mystical aura that would not sit well on smaller men. On each of these Muthalalis, many families depended. Children were educated, parents were taken care of, doctors brought in to treat the sick and infirm....

These Muthalalis did not fight among themselves. They knew that united they would rule. They had Ministers eating out of their hands. The poorly paid police force was just a phone call away to their assistance, whenever needed. Just the other day, Prof Harry Miller, from the University of Pennsylvania had come to Kozhikode, to spend time writing about Kerala, its people and its culture. Prof Miller described in detail about the working of these Muthalalis and their organisations. Suitably impressed, he stated afterwards that the organisational capacity of these Muthalalis could be comparable to the best organisations in the West. Except for one small difference! Those organisations were run, not by the best minds from the best Ivy League Colleges, but the men who graduated from the streets later to run these local businesses. It ran like clockwork on a couple of incentives – unlimited opportunity to grow if one was loyal, dependable and trustworthy, and retribution, if one was not.

The retribution did not always come from their goons or henchmen. It did, but they were not always called to take care of a problem or a problem person. The police could always file a false case and administer a careful beating. Hell to live with, but without the tell-tale signs. Staffing was never a problem for the Muthalalis. Young men would throng to their every beck and call, pledging allegiance and total surrender.

On this day, a young boy, not more than ten or perhaps eleven was holding between his dirty fingers three glasses filled with steaming sweet tea. Balancing this with great dexterity, he walked towards three men, standing with their backs to him, deeply engrossed in a conversation. They were standing around a sparkling, black Mercedes Benz, its door open, and cream leather upholstery with garish purple lining. A familiar and popular tune from a Prem Nazir film playing on its in-built radio....

"*Edha, Chaya,*" he said, "It's hot and fresh, drink it and tell me if you want something to go with it. Velayudhan at the tea stall said that he has just made some *pazham pori*, would you like some with the tea?"

The men looked at each other and said, "No, just stand here, and take the glasses back."

One of them took out a cigarette case. The sun caught the edge of the glittering case and the boy could smell the aroma of the tobacco. It smelt so wonderful in comparison to the *beedis* that the men in Beypore usually smoked.

He looked on eagerly as another man in the trio took out a lighter and held the flame to the cigarette. He seemed to enjoy the combination of the tea with the cigarette. It showed in the way he dragged on the cigarette, holding the smoke inside and letting it drift through his nostrils and his mouth, each word that he spoke garlanded by the smoke. The effect was almost magical on the young boy, as he stood and stared.

"Muthalali, you have to just say, and I will have it done," said one of them looking at the man with the cigarette.

"No, not now, let us wait for another day and see what happens," the smoker said, "Even God lets a man live his entire life to judge him, who am I, a mere man, to judge someone for something that he must have done in desperation?"

"But Muthalali, if we do not punish those who do not obey us, if we are going to have *Dhows* seized by them every time, just so that they prove to the public that they are doing their damned jobs, we can't let them go free."

"I know, I know," he looked at the cigarette one more time, and then almost regrettably he flicked it into the sea, "Go tomorrow to this Customs Officer's house and have a talk with his wife and tell *her* who you are, then ask her to advice her husband. Tell her that if he does not take her advice, he might not live to disobey her again. After that, if he still persists in disturbing our work, we can take care of him."

He looked beyond them at the waiting boy, "Abubacker, take the glasses and tell Velayudhan that I do not want any *pazham pori*. You take this money pay for the tea and keep the change for yourself."

When the boy stepped forward to take the money and glass from him, he held the glass back, reached out for the boy's head and drawing him closer said, "How are you, don't you go to school nowadays?"

Before the boy could answer, one of the men spoke, "No, Muthalali, he works for me now, he runs errands, takes packets for me and generally helps around. He is a good boy, very trustworthy and very loyal."

"Oh, is that so? That is good, very good." He reached inside his shirt pocket, took out a roll of hundred-rupee notes and peeling off a couple, he handed it over to young Abubacker.

"Thank you, Muthalali, thank you," he grinned, and put the money into the pockets of his grimy shorts.

"Don't spend it on unwanted things, give it to Kunhali and ask him to make you some good food."

But he was not there. He had run, first to the teashop to hand over the glasses and then swiftly, as fast as his feet would carry him, to the mosque.

There at its gates, Kunhali, the mosque sweeper, caretaker and janitor all rolled into one, who virtually lived in the mosque, was sitting quietly, a meswak clutched in between his teeth and the feather of some bird in his ear, eyes rolled heaven ward in quiet delight.

"Kunhali, Kunhali, I have something for you," a breathless Abubacker said. Clouds of dust were swirling about his feet as he came to a halt.

Kunhali, rather annoyed at this disturbance, looked up at the boy and wondered what he would have for him. Waving his hands in a feeble attempt to push the dust clouds away, he looked up, peering at the boy.

"Now, what is it, in the name of Allah that you have for me?"

Reaching into his pocket, the boy pulled out the twin hundred-rupee notes that the Muthalali had given him and handing it over to the old man said, "Here, you wanted to get your daughter married, here is some money."

Taking the money Kunhali fondly looked at Abubacker and reaching out for him awkwardly pulled him towards his chest and hugged him.

"Truly, you are a boy with a golden heart; one day… one day, Allah will give you so much that you would be able to give to many more poor people. This is not enough to get my daughter married, but this will help."

Pushing the old man away, the boy said, "One day, I too will be a Muthalali and one day I too will rule over Kozhikode. That day I will give you a car, a house and get you everything that you ever aspired for."

As if he had grown taller a few feet just then, the boy swaggered away, imitating the adopted walk of the Muthalalis, an imaginary cigarette held in between his fingers, puffing away smoke clouds.

In this small village, many others too would vouch for Abubacker's generosity at this young age. It was just a matter of time, they said, before the boy became a man.

4

Dharawi, Bombay

Moosa was born and brought up in the slums of Dharawi, long regarded as Asia's largest slum.

From a very young age, he had been initiated into the world of crime. His father was not at all inclined to send him and his siblings to school. Moosa's was just a typical case of an idle mind becoming the devil's workshop. He had graduated from being a pickpocket to local gangster to a hired assassin. Each promotion came after being convicted of the previous crime. With each promotion came the beatings, first in the local police stations where semi-literate policemen, who had frustrations of their own, would beat the daylights of convicts using bamboo *lathis.* Then inside the jails, either by senior convicts or by the jail authorities.

To get over the beatings quickly, Moosa learnt to taunt the policemen. His usual taunt was to tell those policemen who were assigned to beat him that day that they did what they did because they had small dicks. This enraged them and more than using the *lathis,* they used their boots on his ribs and his stomach. He would not utter a word; he knew that like every nightmare, this too would end. And with each beating, he promised revenge. Someday, someplace, somewhere.... There will be my day, he would tell himself.

To top everything else was his father. A drunk who lived off his children's and wife's meagre earnings, he never was drunk enough to stop his ravings. Morals. He never forgot to drill it into ears that had become fed up of listening to them. About half-baked morals.... Moosa sometimes wondered whether his father's diatribe about his morals would continue if he knew, his mother resorted to prostitution sometimes to feed the family.

And when the frustration of being a poor loser, a lousy father and an empty man crept up within him, the children bore the brunt of his anger. Especially Moosa! It was as if Moosa was born to endure the most of his father's anger at society, at himself and at the ignominy of being unemployed. Compounded with this, he would take it out on his son for getting into trouble with the law and other boys in the area. Sometimes the mother was at home to take a few slaps and a few kicks. But she spent most of her time working, or at least that was what she said she was doing when she was away from home. And the beatings were not the rap on the knuckle kind. They were demonic. Beatings with belts, beaten sometimes by the buckles, sometimes with just plain fists pounded into his face, until the welcome darkness of unconsciousness took over. Or it would be burnings, with pieces of wood from the *Chulha.* On his thighs, his buttocks.... Or sometimes with the glowing butt of a cigarette on his wrists.

Ironically, the beatings would not really be a consequence of anything that he had done. It was meted out with no rhyme or reason. It just happened. The end result of frustrations that his father suffered due to his own expectations from the world and which never materialised.... Unable to hit back at the world and those that promised his father pipe dreams of various kinds and deals, his father drank to quell the disappointments, and when he came home, picked on the easiest at the moment of time to vent his deepest frustrations. Sometimes his mother took it, but for the most part, it was Moosa.

In desperation, Moosa took the trouble of going to the Mahim church every Wednesday to light candles at the Church there. "Kill him or kill me," was his constant unanswered prayer. Mahim church was renowned for miracles and Moosa needed one badly. Or he would go to the *Dargah* in the sea – Haji Ali. There too, he had heard, miracles happened to fervent devotees.

And as each day passed into memory, as each day took on the same monotony of the one before, Moosa knew that it would indeed be a miracle if his prayers were answered. Sometimes, he felt, even the Gods had more pressing matters to attend than answering his prayers. Although, the *peer* at the Haji Ali *Dargah* did not think so.

He'd look up and wonder, on nights when he'd lie on the parapet wall of the Mahim Bridge, gazing at the night sky – if anyone was up there at all? Wasn't this whole thing about God being up there and Man being down here, just a whole lot of muck? He wondered if indeed God were this just, noble and smiling down on humanity. If He was just, why there was a colony called Dharawi almost as if it was created to belie the very existence of a God, defeated Moosa's thinking logic.

He hated Dharawi, its stench, and its absolute, all binding, all pervading poverty. He learnt to identify the overpowering stench and called it the Stench of Poverty. You could smell it a mile away. Poverty had a certain signature about it. You could look at a poor person and instantly recognise his impoverished stature. The body language was notable. The defeated gait, the broken spirit, the eyes that shed not an ounce of hope. And the people, especially the old and the aged, the infirm – they just sat around, waiting for Death to come a calling. You could see it in their eyes. They knew that they would not see a day beyond this ghetto. They were doomed. They were born cursed beyond redemption. And he'd sworn; he hated to accept such a verdict. He would not accept defeat, not even if God told him that he, too, like the million others who lived in Dharawi, was doomed to be born poor and die poor. He would leave Dharawi and he would win. He just did not know how he would achieve that.

One day, coming home early, he heard screams from the direction of their hut. People were crowding around but no one dared to enter inside. Pushing people out of his way, he ran in. Instantly his eyes adjusted to the gloom inside.

There were just two rooms. One doubled as a room for the four children and the other as a room for his parents and it was also the kitchen. The toilet, common to the rest of the entire slum, was outside by the railway tracks. The bathroom was just around the corner. No roof here, just a few thatched leaves tied onto a mild bamboo framework as an excuse for walls.

There on the floor of the hut was his sister, screaming and naked. Atop her was his father, struggling to get out of his pants. The reek of the cheap liquor, mingled with his father's sweat hung in the room. He reached forward and pulled his father off, but the old man was not light. Using both hands, he tried to pull his father off, and just then the older man managed to get his trouser unbuttoned.

Looking desperately around, Moosa saw an old umbrella hanging from one of the bamboo struts on the thatched roof. Reaching out, he grabbed it and using both hands he brought it down with great force on his fathers back, the thwack causing great pain.

The old man yelped in pain and rolled off his daughter. The pain almost brought him out of his stupor and lying on his back, for the first time, he saw his son standing over him.

Moosa ripped the cloth off the umbrella and placed his foot on his father's chest. The old man was cringing in fear and holding his son's feet. Desperate with fear written in his eyes, begging for something that he held dear despite all else – his miserable life. Holding high the umbrella like some spear, he brought the pointed end down and hard - right between his father's rib cage. It went in like knife into butter and probably punctured the old man's heart. For the blood spewed onto his chest and face as if had just exploded.

Stamping on the old man's chest, he pulled it out and once more he brought it down – this time right next to the previous wound. As Moosa pulled it out, another spurt rushed up at him.

The old man screamed one short high-pitched scream, as if it was an excuse for all that he did and did not do for his family. It ended on a small pitiful note. Then, a small bubble rose from his nostril and as it grew larger and larger, exploded.

Taking off his blood spattered shirt, he threw it at his sister, who sat in a corner, cowering in fear. But she was not screaming or crying. She just took the scene in.

Walking out to the street, bare-chested and covered with blood, Moosa said, "Any of you want to call the police, you can do so." Taking a bucket of water, stored there for their baths and toilet, he poured it over himself.

The crowd melted, as if this was something that happened in their midst's everyday. They did not like the police and never cooperated with them. That word was anathema to them. Just then a few of his close friends came through. He quietly nodded indicating for them to look inside.

They came running out just as quickly, a thousand questions on their faces.

Without bothering to explain, he said, "Get someone's taxi. We cannot leave the body here. We have to get rid of it and quickly."

Moosa slept that night a good sound sleep, knowing deep in his heart that part of the nightmare of growing up, the beatings and the terror of his childhood would never come back. A monster that he had willed to be killed was dead, for ever. It would never visit him again.

They never found out where his father had disappeared. No one asked him and he never spoke to anyone about his father. His mother grieved for her widowhood. Like many women martyrs in India, she would take hell and more from her husband but would never talk about divorce. Within two days of her husband's death, she was back to her normal self and for the first time in his life, Moosa heard his mother humming a Hindi film tune while she cooked.

Three days later, he got his first *supari.* A *supari* is the gangland term for an organised murder. While a name is mentioned and a price quoted, the acceptance and the money is handed over to the killer or his mentor along with some *supari* (scented and flavoured betel nut). The kill would then be made within the stipulated time. A man could be taken down in such a fashion for almost next to nothing. The going rate for a *supari* was about 750 rupees. Once a *supari* was accepted, there was no question about its finality.

5

Churchgate Station, Bombay

Churchgate Station is a teeming mass of humanity at around nine in the morning. When someone brushes against you, you don't stop to say anything. You just go on. Or if you are a woman and if someone presses against your body or a shoulder bumps into your breasts, you just curse your fate. But you don't stop to say anything. Nobody stops in Churchgate Station to listen to your complaints, least of all at this time when everyone, it seems, is intent on getting to work or just travelling through the hour.

According to the last estimate by the Railway Authorities, Churchgate handled in excess of a million and half passengers every day.

When a train is announced, this sudden surge of humanity towards the train by the crowd is a unique example of order and control in chaos. There is just this whole crowd of people just bunching up towards a small doorway as if willing the steel train walls to melt and allow them to pass inside.

Nobody notices a young man, dressed in a pair of jeans and a tee-shirt. He has his hands pressed against the back of the man in front, urging him forwards. There are so many like him every day at Churchgate Station.

As the traffic lights up ahead turn amber, the urgency of the crowd intensifies. Some of them are caught in the gap between the train and the platform and they have to haul themselves on the train if they did not want to slip in between. This was an everyday danger, but that did not prevent anyone from taking the risk. You could see hordes of people hanging out of the doorway of the train, their entire body weight taken by a couple of fingers hooked onto the channel on which the doors are meant to run either to open or to close.

The young man pulls out of his jeans a small triangular file. But this is no ordinary file. Its filing days were long over. Its usefulness as a file had come to an end when its sides were ground clean. The three sides converged onto one sharp point. This was a very useful weapon. One could almost call it a stiletto.

His eyes do not look at the weapon. They are constantly darting, looking for someone who might notice what he was about to do. His fingers feel the pointed needle-like edge. Today, no one was looking at him, they were either looking up at the ceiling fans as if by doing that the fans would cool the faces that looked up at them expectantly.

And today, the hands that held it were inexperienced but confident. Feeling the ribs through the sweat-soaked shirt of the man in the front, the hand came up and without much effort slipped it into the man's back, right between the ribs. Leaning on the hand with all his weight behind it, he heard an audible gasp. Quickly he pulled out the weapon and dropped it on the floor at his feet.

Pushing the man deeper into the thicket of human bodies, he pulled back. His action and his body language indicated to the man at his side and his rear that he would not risk hanging out of the doorway. Other willing people took his place and the victim was pushed further inside.

Within seconds, the train began to move and as the young man moved back, he kicked his weapon onto the tracks. No one would notice a piece of metal lying there amongst the garbage strewn on the tracks.

Within minutes, he was at the bank of telephones and dialled a local number. It rang twice.

"Hello?" A voice asked.

"Hello, this is Moosa. The 9.04 has left Churchgate. Your job is done. Let me know if you have anything more." Without any further ado, he put the receiver back and disappeared into the crowd.

Twenty minutes later as the train approached Dadar station, the crowds around the victim began to thin and he was dropped to the floor.

Two seats away a man moved forward and said, "Give him some room, let him get some air, I am a doctor and it looks like this man has had a heart attack."

A day later in a very impersonal, cold morgue, a pathologist in the Government Hospital would make another routine post-mortem. This time on a man who died of a heart attack in a local train.... While he performed his gory task, he made the usual routine observations committing it to memory, in order to write out his report.

While he got to the victim's heart, he noticed a unusual discolouration, a swelling of the heart. He knew a heart attack when he saw one. This one was no different.

He did not bother to examine the heart more closely. Had he done so, he would have found a small hole behind it, through which precious blood had leaked out. This victim would be consigned to the flames without anyone really knowing how he actually died. And, the tell-tale tear in his shirt at the back? Well, they just thought that he had hooked it somewhere on a protruding nail or something. And anyway, by the time he had been taken for the post-mortem, his watch, the briefcase that he was carrying, his pen, why even his lunch bag had disappeared. The Dead don't need anything. Especially material things! His family would get a body, wrapped in a very cheap shroud.

6

Chavakkad, Kerala

Chavakkad is a sleepy little village on the Coast in Kerala. There is particularly nothing here except a glorious beach. Chavakkad is also known as the Indian Dubai. You could buy anything from air-conditioners to imported condoms here. You could order for a particular quantity of gold biscuits or you could order for a particular brand of perfume. Anything was available here for a fee.

You could go to any house in Chavakkad and there would be at least one member of that household working in any of the Gulf countries. Many of these were involved in blue-collar jobs; some were servants in Arab households, some were drivers, some had businesses – Indian restaurants, Indian grocery and spices and vegetables. Whatever jobs they held, you could bet that they were all doing better off than they would have ever been had they stayed back in Chavakkad.

And some had, over a period of time, become Muthalalis themselves doing whatever it takes to make it big in these Arab countries.

But one of the most thriving enterprises here and in other parts was the business called *Kozhal. Kozhal panam*.... Literally translated, it meant 'money in a pipe'. And it was indeed a pipeline. The laundering of money!

Simply put, it was a banking transaction. A man earning a certain amount of money every month in the Gulf Countries would have to repatriate the same to his chosen bank in his homeland. In this case, India and furthermore, in a bank in Kerala. But going to an official bank would ensure that he gets the current currency exchange rate. Instead, going to a *Kozhal* agent meant that his money would reach his beneficiary faster and at a better exchange rate. And more importantly, the money would be delivered at his chosen address. No fuss about waiting for check clearances, relatives unable to write on cheques, no embarrassment, nothing. All it would take was a phone call and someone would make the delivery.

Sometimes it would be someone with a basket of fruit who would ring your doorbell and inform you that he'd brought you fruits from Dubai. When you'd let him come into the house and he'd place the basket of fruit that he'd carried on his head onto the floor. While you'd play the perfect host and offer a visitor something cool to quench his thirst, he would remove the fruit from the basket and below the hay, would be bundles of bank notes.

Depending on how much you were entitled to get, he would remove exactly that much and hand it over to you. No fuss, no vouchers, no receipts. You probably would never ever see him again. Except, if you'd been sent another package.

No one ever complained of money not being sent. No one ever complained of the 'courier' ever giving short. The system worked perfectly. The lubricant that it ran on was fear. Fear of retribution, fear of the unknown…. If there was a problem, it was taken care of and quickly.

But today, those and other murkier things that Chavakkad is famous for did not surface. The sun was at its glorious best. A few temple elephants from the Punnathur Kotta – yesteryears' real palace of a real Maharaja and the present age's Elephant Home where the largest population of captive elephants in the world lived – were being taken to a temple festival at a short distance from Chavakkad in a procession. Most people gawked, some with that absolute dumbfounded expression that people wore when they saw some of these magnificent beasts being serenaded by their mahouts who spoke in a strange tongue that these elephants understood.

Last year these elephants ran riot into a crowd that had gathered to see the spectacle. A few people were gored to death and a few people were badly mutilated. Actually, the incident started off rather funnily. These elephants had been requisitioned for the annual feast at the local mosque that had been built by Tipu Sultan. Most mahouts are Hindus and during the Perunal celebrations at the Mosque, some of the local Muslims got on to the elephants, temporarily dislodging the mahouts. Yes, you could say they were dislodged. Mahouts, used to drinking the local toddy, were given full bottles of Black Label Scotch Whisky. Thinking that the smooth flowing whisky was lighter in alcohol content than their coarse toddy, they would swill on the bottle as if downing a bottle of lemonade. And when it got to their heads, they could not care less about themselves, much less their charges – the elephants.

So these youngsters would get up on the elephants, and believing that they were in control would urge the animals at a faster trot than they can in the midst of the crowds. And intoxicated with the magic of the evening, the noise, the crowds and the mood of the whole event, they would goad their knees into the backs of the elephant's ears and prod them on faster.

Some of them mounted atop these elephants would be smoking *beedis*. And absent-mindedly would stub the *beedis* out on the heads of these animals forgetting that the elephant is not as thick-skinned as it appears.

Unable to bear the pain, the elephant protests vociferously. First it reaches high up and behind with its trunk and grabs hold of the passenger and once it lays hold of the person or persons, it flings them off, as if flinging off a tick off its back. Then with the pain taking hold of its senses, it would go amok. Crowds, thinking that the whole thing is a planned event, stupidly stand in the elephant's path, almost as if saying, "No, I cannot die, not here, not now." Unfortunately, most optimists don't live to tell this tale to their grandchildren and some who do, reminisce with fond remembrance, the right hand they had or the lovely hairdo they used to effect just before their scalp was pulled out! Or indeed the long legs they once had with which they would shimmer up any coconut tree!

But those incidents were far and few between. Today, the elephants walked in single file, almost all of them carrying their own feed. Bundles of Palm Leaves! Long after the elephants left the area, one could always tell that they had been there. The huge balls of excreta they leave behind, like some unexploded canon balls from a bygone era, lie on the roads they walked, almost in mute testimony of their passing. Their mahouts too were impeccable today. Sitting high atop their elephants and talking to each other, they seemed a happy lot.

At the junction of Chavakkad, where the buses stopped, where the Chanda or the main market was, there was this *chaya kadda*, or teashop. There was a little more than tea being sold there. The best *biriyani* that money can buy could be had in this establishment. People came from far and near, swore on the *biriyani* and in 80 years of the place's existence, no one remembers a day when the *biriyani* tasted bad. Or indeed, a wedding without its famous *biriyani* was not a Chavakkad wedding.

Today, four people were having lunch there. They stood apart from the rest of the people that were the customers. They had everything written about them that they were 'foreigners'. Why, they even wore Nike sneakers!! No one did that in Chavakkad. Not even the average Dubai returnee.

They not only ordered the *biriyani*, but also fried fish. And after they had finished their meal, they asked for Suleimanis. A Suleimani is nothing but black tea. It's not the regular black tea wherein a genteel tea bag is placed in a cup of hot water, and sugar added to taste. This is potent stuff. This is tea leaves boiled along with an equal volume of sugar and kept boiling until the very consistency of the water changes till it becomes thick and sweet.

If you knew how to enjoy a Suleimani you'd sip it, and not drink it. And these chaps knew how and more. They lit cigarettes and you could tell from their content expressions that this lot not only loved their Suleimanis but also enjoyed that draught of tobacco going down their lungs after a good meal.

When they'd finished paying for their meal, they walked out to their waiting car, got in and drove off.

They went to the Kadappuram. The Chavakkad Kadappuram or the seaside is very famous. Some of the Americans who came here swore that even the beaches in Miami were not this good. These men knew where to go. They did not search or give away the fact that they were strangers to the area. They got off at a house made of concrete and stone, and with a steel gate.

Opening the gate, they walked in, pushed the doorbell. In a short while, a rather portly-looking man who said, "*Aara*, whom do you want," opened the door.

One of them said, "Hamza. We are friends of Hamza and we came to meet him."

"Oh," the man said, "You just missed him. He has gone to Cochin to meet his sister and brother-in-law. They have come down from Saudi Arabia and he is gone to spend some time with them."

"When did he leave?" The tallest in the group asked. He obviously was also their leader. One could easily see that. It was evident in his manner, in his body language. They called him Alika. They called his name with respect. He was used to being respected; one could also see that.

"Just about half an hour before you came," the man said.

"Okay, when do you think he is going to be back?" this time

the question came from one of the other three. He clearly carried something in his trouser pocket. It was bulging and it was evident he did not want to advertise it. He had covered it with his shirt.

"If he calls or comes back in a day or two, tell him that his friends had come, we'll meet him later."

"*Shari*, I will tell him." The man closed the door and turned back inside.

As soon as the door closed, Alika ran to the closed garage door. Opening it quietly, he peeped inside. There was a Maruti Esteem parked there and bending down he touched the hood of the car. It was hot. Someone had just driven that car in.

While two of them went back to their car, the other two went round the back of the house. Getting hold of a thick GI pipe, they climbed to the terrace on the first floor. Tiptoeing, they went to the first door on the right and tried it. It was locked from inside. The second man went to the row of windows on one side of the terrace and peered in through the clear glass windows. Inside was a decently furnished room and a man on a cot fast asleep.

Signalling to the other man, he pointed with his finger, "Kumar, there is someone there," the other man peeped in, turned around and excitedly said, "That's him! That's Hamza."

Quickly they walked to the side of the terrace where there were a few plants. Kumar took out the bundle that was in his pocket.

From it he extracted a weird looking key and walked to the door that was locked. It was a simple mortise lock and while he played with the lock he prayed that it would not be bolted from within. In two seconds, he had it opened. Trying the handle, he looked up and thanked God. The door opened.

Hamza was sleeping soundly. Apparently, he had driven down in the car downstairs, and exhausted, he had slept. He neither heard them nor felt the muzzle of the gun that now was pressed close to his temple.

Hamza was a courier. Vast sums of money were delivered to his doorstep and all he had to do was ensure that it was delivered. One such mission had gone sour. Soon after he had delivered a large package, the largest that he had handled, the Income Tax authorities raided the beneficiary's house and seized all the money and the accompanying police party arrested the recipients.

Upon careful reconstruction of the events and from information received from various sources in the department it was revealed that the IT boys had received a tip. A tip that came from one of their sources, a source that would receive the handsome reward that the department gave for such information.

When some money changed hands and some more information was sought as to the identity of the source, Hamza's name came out.

Kumar told Hamza, "You can never cheat Moosa Bhai and live to talk about it."

Eyes wide open now, partly with surprise and partly with fear, Hamza pleaded with them. But these gents knew which side of their bread was buttered.

They told him, "You should never have even thought about it, Hamza."

"I will give you all that I got, but spare me my life."

"And that is all we want, Hamza, your life. Now get up slowly and don't make any noise."

They made him stand and with a piece of cloth torn from the bed sheet on Hamza's bed, they tied his hands behind him.

Without a warning, Kumar slipped a nylon rope round Hamza's neck and pushed him back on his stomach to the bed. While the other man held Hamza's feet, Kumar put his knee between Hamza's shoulder blade and pulled at the rope, throttling Hamza.

Struggling against the knot at his throat, and desperate for breath, Hamza wet himself, his feet and hands began to tremble.

Just as suddenly as it began his body began to relax and a little later, his body became still.

They removed the rope from his neck, and turned him round on his back. His eyes had nearly popped out of their sockets and he had very nearly bitten his own tongue through. Without saying anything more, they covered him, walked out the same door on to the verandah, and locked the door, this time with the real key.

Within two minutes, they were sitting in the back of the car and were off to Kozhikode.

Just outside Chavakkad, they stopped the car at the first phone booth with an STD sign.

Dialling a mobile phone number, Alika heard the phone ring once. When the phone was answered, Alika said, "Salaam Alai Kum, Abubacker Muthalali, pigs cannot fly."

"Good, I hope your boys told him that no one walks away from Moosa Bhai after cheating him?"

"Of course, of course, we were told to tell him and we did."

"He should know why he died; otherwise it would have been a waste."

"Oh, he knows, rather he knew."

"Good. What time is it now, oh my God, three o'clock. Have you guys eaten?"

"Yes, Muthalali, we ate. We will see you at Kallai market in the evening."

There was no reply, just a click.

7

Chennai, East Coast of India – 1999

Parry's Corner was a busy section of this town. It used to be called Madras by the British. But recently the Dravidian Party who had come to power in the Legislative Assembly elections decided that Chennai is the right name in Tamil for this ancient town and so Chennai it was. They did that with most of the roads too. This was the Indianisation of India. Renaming with a vengeance all that was or sounded even remotely British.

But most old timers did not bother re-educating themselves. If you needed to get to a particular place and you got into an auto rickshaw or auto as it is called here, and you told the driver that you'd wanted to go to Parry's, he'd get you there!! In reality, the name changes did not bother anyone.

Once you get there, the sheer business-like intensity of the place hits you. Everybody is on the move. Those that are not are just the lepers, the lame, and of course, the ubiquitous street vendors selling everything from Christian Dior perfumes to tacky plastic things.

There are monstrous public transport buses trying to bully their way through the chaos that passes off as the traffic, bullock carts that have no rules written for them and in between all this the tussle for space between the autos and the *meenpadi vandis.* These are essentially the hallmark to an Indian's innovative mind.

Chennai's answer to the Monster Trucks in the West, these were ordinary tricycles, with a sturdy frame, they were fitted with retired motorcycle wheels which were salvaged from junk yards, a 75 or 150 cc scooter engine that might have come from either one or several scooters or motorcycles. And a pair of condemned, but now reconditioned shocks that hold the front fork in place. On top of this contraption is a platform that holds a phenomenal amount of fish baskets and their owners. Careening through the roads of Chennai, they reach tremendous speeds. You could almost see the unseen force that prevents planets from crashing into each other, at work on the streets of Chennai. It's miraculous how one does not see far greater accidents than the current norms.

In the bus stands, you can see the dusty boards on the buses that are parked there. They come to Parry's corner from every nook and corner of Chennai and beyond. Almost all the buses that enter the State from outside have their final destination here. The chaos is total and complete.

In the old days, most companies had their headquarters here. This was essentially downtown Chennai. Old Timers also referred to this place as Madras 1, going by the pin code of Chennai – 600 001.

Being the commercial hub of Chennai, it ensured that most of Chennai came to work here. And the already creaking infrastructure of buses, trains, autos, private vehicles creaked even further. You needed to be in another world when you drive – otherwise the pressure would get to you. You needed a certain amount of immunity to honking horns, autos that come at you almost as if they want your life, cyclists darting in and out of traffic like maniacs and then, the pedestrian who seems to be walking quietly on one side of the road, who suddenly thinks he is Ben Johnson and darts to the other side. The already burdened air is saturated with the choicest of abuse, brakes' squeal and almost like the ebbing ripples on the surface of a just disturbed still lake everything goes back to 'normal' once again.

Architecture varies here from the Mughal architecture of the High Court to the British style of the EID Parry and Co Headquarters, to the teeming vendors and their multi-variety wares. From the omnipresent beggars, the soothsayers who think that they are very smart bringing in the gullible to shell out a few rupees to the prostitutes on the street who promise you the best time you had, you suddenly discover the side streets.

Some of them still have their English names and the one that is just to your right just opposite the Fruit Market looks to be the cleanest one. These streets are all so narrow that two cars coming in opposite directions cannot pass each other. On the sidewalk, people live in dilapidated shacks made of sheets of plastic, palm thatches and cardboard... anything that can stand up and mark an imaginary boundary and create a roof.

Off the main street, you step inside the Stringer Street, there is a certain amount of quiet. And just when you think that you have moved out of the teeming crowds and their displayed sense of urgency, you see another crowd.

This one is just outside a board that says rather proudly, 'English Travels'. Most people are carrying folders, some are well dressed and here in India, especially in Chennai at this place, well-dressed young men or women, carrying folders just mean one thing. Unemployed graduates seeking jobs!

They all are waiting to have someone inside the agency give them the forms to fill out and then perhaps interview them.

Most of the selected ones will have to pay huge amounts of money to the recruiters and after they have paid these amounts, they surrender their passports and other documents for processing. Sometimes, within a few days, they leave for the Middle East. Sometimes, the recruiters disappear with these sums of money and there have been several cases of such incidents.

They all are waiting to see Mr. Johnson, the owner of English Travels. They are willing to pay an equivalent of around 10 to 15 thousand dollars for a travel visa to any destination in Europe or the UK and up to 25 thousand dollars for a business visa to the US. That is a lot of money in India and many an Indian does not manage to save that much money in an entire lifetime!

The catch here is that by the normal means, none of these would be eligible for a visa to any of these countries. They either would not have the requisite documents that these consulates or embassies asked for or even if they did, their communication skills would be so bad, that the officers in these visa issuing sections would presume that the applicant's true intent is not to visit but to illegally stay.

And in the case of all these who were here today, it was indeed true that their intent was not to visit but to stay.

Chennai was the capital in South India for such activities. Here, the inflow of refugees from the neighbouring trouble infested Sri Lanka was high. These refugees came after they had sold all that they had. Most of them were Tamils. They could not mingle with the mainstream Tamil population in Chennai because they were different. They looked different, dressed different and spoke plain different Tamil. And more importantly, here they looked more as terrorists. That is plain ridiculous, but that is how it was after the former Prime Minister of India, the late Rajiv Gandhi was assassinated by a suicide bomber just outside Chennai; and since then the Tamils of Sri Lanka have always been looked on rather suspiciously.

They come here on Sri Lankan passports or just land up on Indian shores at Mandapam, the Southernmost tip of India as Sri Lankan refugees, and manage to contact either an agent or an agency like English Travels to handle their 'travel plans'. That consists of getting a passport organised for about five thousand rupees. Citizenship comes cheap here in India. No questions asked. Just pay an agent the money and provide a photograph.

After that is done, one just sits back and waits for the passport to be delivered. Once they get the passport, the next step begins, to get the visa.

As most of these do not have the requisite documents to obtain the visa and since most of the visas issuing officers are now trained to detect the Sri Lankan Tamil accented English, it has become very difficult to pass them off as Indians.

So the agents target good looking, quite educated Indian males or females. The passport that is about to be stamped with the targeted country's visa will bear the photograph of the bearer. The name on the papers, bank documents, Income Tax details and everything else will correspond with the name in the passport, except the photograph! The photograph will be of the bearer, in this case the educated male or female 'actor' who can handle the questions thrown at them, and most importantly, handle them with ease and élan! For every successful case handled, each 'actor or actress' is paid approximately thirty thousand rupees. This is far greater than any average job that they would get here in Chennai or for that matter anywhere else in India. And this princely amount is for a day's work.

The agents give these people or 'actors' enough coaching. They are asked to memorise their 'names' as mentioned on the papers and passport, dates of birth, names of parents, place of birth, names of children – if any are travelling along, their dates of birth – the whole hog. This is done because some of the consulates have interviews. And once that is successful, the visa is issued.

For instance, the French do not have a consulate in Chennai. They have a processing office in Chennai, where one has to submit one's documents for screening and it is here that one has to go for an interview. Once that is done and the interviewer satisfied, he or she passes on the documents and the applicant to Pondicherry, once a French colony, and where the French consulate is now situated. It is in Pondicherry that the visa is issued.

Once the French or the Germans or a Benelux visa (now known as the Schengen Visa) is issued, the passport holder is free to travel to any part of Europe.

But it is not the applicant who went along for the stamping who gets to travel. The passport goes back to the agent and the photograph of the actor is removed and the photograph of the person intending to travel is pasted. Or in certain cases the entire booklet except the page on which the visa is stamped is re-made.

You see, Indian passports are printed at the Government press in Nasik, Maharashtra, India. They don't come as booklets. They are printed as pages, covers, first page where one's photograph is pasted on, second page where the address etc. is mentioned and so on. Each passport issuing office gets to number the passports in accordance to a preordained series. So if someone were to get a bundle of each sets of pages, that person could put together a passport. Punching the numbers on, using hand-held punches offer no problem to the forgers. And for such people, official-looking rubber stamps are the least of their trouble. Therefore, to punch out the same numbers on the page with the visa throughout the other pages of the passport is very easy.

Once he or she reaches their destination, there are people who are to be contacted. These contacts either provide the necessary accommodation or employment or in some cases both. The jobs are usually in the backs of Indian restaurants, gas stations, and workshops – mostly blue collar.

There in the country of their choice, they apply for political asylum or get into contract marriages. Once they are inducted into the process of political asylum seekers, they are permitted to stay for almost up to three years. In 99% of such cases, permission to stay permanently is given. Or if political asylum is not the intention, they work illegally, save a substantial amount, sending money back through the *hawala* or *kozhal* system and after a period of about four or five years, go home to visit their friends and family and then come back again. Alternatively, they stay with their 'spouses' and slowly blend into the local scenario, processing the local documents and in a matter of four or five years, a citizenship is guaranteed by way of a passport from the host country. The system had become so well abused that there are now Indians, who masquerade as Sri Lankans and get into European, Scandinavian and North America in similar fashion.

This entire operation consists of a wide network of people, and vast sums of money are involved. Paupers have become millionaires and it involves members of the several governmental organisations who actively assist and abet in the procurement of passports, falsified documents and in every other manner in order to assist the agent to access a visa.

These days, many body shoppers in the IT world too, resort to such methods. Many IT professionals cannot speak English well and in their apparent nervousness fail at the interview in the consulates or embassies. Or they have degrees, which do not match their job profiles as in a Civil Engineer turned software professional. These are considered weak cases by most immigration authorities and therefore rather than accept that verdict and stay in India, they use these agents and go abroad using such methods. Once they have worked on a couple of projects, they earn enough money with which they can buy the services of another agent who has access to a solicitor processing immigration cases.

Most smugglers too use this route to push consignments of drugs to Europe, the US, and the UK, although this lot is more organised and very methodical.

This particular organisation in Chennai is in reality Moosa's operation, personally looked after by a trusted and handpicked lieutenant. Money collected from here is used to bribe persons of authority, procurement, and then the transit of drugs, salaries to henchmen, and a conduit for transfer of vast sums of money from his base in Saudi Arabia to India.

From here, Moosa uses his connections to procure arms for his army, through Sri Lanka. Chennai also provides a base of operations in India that is away from the usual gang war infested Mumbai.

8

Parappuram Tharavaad, Thekkemukkil, Kozhikode

Thekkemukkil is a small place. It has just one road running through it and it reaches a dead end at the Tile Factory. On the other side of the road, is Pazhayavattom. Pazhayavattom, which too is a junction like Thekkemukkil. However, unlike Thekkemukkil, Pazhayavattom is on the main road from Feroke to Kozhikode. You needed to either wait for the hourly bus service from Pazhayavattom to Thekkemukkil, or take a leisurely walk down the narrow roads under the natural canopy of the many trees that dotted the roadside. It was not unnatural to see people walking down to Thekkemukkil from Pazhayavattom and in the afternoon, it seemed that the entire stretch of road was deserted. Almost everyone had a siesta after a good lunch in these parts, usually waking up around three to a good high tea that consisted of tea from the Wynad Tea Plantations high on the hills, black Kozhikode aluva and fried banana chips.

But if you took the bus, it would probably take you around fifteen minutes for it to meander down the road, gears crashing in protest at the shape of the roads and the potholes so deep that once, a foreigner to these parts actually wondered if coconut trees were being planted in the middle of the road! Most people headed for Thekkemukkil got off at the towns junction, few people – a tiny majority, waiting for the bus to disgorge its passengers and carry on till the end of the road to the Tile Factory, where it seemed that a conversation had just ended, with the road abruptly ending there, at the massive wrought iron gates. Just beyond these staid gates was the Padumbara Kadavu.

Several governments had come and gone and promises of a bridge connecting Thekkemukkil to beyond the Padumbara Kadavu were not kept. The population of Thekkemukkil waited in hopeless expectation of that magical day when you could walk across the bridge which for the time being, was just a plan in some engineer's head at the Public Works Department.

At the Thekkemukkil junction there was another route also meandering its way past many houses on either side, this route that would also take you to the Padumbara Kadavu.

People would wait for the bus to come back, gossiping, showing off new acquisitions like a new wrist watch sent by a relative from Dubai or perhaps a new sari, perhaps a brand new visa just stamped on one's passport – people standing here made statements of either belonging or proving of their social status and their self-worth. If it wasn't any of these, they boasted of things that were to happen, even if it was perhaps just then conceived in the very mind of the speaker. That wasn't called lying. That was just said to prove to whoever was listening that an effort was being made, earnestly or otherwise to transcend to another level of life, from one's present condition and one could be respected for even thinking that such a migration is even humanly possible.

These veiled games of verbal sword play were allowed here. You could see a couple coming towards you and both of them in the afternoon sun, when the sun was at its glowing best. Lowering the umbrella ever so slowly just so as the sun to touch their faces in order to shower recognition of their identities which otherwise might have been hidden in the gloom of the umbrella's shade, they let you know who was coming.

And having approached you, they would ask you in the brightest of smiles how you were, your family, and incidentally, what happened to that job of yours in Dubai?

You were supposed to have left a few weeks ago, weren't you? And in abject humiliation at the loss of a prompt and believable response you hem and haw and they, knowing that they have just nicked your skin and have drawn blood, lay a hand on your shoulder and ask you to inform them before you eventually leave.

Two steps further on, both of them turn around and smirk at your obvious discomfiture, happy to have embarrassed you and happy that "they put you in your place".

Almost everyone knew everyone else in Thekkemukkil. Moreover, therefore, if there was a romance in this part of the world and if a couple were seen even looking at each other, sure enough the news would spread. Like the hyacinth that was creeping into every nook and cranny that contained water of the nearby Padumbara, gossip meandered into every pore of Thekkemukkil society. Everything was scrutinised; every aspect of behaviour was examined for nuances, subtleties and meanings. Families were broken, reputations tarnished by the sheer viciousness of an otherwise tranquil place, almost as if God had intended the irony to live, in a perfect creation of sheer natural beauty and a smiling, ever helpful population of people.

However, there were few families here that were older than most people could remember, the royalty, as it were of Thekkemukkil. These old families or Tharavaad, were steeped in their own history, creating folklore of yesteryears. The people who lived there were living encyclopaedias and were full of quaintly narrations of those people who had lived in these Tharavaads, and who now smiled down benignly from framed, moth-eaten photographs hung for posterity on ancient whitewashed walls; or perhaps, in the hidden truths of what those eyes had seen but never revealed to a world that had consigned them to flames when Death came! No one would know the irony behind those enigmatic smiles.

One such Tharavaad was Parappuram, which was built in 1607 AD, by the then right hand and confidant of the Zamorin of Kozhikode – Thekkemadom Keshavan Menon – the very man who had welcomed Vasco da Gama in Calicut on May 20th 1498 on behalf of the Zamorin. Vasco da Gama was one of the first Europeans to visit Kozhikode.

Thekkemadom was a man that the Zamorin needed. He was a good administrator, honest and very passionate of what he was doing and never treated his position at the Zamorin's palace as a job, but rather something that he was born to do.

He rarely asked for favours from the Zamorin. In a gesture of his appreciation, His Excellency decided to grant Thekkemadom almost fifty acres of prime land, with almost half of them with a standing crop, in a portion of land bordering Thekkemukkil on one side and on the other the Zamorin's own land and palace.

Thekkemadom built Parappuram in the traditional Malabar Tharavaad style. With a Padippara – which is a kind of gate house particularly in large houses such as Parappuram, the huge house had more than ten bedrooms, a nadumittam – which is an open to sky area in the ground floor, a stage for the recreational arts and where the Krishna Leela was regularly performed by qualified artists of the Zamorin's court. The Zamorin imported each of the pillars and all the other timber at Parappuram for Thekkemadom from Burma. No expense was spared, no artisan was too expensive, no pain too much. The Zamorin was determined to ensure that Thekkemadom got the best and to that end, he did ensure it happened.

Adjoining the main house was a temple with a private pond, where all the women and the men of the household bathed, twice every day. The pond had a structure on one side, with a partition in the middle for the privacy of women changing their clothes after or before a bath. Fish of all kinds, from various rivers, populated the waters of this fresh water pond.

There was also a cow shed with beautiful bovines from as far away as Gujarat. Another building, adjoining the main building was to house the servants, the hired hands and the not too important visitors.

The source of water to the kitchen was from a huge well about thirty feet in diameter, which had clear fresh water from a spring that was 20 feet deep. There was a small opening in the kitchen wall overlooking the well, which allowed the servants to draw water from the kitchen. The kitchen used wood and in Parappuram, there was no dearth for firewood. Firewood was in abundance from the variety of trees, bushes, coconut leaves, coconut husks and more wood from other trees. The vessels for cooking were all made of bell metal or clay and therefore, the food was particularly tasty.

Thekkemadom did not live here alone. He had his four brothers and their families living along with him. Some of them had jobs in the city and one brother stayed at Parappuram and it was his responsibility of running the household and managing the expenses supplied graciously by Thekkemadom.

On the day when Parappuram Tharavaad was inaugurated, all the men and the women had woken up way ahead of their normal times, rushing in the darkness to the nearby pond and finishing with their baths, came back to the main house in the company of servants and footmen carrying flaming torches.

The mahouts with the elephants had come the previous night from the Zamorin's Palace and some from nearby temples. They were busy at the well, giving the elephants a good rub with coconut husks.

While the occupants of the house had all gone in to make themselves presentable, the kitchen had come alive, smoke pouring out into the dawn through the kitchen chimney, rushing up towards a sky that was just beginning to show flecks of the most supreme red.

Thekkemadom had instructed his cook that he would have to excel his best effort. None lesser than the Zamorin was coming to Parappuram for breakfast. No other household in the vicinity was honoured so by His Excellency's august presence, in anyone's recent memory.

The sweepers were out, sprinkling the grounds with a mixture of cow dung diluted in water. This would not only harden the ground a bit but would also prevent the dust rising from the several feet that were to visit today.

Slowly, the other servants had filled out small earthen lamps with oil and wicks and had placed them strategically along the periphery of this elegant house. In a little while one could see the entire outline of the house lit up with these small lamps.

By the time the first cock started to crow, heralding a new day, another chapter in history and indeed a new family lineage, Parappuram was ready to open its doors to the many visitors who were invited today.

The men were all dressed in the traditional *kasavu mundu*. These were typical *dhotis*, spun in a traditional loom using the softest cotton yarn. The *kasavu* is the golden border that when spun into the *mundu* borders, gave it its royal look. The thicker the *kasavu*, the grander the *mundu*, was the average rule of the thumb.

Malayali men were considered a handsome lot if they were not too tall, dark, not the milky-complexioned variety, had a slight balding patch on their head, although that was not a necessity, a slight paunch, hair on their shoulder blades and a lot of hair on their chests. Without a doubt, most of the Thekkemadom males were indeed handsome.

They wore a *veshti* draped across their shoulders. Gold ornaments bedecked their necks and upper arms. Traditionally, the men would wear gold chains, or pearl chains, with a huge medallion or a locket. Most of the men here today wore a pendant made of the claws of a lion or a tiger, encased in gold, and studded with a cluster of both precious and semi-precious stones.

On their upper arms, they wore clasps, a broad band of gold that had either one large semi-precious stone embedded into it or small precious stones bordering the clasp. On their wrists, they wore more gold, either a bracelet or another clasp that either was an heirloom or showed some order of the person wearing it. It was Thekkemadom himself who wore the broadest, part of his 'uniform' at the Zamorin's Palace, indicating his rank and his authority. The clasp was almost halfway to the elbow and clearly carried on it the seal of the Zamorin.

The women were attired in their *kasavu mundu* and *veshti*. They wore their *mundu*, high on their chests, covering their well proportioned breasts, and reaching up to their ankles, exposing beautifully kept feet, fair and pretty.

Their bodies were overflowing with jewellery of every traditional kind. Bangles on their hands covered much of their skin. They wore beautiful anklets, with tiny bells on them, as if to indicate their dainty presence to people.

They wore gold bangles all of various shapes and sizes, some of each were encrusted with precious rubies and sapphires and diamonds. They also wore earrings, beautiful and long one's that sashayed with every movement of their owners' beautiful necks.

Each of them held their ground, assured of their places in the familial hierarchy, no one trying to vie with the other for attention.

Their respective children were tearing around the place, very oblivious of the importance of the occasion, today just another day in their lives.

As the firecrackers erupted, everyone present there knew that the Zamorin's entourage was arriving. A magnificent horse cart, drawn by four white horses, and two horsemen at the rear and two horsemen at the front shooing people away to ensure safe passage for the chariot.

As the chariot reached the Padippara of Parappuram Tharavaad, Thekkemadom and his family stepped out of the cool confines of the house and onto the bright sunlight. Hands folded in reverence of the man who could make or break an entire generation, the ruler of Malabar, His Excellency the Zamorin.

When he alighted from his chariot, a servant put a stool onto which he could put his feet. Elegantly placing one bare foot on the stool, His Excellency stepped out on Parappuram soil.

Immediately Thekkemadom introduced him to the entire family. Thereafter, the Royal visitor was shown the house, the grounds, the temple, and the pond. Finally on the way back to the house, for a sumptuous breakfast, he removed a gold chain with pendant bearing the royal seal, from his neck and turning to face Thekkemadom, placed it on his neck and said, "I do wish you all the very best and may God grant you and your family every happiness."

The many people who were part of the invitees from the various parts of the Zamorin's tiny kingdom, Thekkemadom's own relatives and a select portion of Thekkemukkil, praised Thekkemadom for his taste and for his achievement at building such a truly splendid work of art to house his family in.

They and all the others who saw the house, who knew Thekkemadom, and of his capabilities, were sure that this family would indeed grow and prosper.

Sadly, life has this strange habit of turning around in a manner that one least expects it to and as days passed and as Thekkemadom grew older, there was no sign of a new breed of creative genius that would take over the reins of Parappuram. His brothers were all followers; not leaders and they would take orders, but could not order.

Inexplicably, things change too, when you least expect. It came in the form of a child. Especially when all his brothers, their wives and their children were sure that all that was Thekkemadom's and all of the new Parappuram would surely be theirs. Thekkemadom had no offspring, at least not until now. Moreover, at this age when most people had twenty-year-old children, childbirth was not something conceivable. However, that was exactly what happened.

Parappuram Govindan Menon was born in 1642 confounding most people about both his father's virility and his mother's ability to conceive at such an advanced age. And because he was so small at birth, almost everyone doted on him.

Thekkemadom ensured that his son had the best education and some of the best teachers in the area were summoned for the purpose. His son excelled, and sure earned a name for himself both with the local authorities and the British, who were now establishing themselves as a force to reckon with, and with whom he had a rapport. They trusted his acumen, his ability to grasp a problem and soon enough the Zamorin used Thekkemadom's young son to represent him at the Fort St. George, a fort that the British used first as a trading post and then as a base of Military operations and eventually as the seat of the area representative of the British Crown.

Govindan Menon proved himself invaluable to the British and in their gratitude soon knighted him. Govindan Menon became Sir PG, an instant celebrity and a household name; Thekkemukkil had a celebrity overnight, a role model for every male in the area. Conversationally, if you were from Thekkemukkil and you were to leave the area and mention your hometown to an outsider, you would just have to state Sir PG's name and prompt came the reply, "Oh! You are from that famous village of Thekkemukkil." Sir PG had become synonymous with Thekkemukkil and had firmly put this small town on the map of the erstwhile Madras Presidency. No other contribution or personality had done that to this village, not for a long time it had.

Thekkemadom's only son, Parappuram Govindan Menon, became the most powerful person since his father in the Zamorin's palace, the man who would change the fate of his entire family. His popularity with people sometimes made the Zamorin quite jealous with envy.

Parappuram as a household prospered, and it was Sir PG who persuaded the British to create the Tile Factory at Thekkemukkil amongst many other new additions for both Kozhikode and indeed the Malabar area of the Madras Presidency.

One such was the development of the timber industry on the banks of the vibrant Kallai River. A thriving industry in logging was beginning to take shape when it finally took on a new meaning when Sir PG introduced the British to the timber business and very soon another landmark feature added variety to the growing city of Kozhikode.

When Sir PG passed away in his sleep, during one of the worst rainy seasons that Thekkemukkil had ever seen, when the Padumbara River swelled its bank and flowed half way to Parappuram, he was a grand old man who had seen all of 96 years of life. A star had risen on the horizon of this small village and had risen to its zenith and in his death it lost a charismatic figure, the likes of which would take several generations to replace.

9

Parappuram Tharavaad, Kozhikode – 1962

Saraswathi, a descendant of the Parappuram clan was in labour. The midwife was present, and the men were standing around near the *nadumittam*, the women making themselves busy, preparing, fidgeting, and keeping everything that the midwife wanted ready.

Following the matriarchal system in Kerala, newborn children were named after their mothers. Saraswathi's father was not from Parappuram Tharavaad, but her mother was. Therefore, she was called Parappuram Saraswathi and her newborn would be called Parappurathay, or of Parappuram.

At a little past four in the evening the midwife came out of the room, bathed in sweat but smiling and carrying a little bundle.

"It's a boy," she declared, holding the baby up to anyone who wanted to check.

Apart from smiles and the women rushing forward, there was no other greeting. The men thumped each other on their backs and wished that the infant's father were at hand. However, he was a soldier in the Indian Army and was away.

These days were tough at Parappuram. Gone was the glory, the men had not bothered to be educated and to become specialists. They were content at being "Of Parappuram" as if that generated everything that one wanted in life.

Generation after generation whittled away Thekkemadom's and Sir PG's goodwill of cash, property, jewellery and indeed the fame that they had so valuably built up. And by the time this latest addition was added to the family lineage, there was nothing – not even a shred of gold for the little baby boys' waist. Normally, a gold chain was worn around the waist for the sacred amulets that would ward off the evil eyes and kept the baby healthy.

Today, all they could afford was a black thread on which hung a talisman made of silver, not gold.

In the old days, several days of festivity marked a birth. Today there was not even enough for all the visitors who made grave excuses of very important other assignments and pretended to leave in a hurry.

After all, Hindu custom in these parts demanded that a bride be returned to her father's house for her first delivery. All the expenses, including that of the delivery, were underwritten by the father of the pregnant lady and not her husband.

And on the 28th day after the birth of the child, there is a christening ceremony when most of the relatives are invited for lunch. Just before that the baby is placed in the mother's lap and a small ceremony is performed.

Looking fresh and radiant, wearing a traditional *mundum neriyaethum*, the mother sits on a straw mat. There are traditional lamps lit on either side of her and in front of her. There is a silver glass with milk and bananas with the peels opened. There are small round container's containing *kan mashi* (kohl), *chandanam* (sandalwood paste) and a small *kindi* (a brass vessel with a spout) filled with water and *tulasi* leaves.

At the appointed hour, the mother leans over her child's ear and whispers his or her name into the tiny ears, as if the child would hear and look into her eyes in recognition. If it was a girl, a goldsmith is beckoned and the baby girl's ears are pierced with a tiny pin and a pair of gold earrings are placed therein.

Saraswathi named her baby son Bhaskaran. Parappuram Bhaskaran! Little did she realise that after Sir PG, her son would one day grow to become a name revered, adored and respected in sheer adulation.

Within a week after that her husband, Lt. Bala Govind of the Indian Army's 85th Infantry Battalion, and the father of little Bhaskaran came on leave from his Army job, stayed at Parappuram for a couple of days and left, taking his new son and wife to a new posting and a new life in faraway Bombay. To a new place, a new culture that would be so different from what they were all used to….

10

Diwali Day, Bombay – 1972

Mahim was always crowded. There were either people going to the Mahim Church or people just going away from Mahim to town or further into the suburbs. In a crowded apartment block overlooking Mahim station, a young boy looked out of the verandah of his flat at the passing trains, the cars and the bright kites that were fighting for supremacy over the Mahim skies. Kites were usually flown with a vengeance by their owners during Diwali. These were large paper and bamboo kites, flown with great skill using thread that was coated with a mixture of grounded light bulbs, dog excreta and a whole lot of other things. This when used with the kites in a combat, cut the threads of other kites.

The boy was Bhaskaran – and he spent a whole lot of time just glued to his seat there, watching the duels between the kites – sky dotted with a multitude of colours, some near some very far away.

These were tense moments for the Law Enforcement Agencies – The Police, the Security Agencies of various buildings and apartments – as loose mobs ran amok chasing kites that were either cut during an aerial battle or chasing kites that were drifting into the Dharawi/Mahim area from other areas. These small mobs of street urchins, local hoodlums and petty gangsters gave kite flying an aura or mysticism that prevented the rich kids and even the not-so-rich kids from entering into this colourful world. The rich kids had no stomach for this rough and tumble sport. And although his mother had forbidden him from joining any of the boys in the apartment who used the terrace to fly their kites, Bhaskaran would slip out sometimes, the thrill of holding a high-flying kite, too much to ignore for the ten-year-old.

At times, the youngster watched these petty squabbles erupt into gang wars that exploded without any warning, as one group of kite fliers attacked another with soda bottles, knives, bicycle chains and even razor blades strapped onto overgrown fingernails either with rubber bands or catgut from badminton bats.

Dharawi was famous for its kites. Sometimes you wondered if it was really the kites from Dharawi that was different or the mind at the end of the string that controlled the kite that was different. Kites from Dharawi had a certain method of finding the exact weak spot in the string of another kite using that very same spot to cut it with some superb techniques. Sometimes you could not help but wonder at the survival tactics that were used to keep these Dharawi kites up in the air. It was as if these kites were willing themselves to stay up there despite the odds. In a manner of speaking, it reflected the disparity of living in Dharawi. People lived there despite the odds with some of the population growing bigger than the entire worth of Dharawi. On the other hand, its sheer air of pessimistic nonchalance defeated some. If you were not tough, there was this air in Dharawi that would crush you, suffocate you, and surely, kill you.

Not today, not these kites! They danced in the air, as if to proclaim the spirit that was Dharawi. In this jungle, only the toughest survived. And little Bhaskaran sat there in his perch high up on the fifth floor, his little feet hanging down, his head comfortably perched between the grills of the balcony handrails. His eyes constantly moving taking in the action.

Just then, a minor scuffle was taking place right across the street. A group of boys in their late teens was ganging up on another group – the only thing common between them was that both groups were kite fliers. There was an obvious advantage to one group. They had a visible leader – a boy in his late teens or perhaps even older, Bhaskaran could not say, a strapping lad, quite dishevelled and unkempt alright, but nevertheless the leader of that group. His gait and in the manner in which he held his entire group back with his hands, as if there were marking some invincible boundary for his small gang, told Bhaskaran that he was a leader. Bhaskaran's keen young eyes missed nothing.

It seemed to be another fight and this one was nothing extraordinary either. But just as he had noticed this one boy from the 'visiting' group, for he was sure that this boy was not from the Mahim area. He knew all the major kite flying gangs from Mahim by sight; he noticed another boy. Slightly older than Bhaskaran himself, this lad was Bhaskaran's neighbour and had lived there in the same apartment for what seemed an eternity.

So taking his eyes off the kites, Bhaskaran stood up to watch the contest on the ground. He knew from the high pitch that this was going to be ugly. Suddenly the older boy whipped out a knife and with that one move, he took on an avatar, which seemed to be hidden till then. Bhaskaran just knew that this was not going to be another incident and without a second thought, the young boy ran out of the flat, racing down the stairs, down the driveway littered with garbage and smelling of decomposing sewerage, he ran out of the gate. Traffic plied on, unmindful of the youngster, but he darted in and out the other side, right in the middle of a minor warfare.

For a minute, the suddenness of his appearance on the scene threw everyone off stride. The older boy, seized up the young boy, sneered and continued his tirade. Just then, Bhaskaran, spoke, and almost everyone had their eyes riveted on the boy.

"What is the problem?"

"Who are you and what do you want here?"

"Well, these are my friends and I have been watching you for a while now from up there." Bhaskaran gestured upwards with his thumb indicating the apartment block.

"So, are you going to stop me from taking what is mine?"

"No, I don't understand. What is yours?"

"These boys are flying a kite which was 'stolen' from us. One of our younger boys was flying a kite that I own, and accidentally he let go of the string. It landed here and your friend claims it's his now. I want it back."

"But, isn't that how it's supposed to be?" Bhaskaran asked. By then, he had instinctively assumed the role of the leader of his group, his palm was held outward, fingers pointing upwards as an elder would do in the role of a mediator, one hand resting on his hip.

"Ehhh, don't fool around with me, okay? You do not who I am. Just return the kite and nothing will happen, okay. But if you continue this, I know what to do."

This was the end of the road. Bhaskaran knew that there was not enough time. They either hand over the kite or face the music. And more than all this, his time was running out. He had not told his mother anything; she was probably just awake from her afternoon siesta, and if she did not find him at home, he just about had it when she did.

"You know, I actually, don't know you." Stretching his hand out, he said by way of introduction, "My name is Bhaskaran, I live up there." He again gestured with his thumb, backwards and upwards at his home. "What is your name?" He asked the older boy.

Caught off guard, and momentarily losing control of the situation, the older boy automatically responded, "Moosa, that's my name. I live in Dharawi and you can ask people there – they know me as Moosa Bhai!"

"Well, Moosa Bhai, now I know you too, and this chap is my friend and neighbour." And Bhaskaran clasped the older boy's shoulders.

"Okay, but that still does not resolve my problem. I have to get back my kite. It's a question of my *izzat*. I have to get the kite back." Moosa's large rough hands were holding the younger boy's small smooth ones quite uneasily.

"But, that's not fair. Suppose you got one of our kites, would you return it?" Bhaskaran asked in complete earnestness.

"I don't care; I just want my kite back." Moosa was insistent, almost trying to shake his hand out of Bhaskaran's, the little boy keeping the connection alive, knowing that letting go would mean the end of this dialogue.

"Look, let's have an agreement, okay. From today onwards, any kite of yours that comes into Mahim, we will ensure that we get it back for you. But that's from today, not yesterday. If you say okay to that, you will get many more kites like this, and we all get to be friends. Otherwise, we would not become friends, and will also fight. That, I don't think is a good idea."

Moosa looked at the young boy almost incredulously. He said, "Bhaskaran, you don't know me and you don't know what I am capable of."

"Moosa Bhai, I know you now. I believe that you will be fair."

Almost suddenly, Moosa smiled and said, "Well, it looks like we have a new friend in Mahim from today." With that, he gave the younger boy a bear hug and holding both his shoulders at arms length he said, "I admire your courage. If you had not come, I would have let my anger take over my senses, and probably hurt your friend. I quite like you and I would like our friendship to grow."

The tensed air had changed and almost everyone was palpably relaxed. The kite remained with the 'Mahim Gang' and the boys from Dharawi disappeared behind the row of shops abutting the railway line and Mahim Station, just as quickly as they had appeared.

The younger boys crowded around Bhaskaran, some of them with big smiles on their faces, their relief quite obvious. His neighbour Vinod gave him a hug and said, "You are very brave. Bhaskaran. That boy is quite infamous around here. He is known to have been in and out of jail, police stations and he is not a nice person to cross with. We were actually ready to part with the kite. We just didn't want him to come inside our colony and then look for us in our apartments. But you were marvellous."

"Look, I don't have time for all this, okay. My mother is going to be looking for me and if I don't get back in the next five minutes, I am finished."

With that, he ran back into the colony and up the stairs to his apartment, the door left ajar, just as he had left it. Tiptoeing inside the flat, he peeped into the single bedroom that his mother used, and found his mother still sleeping.

Heaving a sigh of relief, he went back to his perch and began to look at the sky.

Little did he realise that with one stroke, he had walked into Moosa's heart, earned a place there, which would change his life, for ever.

11

Mumbai – Dharawi to Beyond

By the early eighties, Moosa had become a name well known to the police. All the politicians knew him or of him. Ironically, all of them, even his enemies respected him. Money, the lack of which was the only reason his family had chosen to live in a place like Dharawi, was in plenty. Feuds were all around; people wanted skilled negotiators who would not mind flexing and using muscles and weapons, if need be. The legal system was overloaded, creaking and utterly corrupt. In a place like Mumbai, there was not a thing that you could not get done. And one of the rustic elders of Dharawi, who could write reams on the philosophies of life by his sheer experiences in life, once said, "Life and all the opportunities that come across one's path in life are like a fine musical instrument. You need to master it to get the best out of it, and when you do, the world would applaud. But give it to an ignoramus, and no one would give it an ear. Similarly, here in Mumbai, if you are a man like Moosa, if you know the system well enough, its loopholes, well, you could actually orchestrate an entire symphony!" Nothing happened in Mumbai, which Moosa did not know about. It could be the launch of a movie, it could be a *supari* on someone, it could be a new starlet who is also sleeping around with some director. You name it – and he knew it.

He had 'groomed' several youngsters who had lived with him in Dharawi and now promoted to various other areas to look after those operations, or had taken over the operations by sheer cunning and muscle from other operators. His eyes and ears, therefore, were everywhere. People paid him for protection, for favours, for fixing a whole lot of things that they knew no one else could. And for those that could not afford him, well, you'd never know a larger hearted man than Moosa. He gave, he gave liberally to the poor, gave the best medical attention to those who were ill and could not afford the best. The press loved him. His stories of playing Robin Hood gave a sudden boost to circulation figures. The poor from all over the state of Maharashtra and sometimes those who had heard of his generosity came from very far away – no one was sent back empty handed or without a meal.

In a large plot of land that he had 'acquired' from the Government which had converted it into a sort of a dumping yard, he had put up a semi-permanent structure under which every day about five thousand people were served lunch. People called this the "*Khaana Bhandaar*".

From here, his lieutenants heard petitions and were given a priority depending on the urgency of the matter or the illness of the person. And it worked like clockwork. No one complained of bribes, favouritism, underhand dealings – nothing. It just was a smooth affair underlined by Moosa's command that none of his lieutenants or anyone working for him should accept or coerce his poor 'fans' for money or any other favours. People, who did not follow this ethic, were severely punished.

Once, a young man who had worked his way up the hierarchy had been given the responsibility of the *Khaana Bhandaar*, and all was okay for a few days. One day, a couple came to the *Khaana Bhandaar* and the young man took a fancy to the woman and asked the couple to stay back after a meal. He promised them everything that they asked for and said that they could continue to live in Dharawi at a place that he would provide, if only she would be his kept woman. The woman broke down and told her husband, he in turn told another of Moosa's lieutenants who was in charge of acquiring the grocery and provisions for the kitchen, who in turn told Moosa.

Retribution was swift. It came almost immediately. A van arrived and the young man was taken away. None saw him after that incident. No one knew what happened to him. No one asked, no one was told. In Moosa's world, love for the man was the only factor upon which people would do what they were asked to do. If that was violated, there'd be no second chance.

Despite being a much feared underworld figure, there was a side of him that betrayed a very good, large heart. This was why that the other gangs and other so-called dons did not emerge as a viable challenge to Moosa. They too did what he did professionally, but they kept the earnings to themselves and to a small coterie of their henchmen. Therefore, while a system did exist even there, betrayal too was very evident.

However, in Moosa's organisation, all his men were well looked after, if one of them went to jail for any 'work' that was executed for Moosa, everything including the legal advise was provided for. The entire period of his stay in jail was taken care of by the organisation including the person's family.

There were departments within this well-knit organisation that took care of everything. Moosa personally took care of the politicians, the top police officers, ministers etc.

In the meantime, Mumbai's other dons were not relenting an inch of space to this New Hero!! They resisted his every initiative with their own. But somehow they could not ever match his heart. Moosa was known for his '*Dil*', his heart. He did everything passionately, whether giving some gold to a poor girl for her wedding or paying someone's medical bills, or indeed ordering someone to be killed. He never had regrets about anything.

In their desperation to curb his popularity and thereby his growth, they resorted to assassinate him. When a couple of bids on Moosa's life failed, they realised that the more the number of these failed attempts the higher his popularity growth. After each, Moosa would make a dramatic appearance in front of the press, huge numbers of ecstatic supporters and wave to the crowd and then waved a kiss, two fingers to his lips and then to his forehead before offering it up to the skies, to Whoever was up there.

Having tried their very best to take him at every vantage point that he offered them, they now realised the futility of their attempts. Crowds of people materialised out of thin air, egged on by the popularity of the man, and also by the fact that there were those living witnesses to his largesse – people who would slit a throat just for the asking – and this is something that they had not planned for – his ever-growing popularity.

Somewhere along the line, the cunning, the guile, and the street fighter – gifts that he was born with began to fruit. He knew that there was nothing that anyone could do to him, if the people supported him, and slowly, very very slowly, the good stories about him, his acts of charity and his chivalry made headlines – far more than the stories that actually did damage to this reputation of his.

This was not just another Modern Robin Hood. He fleeced the rich not only to further his own lifestyle but to improve the lifestyle of the down-trodden and the impoverished, a legacy that he had left behind. He had the time to think, all those years when society pushed him away at arm's length and never really accepted him, his pedigree or his money – oh yes!! He had lots of time to think. The way to get into the imagination of people and to dwell in their minds was the trick and to do that – you needed to loosen your purse strings a bit – sometimes a lot.

This was also a very important phase in his life, when he began to develop a very core team. He knew that he could never consolidate, build and yet grow on his own. He knew that if he needed to control Mumbai one day, he'd need the finest army. But that alone never guaranteed a victory. It was generals who won wars – and so he was ever looking for talent; talent that was only available in slums like Dharawi. Slums from all over India and the qualification was very simple – poor, desire to become rich and very loyal. Two of these qualities were something that you either became or were born into – but the third was a paramount law. If you were not loyal, Moosa felt you had no right to be called a human being fit to live.

The boy with animal instincts who had mastered survival here in Dharawi was on his way to become a leader in this jungle. Not many people had achieved such status.

12

Lessons from the Peer

Moosa discovered the *Peer* at the Haji Ali *Dargah* during one of his frequent visits there.

The *Peer* was so old that people had stopped asking him how old he was. It was not easy to speak to him in privacy. He was always surrounded by people who sought his blessings, and asked him for advice.

When they met, the *Peer* instantly took a liking to Moosa; and in his company, Moosa found a peaceful quiet. At times, he'd merely let the *Peer* speak while he listened to him.

"You complain about your father, you complain about your situation.... Yet you don't realise that no one can change the situation. You must want that change so badly Moosa that the change manifests itself. Seek the change. God only helps those who are willing to help themselves," the *Peer* would tell him.

"We are mere actors on this Universal Stage, Moosa. You are what you are and I am what I am. It is not that I am better than you are or that you not as good as I am. Each to his own, the road ahead is open and destiny is around the corner, as we walk this journey of life," the *Peer* said.

"In your frantic moments of despair, solitude and abject loneliness – where there is no friend, no foe and all you can hear is the soul-quelling voice that says, not "I Am" but "I Am Here", and you turn around, wondering if it's some long lost friend. Then a weird sense of *déjà vu* takes over you; you wonder now if you're listening to voices that you want to hear – and then again – "I Am Here" and with a quick breath and still heart, you realise that you are in close proximity of God," the *Peer* would say, closing his eyes, and speaking as if he was in the presence of God.

"It does not matter where one is, Moosa, whether in the palaces of Kings or in the bowels of poverty, like you are in Dharawi. Learn to connect within. Seek to understand that which is within. All you need to do is to want to feel the Presence," the *Peer* taught him.

"I am compelled to talk to you of these things. For I believe that you are now seeking this message. I don't normally talk of these things to most who come to me. But I feel that you need this lesson. I don't know how long I will live. And when I feel something as powerfully as I feel the urge to speak to you of these things, then I don't hold back," the *Peer* told Moosa, holding the younger man's hands in his frail ones.

"That which is within you, Moosa, is the biggest Gift," the *Peer* whispered into his ears.

Moosa looked at the old man. He listened intently. Every word that was being told him was absorbed like water into a dry sponge.

"Unless you feel that presence and connect with it, see its magnificence, you will always be small. Thus you have to unravel that which is within you. Then you will come into your greatness," the *Peer* said.

"There is nothing that you can do to change your yesterdays. For they are dead and gone and no man can push the clock back. But if you want to change your tomorrow, you need to do something different today from what you did yesterday. That and that alone will change your tomorrow," the *Peer* whispered.

"Therefore, changing a situation is also about awareness. The more you are aware of how you can change the future by altering what you do today, the more conscious you become of your actions. The more conscious you become of your actions, the awareness of your time increases. Thus you begin to respect time and how you spend it, for you can never stop time or regain time you lost. It is then that these actions become fruitful, because you have now nurtured your thoughts like a careful farmer planting and nurturing seeds he'd sown. In his garden no weeds grow, because of his conscious awareness to what he wants to harvest. Such is the mind, Moosa. Change how you think and you can change anything." the *Peer* smiled his cheerful smile at Moosa.

Holding his hands in prayerful respect, he said, "It is with a deep-rooted conviction of Faith, that the seeds of our own desires come to fruition in the form of miracles that we never thought would materialise. So keep the Faith," the *Peer* said.

"Do whatever you can for another human being. Be extra kind. We only get what we give. So give lavishly. Not because you expect anything, least of all gratitude. But give because we have only been given all of that we have got, to give," the *Peer* taught him.

"Go in peace, Moosa. Realise that you are where you are only because you have to progress, your journey to your destination is not done. We all change in life. Once upon a time, I was a young child. Then I changed and became a young boy. I was full of mischief and playfulness. Then I became a young man. And I have continued to change and as I have, I have learnt. My knowledge is not mine. It is what I have been taught. It is what I have learned. My experience has been my teacher. I have been taught humility by the presence of something that is much larger than I will ever be," the old *Peer* said, with tears in his eyes.

"The knowledge that what is within us is so much bigger than we will ever be! We are tiny and so human compared to its magnificence. We can only bow down, touch the earth with our foreheads, for we can only worship to The One that is, and that will always Be," he said in a low voice.

"Never ever be distraught at what life has given you. Realise that everything changes. Nothing remains status quo. Reach within, Moosa, more and more – and trust that which is within. You will be amazed at what you become," the *Peer* said.

Moosa listened in silence. These were life-changing pronouncements. He knew that whoever was up there had brought the *Peer* into his life and made these revelations to him so that he'd benefit.

Only time and the practice of the *Peer's* advice would prove him right.

One day, when he sat with the *Peer* and the *Peer* had not said anything, Moosa asked him if he was sad.

"Why do you ask Moosa?" The *Peer* asked rather amused.

"You normally speak to me at length. Today, you have barely said a word," Moosa said.

"Perhaps whatever needed to be said is already said?" the *Peer* answered Moosa with another question.

"What do you mean by that?" Moosa asked the *Peer.*

"There is a time for talking; there is a time for silence. There is a time to listen. There is a time to do. You cannot do the same thing over and over. You cannot be a listener for too long. At some point, you become the speaker, because you have listened, and therefore you know. Who is the listener? Isn't he a seeker? And who is the speaker? Isn't he the knowledgeable one?" the *Peer* asked him.

"When you have found what you are searching for, you stop. You don't continue searching after you have found whatever it is that you seek. As much as I was filled with the desire to tell you what I told you, now I have nothing else to offer you," the *Peer* told Moosa.

"When the nestling young chick's wings grow, it flies out of the nest into the world. It is no longer afraid. Its world was small yesterday when its wings were frail and weak. Today as it soars in the sky, its world too has enlarged. It will define its own world and seek its own destiny, as much as you have to now seek yours, Moosa. I believe that you will, now that you know what you want," the *Peer* said patting Moosa's hands.

"All that you must learn, you will be taught. Now you know where to seek your lesson, where to turn for advice. Seek it diligently. The paths that you walk will be made open to you. That which you seek will be revealed to you. Don't be afraid, Moosa. All that you dream are the dreams that are meant for you. For I cannot dream what is meant for you as much as you cannot live my life and so it is written – each to his own," the *Peer* said.

"Go in peace, my son," the *Peer* told Moosa as he got up from where he was sitting, walking away from Moosa.

Many times after that, Moosa went to Haji Ali, but it was almost as if the *Peer* had disappeared. Someone said that he'd gone on a *Hajj*. Others said that he'd finally gone back to Ajmer, his hometown.

Moosa felt that the *Peer* had come to his life to teach him, to make him aware of the presence of something larger than he'd ever be.

Only time would stand testimony to that, he knew.

13

The Beach Hotel, Kozhikode – 1975

The smuggling of gold had reached a point where it was no longer sufficient to bring in a few pieces through transit passengers. The demand was for bulk quantities. Bombay was not an easy port of entry for the contraband gold. Most of the gold for Bombay came in through the small ports of Diu, Daman and Gujarat. But Bombay was still very difficult and even if one managed to get some in the difficulty of actually delivering it was even more, with several gangs trying to nab it before it was finally delivered.

Moosa had known of the Kozhikode, Gulf connection and had actually witnessed a transaction. Somehow, he had never made an actual deal happen.

He knew several people who would offload the gold from him, once he had it. Ministers who wanted to convert ill-gotten wealth into bullion, merchants who wanted to cater to the ever-growing population of gold users – the list was endless. Demand was never Moosa's problem, but it was supply.

He knew that if he wanted to emerge on top, he had to become the number one supplier. If he could not, then the rest of the others would combine to form a cartel and would take the largest pie in the market, or he would have to be content with becoming a minor supplier.

In a bold move, he decided to explore the Kozhikode connection. The other major problem was that Kozhikode was not connected to any other city by air, except those that could afford their own private aircraft. Just outside Kozhikode, a little away from the University, a small town called Chelari played host to a ramshackle runway, that was built there for the Birlas, the other name in Indian Industry than the Tatas who had their fingers in just about every pie. The Birlas had quite recently put up a huge plant outside Kozhikode in a place called Mavoor, a plant that would manufacture paper out of bamboo. And once in a way, one of the Birla Bigwigs would fly down to Kozhikode from either Mumbai or Calcutta to inspect the factory work.

And there was no one else who had business in Kozhikode that warranted the arrival there by air.

Moosa could charter an aircraft from Mumbai and fly down to Kozhikode. He hated flying, especially the smaller aircraft. But he had to make an impact on the Muthalalis, who he was told controlled the gold trade in Kozhikode. He knew that if he was going to come back to Bombay with a deal, the Muthalalis had to be impressed that they were dealing with a real big shot.

To further the image building exercise for his forthcoming trip to Kozhikode, he used the services of Akbar Ali, the famous Bombay-based Guide-turned-Travel Agent, to find out about the best hotel in Kozhikode town. Akbar Ali not only found out, but made a booking in the suite of the best hotel in Kozhikode – The Beach Hotel.

The Beach Hotel was just that – a hotel on the beach. A colonial building that was one of the remnants of the British Colonial legacy, and which somewhere down the line had become a hotel. The finest in Kozhikode, the hotel boasted of turbaned English speaking waiters, the restaurant had an undisturbed view of the Kozhikode Beach and the Arabian Sea and the food – well, you couldn't find finer food in Kozhikode. The best chefs were employed and the fare was a Kerala food connoisseur's absolute delight. The hotel was a veritable pilgrimage to those who enjoyed such a cuisine.

The hotel's rooms, most of the best, faced the sea and if you were an early riser, you could pull up the lace curtains and the bamboo blinds and look into the ocean, where trawlers were busy pulling out of the harbour, small ocean going boats with fishermen carrying nets and hopes of a decent catch all plying out to sea in a rush to bring back to this seafood-craving populace a taste of the sea.

And last but not the least – a very well stocked bar! If you loved to drink, you'd come here as often as you could. What was once a very stately ballroom, with teakwood flooring, it now echoed the muted footsteps of the canvas shoe-wearing, white-uniformed, turbaned waiters carrying drinks on ornate silver trays, bearing drinks, ice buckets and ice spoons also made of silver with appropriate cocktail cut glasses of the finest manufacture.

The muted lighting from an ancient chandelier also of cut glass and elaborate design threw shadows of the walls and caught the glint of steel forks as they dipped into mouth-watering short eats, that seemed to appear as if by sheer magic.

The cream of Kozhikode came here to relax, to meet on business deals and a few just came in to savour the atmosphere, which when mixed with the cigarette smoke, the humid sea breeze and the service, did give a heady sense of old world power and new world money.

Then, there was the Cards Room where Bridge or Gin Rummy was played and this room attracted some of the best Bridge players from further west, some coming for the pleasure of playing at the Cards Room from as far away as Mangalore.

And for the women and children, more than an acre of the rolling green manicured lawns was maintained in such fine shape by a perfectionist of a gardener. The hedges bordering this lawn, very well maintained a sort of a green wall, preventing people from walking onto the lawn except for well-appointed archways, through which winding pavements made their way across through the green grass, almost as if someone had carelessly strewn a ribbon on the grassy surface. On summer evenings, it was customary to see couples stroll the path or perhaps in pensive thought.

And so today, the staff and management of this august hotel were awaiting anxiously, the arrival by air of a 'Gentleman Businessman, from Bombay'.

They had reserved the best and only suite in the entire hotel. Sometimes, it was occupied by visiting dignitaries who found the local Public Works Department Guest House bad on upkeep and maintenance and so preferred the opulence and the style of the old world that was offered at the Beach Hotel.

The living room was huge. There were no two ways about it. The entire flooring was parquet in teak and from the look of it, quite old teak. The sofas were made of a combination of rosewood and teakwood. There was an easy chair with a wooden tray upon which you could either lean forward, have breakfast or if you prefer, write something. Otherwise, you were meant to lean back and lift your legs onto the extended arms of the chair. This occupied quite a lot of space in front of an old and empty fireplace. The irons were still there, some soot and a grill – but it was more of a show piece of antiquity than for any utilitarian value. In what seemed a deliberate thought to separate the drawing from the dining – a carved wooden partition was put in place. Without a doubt, someone had done this a whole lot later. The partition was a cheap imitation of a Kashimiri room wooden divider and it seemed out of place in this otherwise beautiful room. The dining table again in rosewood, with eight massive chairs, formed a beautiful and handsome set. Above this was yet another old world beauty – a real cut glass chandelier, which was, shipped in all the way from England.

The massive rosewood made four poster cot, with an original GE ceiling fan suspended from the high ceiling, the Belgian mirror dressing table, the silk cotton lace and bamboo blinds, chandelier in a riot of tropical colours on the smoked glass. The entire suite was air-conditioned and maintained at a comfortable 22 degrees Celsius by three massive room air conditioners. This was the only recent change in the suite, and apart from it, hardly anything except the sheets, the curtains and the paint, had changed here in about 50 years.

The inviting French windows, which when opened out, gave the best view of the beach and the sea from The Beach Hotel. It was a fabulous site, almost a thousand square feet of yet another perfectly well-kept lawn and rooftop garden, with a sun umbrella in the middle under which were white wrought iron painted chairs, a lounge chair made of cane and wood, on which several a suntan seeker had sunned.

The bath in the suite was also excellent. Done in white, it had a metal tub coated with enamel, and it rested on legs, which looked like the paws of big cats, made of brass. The pipe fittings were from Yardley's of England, manufacturers of such high-quality bath and toilet fittings and a supplier to the Queen of England. The paintings on the wall, several of them and all originals painted by some bygone Englishmen of a woman disrobing, in various stages and finally of the same woman, nude with one foot in the bath....

"Everything has been checked and re-checked for the mysterious VIP guest," the head of housekeeping informed the manager of the hotel. The manager was waiting with a few of his trusted staff amidst small chatter and idle gossip on the portico, whose conversation suddenly ceased as the security guard from the driveway entrance blew a sharp whistle, as if on pre-planned arrangement.

Almost immediately, he saluted a car that swept into the driveway, a 1973 Mercedes Benz; in the rear, a man sat – dressed in a white shirt, his hand on the door, a cigarette held very casually in two carefully manicured fingers. Two seconds later, there was only the red dust blinding his vision.

Moosa had arrived in Kozhikode.

14

Moosa in Kozhikode – 1975

In just a couple of hours, the telephone in The Beach Hotel was constantly ringing. Trunk calls were flying back and forth, at a pace that the hotel had not witnessed in a year.

Using his existing connections in Bombay, he had made contact with a few Muthalalis. In particular he was interested in a couple that were based out of Beypore and he invited them to The Beach Hotel, where in the air-conditioned comfort of the suite, Moosa could talk business.

And come they did, each with an entourage of about four people, two of whom waited in the humid lobby of The Beach Hotel and two came to the suite along with their boss. Moosa immediately knew that these were just paid bodyguards and were here to prevent anything ever happening to their boss.

Both of the Muthalalis who came to see Moosa apparently knew each other but there was no bonhomie between the two, just the casual acknowledgement of each other.

They sat facing each other on the sofas in the drawing room, their respective cronies standing behind them; and to their left, in a single seat, Moosa. One of the other Muthalalis had supplied an interpreter, a young man and they were waiting for him. Conversation otherwise would be very difficult, with Moosa speaking only in Hindi and these Muthalalis speaking only in Malayalam.

Just when the silence was getting awkward, there was a knock at the door and Moosa leaned forward to get up. But one of the men was faster. He moved forward and opened the door, putting his body in between the door and the man who knocked.

"Is Moosa Muthalali here?" the visitor asked.

"He is Moosa Bhai and not Muthalali," said the bodyguard.

"Ah! That does not matter to me. I was asked by my Muthalali to do some interpretation work and that is why I came here."

With that, he raised himself on his toes, to look beyond the bodyguard's shoulder to get a glimpse into the room.

The bodyguard moved aside and let him in.

He moved in, hand outstretched and wished Moosa. "Assalaam Alaikum, Moosa Bhai! My name is Ahmed, your interpreter."

"Waalaikum Salaam, Ahmed! I am grateful that you came," Moosa said and shook the offered arm.

Ahmed stood behind Moosa and the conversation began.

One of the Muthalalis who had come first, said he would begin. He began with a description of himself. Then he spoke about his operation – liquor imported from the Middle East and the *kozhal* operation for Feroke to around Kadalundi.

The other, more authoritative of the two, began to speak. He talked of his father, his father's father and how they were a well-known family of *Dhow* makers. He spoke of his current business, his contacts not just in Dubai, but also in Muscat, Jeddah, Tehran and Baghdad. He spoke of the volumes of the gold that he was bringing in and finally when he told Moosa that he thought that tying up with him would make good business to Moosa, Moosa knew that this man had potential.

Just then, there was another knock at the door. This time, it was a liveried waiter who announced that the chef was happy to serve lunch either downstairs, or perhaps in the suite itself?

They pondered amongst themselves and decided that they could talk a little further and have lunch in the privacy of the suite.

The hired help would not leave a Muthalali alone even when it was lunchtime. He would wait. Sometimes, the Muthalalis would be kind enough to offer these men lunch or dinner or breakfast, but that depended on the circumstances.

Today, they were in the company of a Prince of Heart and a Prince of the Poorest of the Poor who knew of hunger firsthand. And today, he was at his magnanimous best. He asked them all to join at his table.

And while they talked a while more until they brought lunch in, Moosa was introduced to the bodyguards. The Muthalali who 'imported' liquor introduced his bodyguards, and then with the other Muthalali whose family were *Dhow* makers and 'importers' of gold.

Moosa was not particularly impressed with the first one's men. They sure had muscles, but not the street fighting sense of survival skill and in a bind they would go with whoever offered them more. He just knew. And Moosa's feel for people was good.

The second Muthalali, who introduced his two bodyguards, fared better than the first. Moosa immediately liked one of them and asked him for his name, through Ahmed the interpreter, once again.

"Abubacker," the strapping young man said, in a confident voice, looking straight into Moosa's eyes, "I have been with Muthalali since I was a young boy."

And just as quickly the young man's face became impassive and he went back to his posture – hands folded across his broad chest, feet spread out and head held high. His thick black moustache rolled skyward at either end.

Lunch was served and once again, Moosa insisted that all the men sit down and eat.

He knew deep down that the assignment for which he had come to Kozhikode was successful. He had found the man with whom he would do business. It was just a question of how to play this right.

Moosa was now confident that not only would he do business from Kozhikode but that the man whom he would do business with was Abubacker.

By some quirk of fate, life for Abubacker would never be the same again.

15

Velliangadi, Kozhikode

Angadi meant Market and Velliangadi in Malayalam meant Big Market. And Big, if not anything else, it certainly was. Everything, just everything that one might need was here. It was in Velliangadi that you could find the largest dry fish market on the West Coast. It was here that you could find the largest market for fishing goods that any fisherman fishing these waters ever would want. Bright rolls of nylon lined the sidewalk that once used to boast of window shoppers. Now the shopkeepers had taken over the sidewalk, pushing the gawking pedestrian and serious customer onto the bustling street. The street was overflowing with hand-drawn carts, cars, lorries laden with produce and more pedestrians.

There was an air of sustained chaotic nonchalance, but on the other hand, you could look at it very carefully and there was an order. Everyone was doing something specific. Everything had purpose. Nothing was haphazard. This was the way it was always here. The clothes might have changed, the traffic might have increased, but the bustling of the market had somehow, increased its tempo a couple of notches, retaining the drama and the pace of life. There was another thing that you could find obvious – the smooth flowing river of commerce and money. Such an activity could not have sustained itself if not for the money. It was always changing hand from a merchant who had just received his stock of dry betel nuts or copra or chests of tea. Money was the pulse on which this market vibrated. The rest of the transactions were there because they added to the hue and variety of the trade.

There were people, who came to buy provisions at wholesale prices in order to save that wee bit, and it was very tempting not to buy more than the list that your wife gave you. Red chillies from the plains, black pepper from the highlands, yellow pumpkins and bitter gourd from the foothills of the Western Ghats and every tea estate worth its name was represented here, large and small alike. Yes, you could also buy coffee here. Coffee from the Coorg, coffee from the highland plantations of Ooty and from further north.

Rice from various fields had made its destination to the shops of Velliangadi, representing a season's worth of hard, backbreaking work. When you ate rice that you bought from Velliangadi, there is an old Malayalam saying that you taste the soil and the tears of the farmers who had bred it, from sapling to harvest, through the various hands that dealt with it as a commodity and right to your plate. The non-resident Malayalis of Kerala, especially the ones in the Middle East, swore that although they got some of the best rice in the world there in the Middle East, but it certainly was not quite like the rice that you would get in Kerala.

And there was the section where you had some of the best tinsmiths this part of the world. You name it – and you could have it made here. Curiously, the other day someone had come up with this brilliant idea – why not ask these tinsmiths to make a peg measure that would be all at once ethnic and at the same time – different? Therefore, the Velliangadi peg measure is available. Looks like any other peg measure for sure, except the measure was slightly higher than your usual peg measure. This was the tinsmith's way of ensuring that people never forgot where they bought *this* peg measure. You could almost smile at the thought process of the tinsmith as he bent over his anvil shaping something that would leave his signature there for many years after the actual purchase.

It was in one of these streets, that a white Ambassador car carried Moosa in the rear sit and Abubacker in the front next to the chauffeur. It slowly meandered its way to a back alley where it seemed almost the entire traffic was headed one way. Mohammed Kutty and Sons, Tea Merchants – the board declared. You needed to look closer. There seemed to be a mistake. Unlike the rest of the shops that sold tea leaves and tea dust in Velliangadi, this one seemed to be catering to the tea drinker by supplying piping hot tea, in glasses and not in cups.

There were people from all walks of life there. There was something magical about the atmosphere. Although most of the tea drinkers were out in the open – this being a dead end street, you could sit on gunnysacks, parked handcarts, on scooters – on anything you could park your backside on. Alternatively, you could sit on the round stools that the establishment offered around equally round tables.

You could order regular tea with milk and sugar, you could order Sulaimani tea which some of the customers preferred, you could order tea with mint in it, tea with lemon in it and tea with *masala* powder in it. The choices were plenty and you could buy either a cup or a jar that was brought to you in an earthen pot that was kept hot by setting it on a bed of hot and burning coal embers.

It was here that Moosa and Abubacker finally came to. The best part of the Velliangadi teashop was that despite it being in the heart of a thriving market, it offered complete anonymity. If you did not mind the slightly humid, *beedi* smoke filled air, then you could sit inside the large shop with no one giving you a second glance.

Moosa had discovered that Abubacker could speak a stammering of Hindi, which, Moosa learnt, Abubacker had picked up from working on the vessels and the Arab *Dhow* sailors who were not all Arab and were sometimes from Bombay and Gujarat, too. And the young man could easily communicate his mind, without creating too much of an ado about the language being a barrier between this strange, yet hauntingly overpowering character who had just walked into his life at The Beach Hotel.

Just after lunch that day, when without looking at the order of which Muthalali went first and who went second, they found themselves alone for a brief second when the others had gone either to the verandah to wash their hands at the tap there. Instantly Moosa had leaned over and told Abubacker, placing his hand over Abubacker's, "Call me on the hotel phone the moment you are alone." Increasing pressure on the hand, and looking directly into Abubacker's eyes, Moosa asked once more, "Do you understand me?" Without blinking or looking away, Abubacker said, "Yes I do, and I will call you before the night is over."

Almost immediately, they moved apart, as if each was lost in his own thought. No one suspected anything and after exchanging a few more pleasantries, they parted. Moosa promised the Muthalalis to get back to them in a couple of days with some news of his decision.

Sure enough, Abubacker called. Moosa asked him to come over at midnight and said they would talk. They took an instant liking to each other. Abubacker liking Moosa for saying one thing that would set the tone of their relationship – Give me your self completely and I will never ever let you down. That was not like working for the Muthalalis with whom you never knew if a request for a favour would ever be granted till it was either done or not. He liked Moosa's approach to managing his people. Ruthless, yes he was, but at the same time, gracious and benevolent. No man who worked for Moosa could ever complain of going hungry, or that he was not looked after well.

Abubacker told Moosa everything about his life. Growing up in Beypore, working for one Muthalali or the other from the time he could remember. Killing someone whom he never knew who had betrayed one of his Muthalalis, a man who once was considered close to his Muthalali when he was just 17, and how he had worked himself up at the thought of betrayal of a Muthalali and not worried about going to jail for a murder.

Finally, Abubacker told Moosa about his lifelong dream of being a Muthalali, how he had laid awake long, lonely nights on the Beypore beach, dreaming of being one. His dream of marrying a woman, having a family and his children not having to do half the things that he had to do as a child – just because he had no choice. He told Moosa about his dream of living one ordinary day as a carefree child, playing on the sands of Beypore Beach without a thought in the world of hunger and having to work.

And somewhere, neither knew when, but during the passage of night into early morning, they had crossed a mental bridge and one of them had touched the other's mind, occupying it perhaps for a lifetime. Only life, the test of time and the ironies of the lives the both men would lead would answer that. However, now sitting under the moonlight, cross-legged on the lawn overlooking the sea, the French windows open, and the lace curtains drifting lazily, it seemed that nothing would part these two. And if you were God just then, and you saw the affinity that the two had developed for each other, it was magical and you would have wished them well. Across a lifetime, two men had discovered a soul mate.

Early in the morning, the boats across in the harbour were pulling out for another day in the sea. Abubacker lighting yet another cigarette and sipping the nth cup of tea, told Moosa that he was dying to get some sleep. Clasping the younger man's hand in his and bringing it to his own heart, he said, "Help me run this operation from Kozhikode, I promise you Abubacker, I will help you become the most powerful Muthalali not just in Kozhikode, but in the entire state."

They hugged instinctively. With the sheer bonding of love, mutual respect, and admiration for having crawled out of the gutter that society, family and circumstance had thrown each of them into and for having crawled out of hell and to live....

Just before he left, Moosa once more told him, "Call me around noon today. Let's meet somewhere else. I would like to leave around noon tomorrow and before I go, I would like you to take over my operations here."

It was at that moment that Abubacker decided that he would take Moosa to the Velliangadi Teashop. No one would recognise them there and they would be able to talk.

For perhaps the first time in his life, Abubacker saw hope as a visible ray of light which was within his grasp.

16

The Deal Sealed

Sitting there with a dozen voices, strains of conversations drifting into the air and muted laughter at some poor sod's expense renting the air, Moosa and Abubacker chalked out the operation plan for the new business venture.

Moosa gave Abubacker one clear option. Knock out your competition or start from scratch. Abubacker owed too much of his life to his Muthalali and not just that – Abubacker operated on a different platform. He knew that if he could take the minds of the people of Beypore and if he could gain their trust, no Muthalali worth his salt could compete with Abubacker. He wanted to duplicate Moosa's operation in Bombay and he knew that if he won, it would be because people supported him.

He did not want to spill unnecessary blood. Of that, he has sure. He told Moosa that he was not intent on killing competition but that he would overtake the competition.

"How will you do that, Abubacker?" Moosa asked.

"Well, first thing – I am going to my Muthalali and tell him that I am getting into business with you. That you are going to supply me with the necessary money and infrastructure to get the gold here to Kozhikode."

"Don't be so naïve. Do you think that your Muthalali is so gracious that he will bless you and ask you to grow and cut into his own profits?" Moosa asked angrily. Moosa would have preferred a coup. Bloodless or otherwise, he really did not care. He would have preferred to have staged a complete takeover and was surprised at the younger man's lack of absolute ambition.

"He fed me when I was hungry, looked after me when there was none to look after me, taught me all that I am today. I cannot do this any other way."

Moosa shook his head, puffing on his cigarette deeply.

Abubacker continued knowing that Moosa was listening, if not agreeing entirely with whatever he said.

"I will go and tell him that you and I are beginning a new operation. I will seek his blessings. If he agrees then half my problems are over. I will not interfere with his existing clients as I need to only do business with you. But if he interferes with me, he is waking up a sleeping giant in me that he would not like to see. And he will then know what I have to do. Have no doubts about that."

Moosa looked up at Abubacker, surprised a bit at the intensity of the young man's intention and clarity of action.

"Okay then, I will not interfere in how you are going to handle your business. But I will not have you come to me at any point to say that you have failed. Whatever you need to get, get it done. Men, cars, boats, telephone – whatever you need. I do not want a single order that you give to be taken as nothing less than seriously. And I want you to buy a good home for yourself. Slowly we can look at getting you a good wife. Buy yourself a car. I want you to walk, talk, and act with an authority that you have only dreamt of until now. I do not want any dispute in the fact that from today, the moment you and I shake hands on a gentleman's agreement – you have transformed yourself into Abubacker Muthalali. And unless I tell you, no one, not even you are going to believe that you are anything but that."

Moosa paused to sip at his tea and extract a last puff out of his cigarette.

"I want you to go to your Muthalali today and tell him about our deal. Mark my words here, Abubacker, I said go and tell him about our deal and not ask him, okay?"

"And tomorrow when I go back to Bombay, I want you to come with me, to meet my people, see my roots and come back here with money. You are going to build me an empire Abubacker and I want you to remember always that you are part of a kingdom."

Abubacker looked, as always, directly into Moosa's eyes. And he never said a word, just clasped the older man's hand, and shook his head.

He just knew that he would rather die than give up on Moosa.

17

Beypore, Kozhikode

The lights were on in the house of Syyed Mohammed Ibrahim, Abubacker's Muthalali. Syyed Mohammed had one of the biggest houses in all of Beypore and people always remembered this as 'The Big House'. It had been that way for as long as one remembered. Unlike many new rich families in Beypore and indeed Kerala, 'The Big House' was always so.

Abubacker was a frequent visitor here and he could go into the kitchen, which was off the limit areas for visitors, except family. Sadly, Abubacker knew that it was a matter of days before he might ever be able to step into this household again. They would brand him a traitor; an enemy of the hand that fed him and most families in Beypore would never again name their sons Abubacker.

He knew that he would never do this any other way. His Muthalali had been a kind man, at times treating him like a son. Having said that, Abubacker knew an opportunity when he saw one and not even God would forgive him if he did not seize this opportunity.

In the kitchen, he saw Saffiya, Syyed Muthalali's youngest daughter. She was cooking something for the evening supper. Whatever it was that Saffiya cooked, it usually was mouth-watering. Abubacker loved Saffiya a great deal for her extreme kindness, absolute lack of arrogance – for she was indeed the rich daughter of a very rich father – but never once spoke badly to the servants or her poorer friends. She had always been kind to Abubacker, feeding him whenever he was hungry, giving him clothes other than the ones that her father gave him for Eid and on Syyed Muthalali's birthday and on certain other religious occasions.

Despite the love he had for her in his heart, he never mentioned it to her even once. He knew that if he wanted to live he could never marry her. His stature was far too lowly than even a hired servant that this household had. Therefore, instead of the cinematic *Laila Majnu* heroics, he chose to crush his love for Saffiya right there in his heart.

Muslim women normally wore the traditional *burqa* over their clothes, but in the house in the midst of family, there was no need for the *burqa*, but women usually covered their head. Saffiya had worn a *dupatta* over her head, and seeing Abubacker in the kitchen, her face lit up and she greeted him, "Salaam, why are you so tensed?" Usually he would greet her first and begin chatting with her, until she sensed his hunger and gave him something to eat. But today, what was wrong? She wondered. It was not a worry that she sensed on his usually stoic face; it was something more than that. She looked at his downcast face and hit upon it. Abubacker was sad. That was it. Now, why would he be sad? She again wondered.

She waited for him to say something, but he was quiet. He had not even greeted her in return. Yet, she said nothing. Asked him if he wanted to drink some tea and he did not reply to that either, just asked her if her father was in. She again looked at him, but seeing no reply or conversation forthcoming she ran into the house, looking for her father.

Syyed Muthalali had just finished his last prayers of the day and was playing with one of his several grandchildren, when his youngest daughter rushed into the room and said, "Abba, Abubacker is here to see you." He looked up at Saffiya and said to her, "You look after the child, let me go and ask him what he wants. By the way, where is he?"

Saffiya told her father that he was in the kitchen and without a glance at her father, began playing with her nephew.

Syyed Muthalali was not a big man. He was of average height, his hair still thick on his head, a darkening of the skin around the forehead, which touched the ground during the five prayers a day that he rarely missed. He had the typical good looks of the Malabar Mappila who were descendants of the Arab traders who frequented this coast, some time long ago. Nowadays, no one quite remembered if the Arabs had come here or vice-versa. Nevertheless, whatever it was, the similarities of looks were unmistakable. As his hands reached inside his shirt pocket to fetch his prayer beads, he wondered what it was that was so urgent that Abubacker wanted to see him at this hour. It was unusual.

Somehow, he never suspected treachery. He knew that Abubacker way beyond that. He knew that should he trust one last person on Gods' Earth in the very end, it would be Abubacker. Repeatedly, Abubacker had demonstrated his loyalty to Syyed Muthalali and there was no need to question that anymore.

However, curiosity is another thing and just before he turned into the kitchen and came face to face with Abubacker, Syyed Muthalali thought of Moosa and wondered if the Bombay Don had sent word for him through Abubacker.

Seeing Syyed Muthalali, Abubacker got up from the threshold of the doorway where he was squatting.

"Salaam alaikum, Muthalali." He raised his right hand to his heart when he said that.

"Salaam, salaam," Syyed Muthalali said, "I wonder what is so urgent that it can't wait till morning."

"I need to speak to you tonight. Tomorrow I won't be here, Muthalali."

"Okay, okay tell me, what is it?" Pulling up a chair, Syyed Muthalali sat down and faced Abubacker. He beckoned Abubacker to sit and he took his seat once again on the threshold of the door, squatting on his haunches.

"I am going to be leaving you, Muthalali." The words came out as if in pain.

"What do you mean – leaving me?"

"Yes, I mean exactly that," Abubacker said, looking up at Syyed Muthalali's eyes for the first time.

"I am going to be working for Moosa, the Bombay Don whom we went to meet."

Slowly Syyed Muthalali stood up, looked down at Abubacker, and asked slowly, "How could you do that to me? I am more than your entire world."

"Sometimes, Muthalali, another tree cannot grow in the shade of the banyan."

"Oh come on! Do not talk to me about philosophy now! Where did you learn to philosophise? At my feet, right? Now, you throw it back at me? Well, well, that is simply great."

Abubacker took one step forward trying to reach out to his old master. But Syyed Muthalali was adamant. Here was a man who just committed something *haraam*, something sacrilegious, and that person could not touch him. It made him want to cringe.

Still backing off, with an expression of deep hurt in his eyes, Syyed Muthalali said, "Go away, never come back."

Abubacker was not going anywhere. He had to tell Syyed Muthalali that this was his way of doing things. For the food that his Muthalali had provided him with, for the clothes, and for the respectability that Abubacker had today in Beypore, he owed it to this man. But he had dreams of being a king and no one would take that dream away from him. Not even a hurt and upset Syyed Muthalali.

"I could have come in here and killed you, gone back to your lieutenants and gained control over them," Abubacker told Syyed Muthalali in a matter of fact tone, "But instead, I chose to come here, see you – look you in the eye and tell you upfront that I am leaving, going my way, seeking my own destiny. I will not bother you, your family or your business."

He paused for breath, looking up the man standing across him, pitying him, and at once hoping that he would never have to face another man like this, sometime in the future.

"I am going, and I don't want you to look for me."

Syyed Muthalali, stunned beyond anything that he had faced in a long time, simply shook his head. Disbelief at what he had heard belied totally by the look in Abubacker's face and the fact that he knew that the young man standing there in his presence was deadly serious. "Yes," he thought to himself, "If he wanted to, he could have come in here and killed me. I would have never even suspected the motive before my last breath left me."

Sadly, the pressures of being a Muthalali and the gravity of the moment overtook Syyed Muthalali and he aged, in a seeming instant. He looked at Abubacker, with almost deep compassion and said, "*Podo moneh*! God bless you and keep you happy wherever you are."

"I just want to tell you one thing more, Muthalali, and I will leave. I will never ever interfere in your business, never poach your people or your clients and I will never compete with you." Abubacker told him, as if reeling off from a well-rehearsed speech.

"And I will always be at your call, should you need me." He looked up at Syyed Muthalali. He had just told the man who was his mentor something phenomenal in the law of the jungle. You let me live and I will let you live. Break that law, and then don't blame me if I behave like an animal.

Syyed Muthalali was not able to say anything; he just looked devastated as he thought of his own progression to becoming a Muthalali. This was not the way he had become one, he had inherited it from his father, who had from his father before him. These days were different. You needed to seize power. Power was not inherited anymore, you had to fight for it – if you wanted it, he thought to himself.

The next day, before leaving for Bombay on the first of his several plane trips, he went to Kallai fish market and took a small room at the back as his office.

In one stroke, he realised that he had achieved what he had set out to do – that he would affect a bloodless coup, retained Syyed Muthalali's remaining respectability in Beypore, and effectively became one step short of being 'The Muthalali of Muthalalis'. In order to achieve that, he would need the blessing and funding of Moosa Bhai. By tomorrow, he knew that the whole of the underworld and through the grapevine, the market in the Middle East, would know of the coup. He knew why Moosa had told him to come along to Bombay. He had to consolidate, and consolidate quickly. If he did not, someone would play another coup on him and it might not be as bloodless as the one he had just engineered.

He spent one full month with Moosa in Bombay. For a young man who had not seen anything bigger than Velliangadi, Bombay was awesome. It seemed to him that almost every state from India was represented here. Moosa was patient, a wonderful host; and he wanted Abubacker to understand how he ran his empire. Moosa sent Abubacker around in a car along with a driver who was working for him all over town. Abubacker met all the 'lieutenants' in Moosa's army and understood the power that Moosa wielded over them. He knew what he needed to do in Kozhikode if he wanted to grow in Moosa's empire. Moosa was sure that Abubacker was learning, and learning quite fast. He needed Abubacker to learn the ropes and he knew that once Abubacker began to work, he could not afford any mistakes.

With all the necessary tools provided, it was up to the man on the job to make an assignment work. There was no room for slip-ups.

One morning, Moosa called Abubacker and asked him if he was confident of going back to Kozhikode. Abubacker realised that Moosa had thought him ready, and so he said yes.

On the train back to Kozhikode, Abubacker thought to himself of how people come into your life as someone and continue to remain in your life and your memory not as the very same person as you had met but as someone on whom you have just bestowed a lot of respect and undying loyalty.

18

Mahim, The Growing Years

Lt. Bala Govind had successfully produced two more children. One was a boy and the other a girl. He was a hardworking man who was progressing in the army, or so he told his wife but could never explain why his rank never went up!

The flat in Mahim was tiny and crowded. Sometimes Saraswathi's parents made a month-long trip to stay with them, and 'to be with the children' they said!

His eldest son was always into some kind of mischief or the other, always being thrown out of school, always caught being naughty with the girls – the boy's troubles never seemed to cease.

In the end, Father Dominic, the Jesuit priest and principal of the St. Michael's Boys High School, called Saraswathi to the school and handing over Bhaskaran's certificates, he sadly explained to her that he was having trouble routinely with Bhaskaran and that he would have to leave school.

Having no other option, she tried to get him admitted into a 'parallel school', which offered a High School degree from the State Education Authority without her son having to repeat another year in school. She managed to put up enough money and made her son promise her that he would complete High School.

It seemed that the new environment did wonders to Bhaskaran. Not only was the new environment full of school dropouts like him, but for the first time in his life, he also met naughty girls. Nothing could have made him happier and he left home every day without a complaint to his mother, who thought quite naively that her son would finally take his High School exams.

For the first time in his life, here he was freely mingling with girls of his age, teasing them, chatting with them, and being aware of their sexuality.

Bhaskaran had been noticing that in his class there were about fifteen boys and about eight girls. In his previous school, there was a strict dress code – you came to school in uniform. White shirts and charcoal grey trousers!

Here it seemed like another world. Most of the boys would come dressed as they pleased and the girls too adapted this code of conduct. Most of the teachers were retired from various educational institutes and coming in every morning to a job that paid a monthly salary over and above their pensions was more important to them than imparting any quality education to these youngsters.

Invariably, a gang of boys and girls would often bunk classes, going to the Juhu Beach or perhaps to a morning show in a theatre. Some of the girls became attached to some of the boys and soon, the group became further classified on the lines of couples.

In two months of going around Bombay city with several of his new girlfriends, Bhaskaran was quite confident that he could go to a movie theatre with one of them. He knew them all well enough. The girls too were comfortable with him.

Those things suddenly took a backseat in his life when for the first time, he and a bunch of his classmates got involved in a street fight.

It was all due to a girl who lived in same building as Bhaskaran did. She was known to have several boyfriends; she would frequent most parties, and was seen on the terrace smoking cigarettes with guys.

Also, other guys wanted to befriend this girl. Shabnam, was that her name? He couldn't even recall her name properly.

Shabnam used to go to college in town taking a train from Mahim all the way to Churchgate. Sometimes, some Romeo thinking that she was an easy-picking would follow her all the way from town. She was not one of those types. Try saying that to dissuade a street side Romeo. Gosh! These people were die-hard optimists.

So this guy bought a nice-looking rose, got it wrapped in cellophane paper and was waiting for an opportunity to catch her eye, when all at once, he saw another guy trying to do just that. Not for a moment, did he stop to think that Shabnam already knew this guy. His primitive brain running high on sensual pictures of a nude Shabnam would not see reason or logic.

He just presumed that his 'property' was being poached from right under his nose. In disgust, he threw the rose wrapped in cellophane paper in the path of an oncoming train, sensual thoughts now replaced with a menacing thought of revenge.

He had followed Shabnam to her apartment block a couple of times when he thought that he had made mental contact with her. She, oblivious to the fact that she was being followed, led him straight to where she lived.

And today, the man who had 'poached his Shabnam' went into the same building with her. The stalker noticed that they were holding hands while crossing the busy street separating Mahim station and the apartment, and were laughing at each other, walking close to each other.

He ducked into the apartment and for the first time got a glimpse of the complex. The apartment was rather a series of dilapidated buildings built on a large plot of land, as if someone had this wonderful idea of building a wall-cum-apartments; in the middle was a huge open space, which was meant to be the vehicle park. All he saw today was a bunch of young people playing cricket with a tennis ball.

Slowly he slipped out of the complex, went to the nearby phone booth, and made a call.

Within half an hour, six other rough looking gents had come to the apartment block and were casually lounging outside. The stalker animatedly told his friends about what had just happened, and they told him not to worry and that everything would be sorted out.

They had to wait another half hour before the guy who had 'poached' Shabnam appeared at the gate of the complex with about four or five other guys. They seemed to be sharing a joke and to the stalker it seemed that his 'enemy' was telling his friends about how he had enjoyed Shabnam.

Without a word, he walked up to the group, knowing fully well that his group would back him. He asked the man who started it all, point blank – "Who are you, I say?"

The guys who'd just come out were quite startled at the rather rude interruption in their conversation, and one of them asked back quite automatically, "Who are you?"

"See, that girl who lives here with whom you came in today from the station, is mine." The stalker said, motioning with his finger at the guy who seemed to be Shabnam's friend.

"Yeah? Who told you she is your friend? You don't even seem to know her name."

"Look, just back off, okay? I do not want to hurt you guys, but if I have to, I will. Just don't mess around with me," the stalker said.

"Listen, we are four of us here and what is that you can do to all of us," asked Bhaskaran, speaking for the first time.

Suddenly without warning, the other guys in the stalker's group rushed forward and started beating and kicking Bhaskaran and his friends.

Without realising that they too were armed with cricket bats and wooden stumps, this group began to fight back. Bhaskaran first thumped the cricket back hard across a guy who was just piling his huge fist into one of his friends' stomach. The chap just let go of his friend and slumped onto the pavement, crashing like a sack of potatoes.

Another of his friends used a cricket stump and hit one of the attackers on the head, sending a fountain of blood gushing up.

With two of the stalker's army down and all the others in the other group still standing, they suddenly decided to withdraw and carrying their wounded colleagues, hailed a passing taxi and all of them piled in, not before yelling a warning that they would come back.

These boys knew trouble when they saw it and did not know what to do.

By then a small crowd had gathered – curious onlookers and some of the apartment residents. But the group decided not to educate anyone and walked out of the complex to the nearby Irani Tea Shop to discuss further their next move.

Bhaskaran sensed trouble. He knew from the looks of those guys that they would come back and finish what was not completed. They sure were a mean lot.

For twenty minutes, they began to argue about a whole lot of ideas, and he shot them all down.

Finally, he had an idea. His friends, seeing the intensity on his face, fell silent and urged him to continue. "I am going to leave you guys right now. I am going to Dharawi. I am going to meet Moosa Bhai and seek his help. We cannot face these guys on our own. Moosa Bhai will help me. One of you guys cover me at home. In case my mother yells for me, say I am studying with one of you. I will be back before she yells for me again."

Saying this, without waiting for a quorum, he ran out of the Irani Tea Shop, crossed the road and slowed down to a quick walk. It would take him approximately ten minutes of walking to reach Dharawi cutting through the railway lines.

He had not been here before. He had met Moosa and they had become fast friends. But it was always Moosa and his gang who would come to Mahim or they would meet up travelling on the train to the city. He had never been to Dharawi. Somehow, it had never happened.

Today, he felt lost in this seedy and grimy world. He did not know where to find Moosa. All Moosa had told him was that if he ever needed to find him, just come to Dharawi and ask for Moosa Bhai; anyone would point out his *adda*.

The moment he sensed that he was in the bowels of Dharawi, he meekly asked a passer-by if he knew where Moosa Bhai lived. The man shook his head and carried on walking.

Bhaskaran went ahead and came to a taxi stand. He thought this might be a good place to enquire. He went to the first cab in the rank and asked the driver who was reading something in the dim light of a fluorescent street bulb, "Excuse me, do you know where Moosa Bhai lives?"

The cab driver cast one look at him and returning back to his magazine said, "Go further North and look for a signboard that says, Jaffer Tailors, ask there, they will tell you."

Bhaskaran wanted to ask the cabbie what he meant by North, but he sensed that this was all the information that he would ever get.

So he went ahead and the first friendly looking passer-by he encountered, he asked him, "Do you know where Jaffer Tailors is?"

The man looked at Bhaskaran and asked him, rather suspiciously, "Why do you want to know?"

"I was told to go to Jaffer Tailors and ask for Moosa Bhai. I am his friend."

The man looked once more at Bhaskaran and reaching out took his hand and said, "*Arrey Bhai*, you should have said so in the first place. But you were asking for Jaffer Tailors. That is why I was reluctant to give you any information. You see, there is no tailor there now, just a signboard. That is Moosa Bhai's *adda*."

"But never mind, come with me, I am going past there and I will take you myself."

In five more minutes, he was in a dimly-lit shack. It was covered with tin sheets on the outside, lined with jute and cinema posters of a whole lot of movies like some macabre wallpaper on the inside. There seemed to be carpet on the floor, but he was not able to see clearly beyond his arms.

He was shown in and asked to wait alone perhaps for a moment, when the man who brought him here went to inform Moosa or one of his several friends. Then the lights came on. There were sofas of a garish red, some plastic chairs, and a few *gaddis* on the floor. Surprisingly, the room had an air-conditioner.

Turning around, he saw Moosa standing with a big grin on his face. Arms outstretched!

In sheer relief at having found his friend, he ran into Moosa's arms and hugging him, could only say, "Thank you Moosa Bhai, thank you."

Moosa looked at Bhaskaran and asked him, "What brings you here at this hour?"

"I will tell you, first I need some water, and can I sit here?"

"Of course, I have already asked someone to bring you something cold to drink."

He sat down and related everything to Moosa, without missing a single detail.

Moosa smiled, almost relieved. "That's all? I thought you must have got yourself into serious trouble. Don't worry I will send you two of my boys and they will accompany you to your apartment complex. They will spend all of tomorrow and the day after there."

Thanking Moosa once more, Bhaskaran got up. Immediately two villainous-looking characters that he last saw in some bad Hindi movie, appeared out of the darkness and asked him to follow them.

He was back in Mahim in half the time that he had taken to walk to Dharawi.

Two days later, while the gang was playing yet another game of cricket inside the complex parking lot, the stalker arrived, this time with four of his friends, all carrying hockey sticks.

Before they could enter the complex, one of Moosa's men stepped forward and asked him where he was going. The stalker knew that this was no ordinary customer and told him that he had some difference to settle with some boys here.

"We are Moosa Bhai's people. Moosa Bhai has provided protection to this colony. If anything happens to anyone here, I have been instructed to kill first and ask questions later."

The stalker paled at the cool response. He had not anticipated this at all.

"No, there is nothing that serious. These are just ordinary *chokras* and I want to just tell them not to mess around with my girlfriends, that's all."

"Where do you come from?" One of Moosa's men asked.

"We come from town," came the indifferent answer.

"*Abbey*, I know that you have not come from the moon, which part of town?" he growled.

The stalker said, "Churchgate."

"Tell me your name and your father's name."

"My name is Raju. And why do you want to know my fathers name?"

"*Abbey*, if you don't leave here in the next three minutes, I will need to change the shape of your face, and that of your bloody lousy friends here. Then we'll have to call your father to identify you. That is why I need your father's name. Any problems with that?"

With that, he grabbed Raju-the-stalker's shirtfront and almost lifted him.

"No more *bakwas*; if you say anything more, I will drag your backside into Dharawi. I do not want to see you anymore and if you decide to come back and trouble these people, I will personally come to Churchgate, to introduce you to Moosa Bhai's Churchgate man Francis. Together we will redecorate your face, and leave you with enough life so that you can scream when the gutter rats begin picking on your useless flesh. Understood?"

They just backed off. Mahim never ever saw Raju-the-stalker ever again. Moosa never told Bhaskaran or ever reminded him of how he came to his 'rescue'. Although Bhaskaran came good in the eyes of his friends, he never bragged or boasted of the incident. He knew whom he needed to thank.

He just knew that his relationship with Moosa Bhai had not ended there. It had just took on another meaning, escalating the relationship to a higher plateau.

His relationship with his father was barely okay. After more than two decades in the army, he was finally made Captain. By then, he was sick and tired of army life and had decided to quit.

With three children and a wife to feed, living in Bombay was going to be difficult. Yet, he managed to find employment at the offices of KRK Menon. KRK was one of the richest Malayalis in Bombay. He had come to Bombay about three decades ago, hungry and without money. He had worked in restaurants, cleaning dishes, chopping vegetables and cleaning the floors. KRK then came up with the idea of a cash fund that would involve an individual putting up a certain amount of money for a fixed period and then through a system of lots, the person would get his money with a minimal interest at the end of the fixed period. In case the individual wanted to encash of the amount that would be his upon maturity of the fund, he would have to pay a premium to purchase the fund.

KRK decided to call this unique starting point in his life Pankajam Chit Funds. He decided on the name in perpetual honour of his wife, whom he adored.

At the time of KRK starting Pankajam, this seemed a novel idea for the scores of South Indians who had thronged to Bombay upon hearing of fabulous stories of opportunities in this metropolis often referred to as India's Manchester.

In a few years, Pankajam had grown so large that KRK needed people, trustworthy people whom he could trust. And when Captain Bala Govind was recommended to KRK by none other than his own trusted lieutenant, Purshottham Das – a man who had come to Bombay along with KRK, worked in the same kitchens and had slept on the same footpaths of Bombay, KRK did not hesitate. He hired him on the spot to look after his operations in the Mahim, Sion, and Chembur areas. All these places were becoming bastions of the middle-class South Indian families.

When he got this major breakthrough in life and that too so soon after his discharge from the Army, Captain Bala Govind literally threw himself into the job, earning him quick accolades. For someone who had served the Army for so many years and for someone who had to really perform to get recognition, this was music to his ears.

Quickly his reputation enhanced and within a short while he found himself inducted into the coterie of decision-makers, that KRK surrounded himself with and consulted on all major decisions. Once you were through this coterie, you were on your way to becoming a name to reckon with. Already in the Captain's limited social circles, he was being called Pankajam Bala Govind. He was enjoying this life, the importance of being known to be close to KRK, be seen at his parties and hobnobbing with the rich and powerful in Bombay city.

On the other hand, for Saraswathi and the children, it was not so great a life. The children began to develop an aversion for these 'high society parties' as they called it. This was primarily because they never had the fancy clothes and the fancy shoes that the other children had. They never went to the high snob value schools that the other children had the privilege of studying in. Sure, all three of them could speak well – in Malayalam, which of course was their mother tongue, and in English and Hindi. But the schools that they went to were steeped in middle class values and traditions and this showed up when the children went to the parties that KRK, and his coterie threw, it seemed, always. There was no reason for a party – just the smallest excuse was good enough for a party. Then of course, expense was hardly an issue.

Saraswathi too felt as the children did. She could not speak English as fluently as the other wives did. She did not have the kind of jewellery that the other wives wore and she did not have the very expensive saris and never had the perfumes that the other women doused themselves in.

Rather than complain to her husband, she pretended to be busy with the children and their education. Her only concern was Bhaskaran. He seemed to have his own agenda in life. He was not bothered about his father's advice. He never made friends on the same criteria that his brother chose friends – English speaking, good family, and no *lafda* type of friends. His friends were mostly from the slums, could never speak a word of English, and were the kite-flying, hell-raising variety of kids. His sister was constantly tagging along with him and so a lot of his character rubbed off onto her. His brother and his sister were the studious types. They had only one agenda – to stay on top of the class – always.

Saraswathi remembered speaking to a tuition teacher once who remarked, "I find it difficult to believe that you have these two excellent students and that you are the same mother of a ruffian too!"

Every year she had to accompany him to Father Dominic's office and she would promise that she would ensure that he would get good grades so that the school would promote him to the next class.

But threats and coercions would go a short way, if one did not exert one's will to change oneself. Within a short while, Bhaskaran's grades would again plummet.

Slowly, Bhaskaran's dad became increasingly involved with his duties at Pankajam and the distance between him and his family increased.

Bala Govind told Saraswathi clearly that she would have to join him on the social circuit as he was fed up excusing her from the various social events that he found himself being invited to, saying that she was home looking after the kids. In desperation, she wrote home to her parents and they, knowing that this was also a way out of their financial predicament on the one hand and a face-saving formula out of their poverty, 'reluctantly' agreed to come to Bombay to stay with their daughter and son-in-law 'to look after their grandchildren'. After all, they had never lived in a cooped-up apartment all their lives and leaving the plush Parappuram Tharavaad, with the surrounding gardens *et al*, was something unthinkable! However, since it was for their daughter, well, they would oblige.

Speaking to KRK, explaining the circumstances about the fact that he, Bala Govind, was not able to spend quality time with his children, had decided to ask his in-laws to come and live with him in Bombay so that his 'worry' about the children's moral and traditional upbringing, would come to an end. KRK knew where this was leading to – an appeal for a larger flat and perhaps an increment in the salary. He knew a good man, without a doubt, Bala Govind was doing a good job, and had he found a rather professional kind of an employee, he would be paying him much more than he was paying Bala Govind. Without further ado, he promptly made a decision.

A promotion and a substantial increment was announced for Captain Bala Govind, along with a car for himself and for the use of his family. The family had for the first time in their lives a company provided car.

It was to these 'luxuries' that Saraswathi's parents were brought to, and from here on, life would change for them all.

19

Moosa

Bhaskaran began to see more of Moosa Bhai. He began to get to know him better and better. Moosa developed a feeling of affinity towards Bhaskaran and something in the young boy drew him closer to him.

He urged Bhaskaran to study well at school. Bhaskaran would look at him, "Now, you don't give me the same lecture."

"See Bhaskaran, I am only telling you from an older brother's perspective. I did not have anyone to guide me or mentor me. I just became what circumstances made out of me."

"But what's the point in studying when so many who have already graduated have no jobs?" Bhaskaran would ask.

"That's because, in life, it's just not enough to have a piece of paper that says you have graduated," Moosa would patiently explain, "Life is more than that. You have to know what you want to do in life and then when you aim for that one job with your heart and your mind and your soul, believe me when I tell you, you will get it and don't let anyone tell you that you cannot." Moosa advised.

"I have learnt the hard way that intention is important. If you don't have any intentions, an underlying intent in your life – how can you blame anyone if you did not make it in life? After all, you yourself did not have any keen intent?" Moosa would say.

"I have become what I have become because I intended to become the Number One in my business. I have no shame to tell you that. I was tired of being poor. I promised myself that I'd never be poor again. In a manner of speaking, my dear boy, when the intent is strong enough, the will is shaped," Moosa told Bhaskaran.

"There was never a time that I was not aware of my intention. Such was my awareness of my intent, such was my total mindfulness of my intent and such was the power that it created within me, I had barely any time for anything called fun and games," Moosa said reminiscing about his growing up years.

"These things I felt. I knew a long before I became the man I am today that I would be out of Dharawi. I knew even before I left Dharawi that I would someday have enough money. Such was the belief of my intent and such was the intensity of the faith that my intent caused in me, that I'd no doubt that I would make it in life. And then I came across a teacher who taught me that one only dreams of what one can fulfil. I don't dream of being an astronaut. Life calls me to do what I must do. If I have the guts to follow my dreams, then I will touch them," Moosa said.

"And that is why I want you to become the stuff of your dreams. You should not become another street urchin. You come from a good family. That is your environment. Sure your father may not be the richest man in the world today – so what? You can become better than he ever did in his life? But how can that happen if you are not seeing the future? And let me tell you this Bhaskaran – the future is nothing but what you see of it. If you don't see it, then you have no future. If you see it and if you see it in the manner, in which you want to see it, so will it be," Moosa told Bhaskaran.

"I remember hearing the tale of Aladdin and the Magic Lamp. Have you heard the tale?" Moosa asked the young boy.

"Yes, I've heard of it," Bhaskaran said.

"What does the genie of the lamp tell Aladdin?" Moosa asked Bhaskaran.

"Hmm... Let me think... Yes, I know. Your wish is my command is what the genie tells Aladdin," said Bhaskaran.

"Right you are, my friend. And so it is with your mind. You must command it. You must control it and you must order it. Then your brain will do what you want it to do. Never ever doubt the capability of the brain. Never ever doubt that there is not an iota of difference between the greatest man that walked this earth and you. For you are both cast by the same Hand that created this Earth and for it is said that He created Man in His image. What you are capable of doing is more than you will ever know, till you have discovered who you are," Moosa told Bhaskaran.

"I have heard that the greatest athlete and the greatest of businessmen say that they believed they could do what they achieved to do it before they actually did it. I've wondered at that. So is the athlete saying that he actually ran that special race in his mind before he actually ran it? If that's right then what I believe is also right – That your thought is what causes the action. So in a nutshell – unless you think it, it does not happen," Moosa said to Bhaskaran.

"And then the biggest question that I would like to ask you and which you should ask yourself time and time over again is simply – Who do you want to be? That is the biggest question that you can ask yourself, in my opinion. That quest will take you to places that you'd never dreamt you go to; it will take you to people whom you'd never thought possible of meeting, and it will finally take you to where you wanted to be," Moosa explained to Bhaskaran.

"For the moment you answer that question in all the honesty of your being, knowing who you are and having an inclination of where you want to go – there is no way that it will let you become anything else than you wanted to be," Moosa said.

Sometimes when time permitted, Moosa would take Bhaskaran to the imposing Gateway of India. From there, sitting on a convenient perch, looking up at the swank Taj Mahal Hotel, he would put a hand on Bhaskaran's shoulder and tell him, pointing at the Taj, "One day, I want you to be able to sit there. Enter that lifestyle! Not stand here and look from the outside with envy and a fond hope on your face. If you want to make that happen – then you need to do something. You can make a lot of money, either as I am doing now or you become successful in the traditional method – get a good job or be employed in a good company. I do not want you to become another me. I will help you – pay for your education, clothes, whatever. But you have to do it." Moosa said, looking deep into Bhaskaran's eyes. Moosa looked down at the concrete bulwarks that were strewn around the Gateway of India to prevent soil erosion.

Just beyond them, the Arabian Sea lapped at these bulwarks, in giant gurgling sounds.

"Look at that," he said pointing at the seawater.

"There is a rhythm and movement to everything – including life, the breath we take, the moves we make, the things we think of, and the things we want," he said to Bhaskaran.

"You need to touch that rhythm and movement, discover it and then life's Pandora Box becomes less of a mystery."

"It's beautiful, when you can feel the rhythm, the movement. Then nothing puts you off. You know just like the dry bed at the beach which was only full of water last week, that the water will come back – with the rhythm and movement of the earth. There's no need to feel any disappointment, if you will only understand," Moosa told Bhaskaran.

"But it's important to establish one's intent. And with undying commitment, hold onto that intent till it has become established. Till it has become what we sought, seek it without rest, and work towards it. Your intent, as I have proved beyond any reasonable doubt in my own life, will become your life," he said.

"I agree," Bhaskaran said wholeheartedly.

Moosa smiled at the younger man. "The point is not to agree but to simply see. You see, when we do we begin to listen. When we begin to listen, we begin to open. When we open, our world becomes limitless. In that state, everything can teach us to see more than we in our adultness have ever seen or comprehended. That is the awareness that you need to develop, Bhaskaran. Coming into our own is not about luck or destiny or fate, it is these things that I have told you about."

Moosa said, "Yes, awareness, being aware of the rhythm and movement, listen to it," he said putting his hand on his chest, "You can even hear the thud of your heart, in the stillness of your breath... listen... we make too much noise.... For everything comes softly and quietly – such as life when it is breathed into a baby and as death when it comes in its deathly quiet."

Bhaskaran had never seen Moosa like this… in this avatar. It seemed to Bhaskaran that an ***Angel of God*** had just appeared in his life, taken hold of his hand and said to him, pointing to a strange path ahead of him, "Go, that is the path that you have to take, walk along it. Never turn back and never give up. You have to win."

He threw his hands around Moosa and told him, "Moosa Bhai, I love you with all my heart. I promise you that I will never ever disappoint you. Here is my life, take it and make whatever you can of it. I just want to win. I do not want to live in Mahim for the rest of my life and I do not want to make do, every day."

"*Arrey Raja*, you don't have to do anything. Have the desire to win, have the optimism to go on despite the odds, knowing deep in your heart that even if there is something that Moosa cannot do for you, he will get it for you from somewhere else. Just win. You have to conquer the world," Moosa said with a smile.

Buying themselves some *chana* from a vendor, they would walk down the waterfront, deeply engrossed in conversation, each leaning on the other, not using each other, but just feeling each other's hearts, each other's souls and the trust between them developing into a bonding harmony of one thought, one emotion.

They both knew very well that some strange quirk of fate had brought them together, the thought crossing their minds simultaneously, they looked at each other and they held hands, only a smile on their faces, the setting sun throwing shadows way ahead of them, their thoughts bonding them better than any conversation that ordinary human beings passing by would never comprehend.

20

The Final Metamorphosis

Bhaskaran's attitude saw a sea change. No longer was he bunking classes, he became a top ranker and people wondered at this change. Suddenly, life had a purpose and he knew that he was wasting his life until then – only because there seemed to be no purpose. Just the other day, his Maths teacher wanted to know the name of his private tuitions teacher. Bhaskaran only smiled because he knew that he had no private tuitions at all.

Today was a day that most Bombayites hated. The rain was lashing Bombay and traffic was crawling, the trains were late and yet, Bhaskaran made it to school. He knew that most of the students would 'know' that there would be no school today; the teachers would absent themselves knowing that the students were not going to come.

After a difficult journey and an hour and a half later, he was in class, which, as he had guessed was deserted.

He peeped into his class and there was not a soul there either. As he came down the stairs, he saw Eddie, the Anglo-Indian peon, clerk, part-time cashier, lunch boy, the head master's eyes and ears and as far as Bhaskaran was concerned – a nice guy who did what he did because he had no other choices in life.

Eddie had a huge plastic sack slit down the side, which he used as a cloak to cover his head and back. Not that it did much good, because he seemed to be wet – and still that did not dampen his smile, exposing all of his tobacco rotten teeth despite a shudder now and then running through his thin frame.

Eddie spoke to Bhaskaran in perfect English, the language being his mother tongue. Bhaskaran always spoke to Eddie in English and that too, respectfully. Never abused him as the others did, never teased him, never taunted him, and never insulted him. Eddie liked Bhaskaran. The boy, he thought, had some class.

"Ole man has declared today a holiday, Basky," Eddie was also the only person in his life that called him Basky.

"Couple of your mates were here, but they left a while ago. I am going to be leaving in a while. I am just waiting for it to clear up a bit before I walk to the station."

"Okay Eddie, you go on and leave the gate open. In case someone else comes along, I will tell them."

He walked around absently to some of the other locked classrooms and on the library padlock, he found the morning's newspapers tucked in. Eddie had forgotten to open the locked office doors and place the newspapers inside.

Sitting cross-legged on the floor, which was actually a corridor, he opened the soggy newspapers and began going through the headlines.

It screamed at him, 'Underworld Don Moosa Arrested' – he scanned through the news.

In a sweeping raid that the Police had conducted under the aegis of a new Commissioner of Police, Moosa was taken into custody. The Police had arrested them on a specific charge of extortion. It said that their kingpin was arrested last night. Bhaskaran knew that the Police had arrested Moosa instinctively. He scanned through the news item again and realised that the police station mentioned was not far from the school.

Standing up slowly, reading the rest of the news without digesting anything, Bhaskaran headed for the staircase.

He ran most of the way to the Police station and then he did not know what to do. He just stood opposite the police station and hung around a teashop. There was not too much of a crowd in the teashop and he just stood there, pretending to take shelter from the rain, like a few others before him.

Some of them were talking in hushed tones, and Bhaskaran latched onto every word, listening to a conversation for a few seconds and if that made any reference to Moosa continued listening, otherwise moving onto the next group of gossipers.

"*Arrey Bhai*, they are going to make that Moosa Bhai retire," one of the speakers said, confirming what he'd feared most. That Moosa was arrested and was held here in this police station.

"But, what is the police's problem, *yaar*? Moosa Bhai is doing good for the people of Dharawi, there are no problems there and sure he takes money from the rich, but he is giving most of that to the poor, *yaar*," another speaker said.

"That's the main problem. He should have given the police also a cut. You cannot survive in Bombay without taking care of the police," a third speaker said.

"Anyway, let's just wait and see what happens now."

"This new commissioner is a real daredevil; he does not care for his own life, they say?"

"A new broom always sweeps clean, *yaar*. But for how long?"

"Quiet, here comes a policeman. Don't say anything more unless you also want to be inside the cooler!"

Just then, the sound of boots hitting stagnant water puddles and a voice that sounded very important, or at least was trying to sound important said, "*Arrey*, send half a dozen *chai* to the *thaana*. And send them all in good cups. Don't send them in your usual lousy glasses."

Before the tea master could say that his usual *chai* delivery boy had not turned up for work, Bhaskaran edged forward and holding the tea master's hand said, "I will take it across, master."

The tea master never asked him who he was and what he was doing there, he was just relieved that someone was available to deliver the tea.

Putting six porcelain cups on saucers, he measured tea and mixed it with the watered down milk. Holding an aluminium mug taped with coir rope on the handle in one hand, he measured twelve spoons of sugar and taking another mug in his other hand, he raised the mug containing the tea high above his head.

With one swift action, he poured the tea into the other mug with a flourish. Then once more, back into the other mug and then briskly, he poured it into the cups.

Placing them all onto an ancient chopping board that also doubled up as a serving tray, he used a piece of a cardboard box to cover the tea from the rain and gave this to Bhaskaran. "Go, cross the roads carefully, wait for the cops to finish and then bring the cups back. Don't talk to anyone and if they ask for the other boy, say he did not turn up today. And remember, don't ask them for money either."

Bhaskaran just nodded, his heart, his mind, and his body already inside the police station.

He entered the police station, and saw the constable who had come to place the order. He in turn saw the boy and called him over.

Taking one cup, he told Bhaskaran, "Go inside and give one cup to the *Sahab*, then the other two sitting adjacent to him. Go inside the room and there you will see a man sitting on a bench by the wall. Give him a cup and wait for him to finish and then come back with the empty cups."

Without looking up at Bhaskaran to find out if he had understood the instructions, the constable was already busy pouring the still steaming tea onto his saucer from where he would slurp it – drinking tea in the typical fashion of the rural tea drinker.

Bhaskaran went in, his heart hammering. This was the first time that he was in a police station. He knew that if someone, anyone, asked him what he was doing there, he would not be able to speak because his mouth was dry, his tongue sticking onto his palate, and he just knew that his teeth were glued to the insides of his mouth.

He walked on inside where he saw a tall man sitting at a desk with his feet on the desk and two other constables sitting on tables opposite the tall mans table. In one glance, he knew that this tall man was not a constable. He just knew that. He walked to him first and said, "*Saab, chai.*" The words came out in a voice that even Bhaskaran did not recognise.

The man was reading a newspaper and he put that down, swung his feet off the table, and nodded towards the table. Reaching into his trouser pocket, moving his holstered revolver out of the way, he reached into his pocket for a packet of cigarettes.

Tapping his hands over his trousers and then his shirt pockets, he looked at the constable and said, "Pandey, give me a match."

Pandey jumped and rushed forward, a lighter magically appearing in his huge hands, already lit and the flame totally hidden in his fist and leaning reverentially before the tall man, lit his cigarette.

The man reached for his cup of tea and sipped it. He then looked at Bhaskaran and said, "Well, what are you staring at? Give them their tea before it becomes as cold as you are."

He moved over to the other two constables who took a cup each and then one of them getting up, told Bhaskaran to follow him into the other room.

There, lying on a bench was Moosa. The constable said, "Moosa Bhai, have some tea." He then left the room.

Moosa Bhai did not get up. He just turned on the narrow stool and looked at the boy. He stared, not believing his own eyes, then looking past the boy at the doorway and seeing no one there, sat up. Still bewildered at Bhaskaran's presence in the police station, he asked in a whisper, "How did you get here?"

"Shh..." warned Bhaskaran, "Drink your tea and tell me if you want me to do anything."

Moosa's mind was racing. He had covered this police station in his monthly handouts. He had tried talking to the new inspector. Handpicked by the new Commissioner, he was hell-bent on showing the Commissioner of Police what he was capable of achieving. Despite Moosa's continued pleas, he was adamant. He said that he would be satisfied only if Moosa was arrested and produced before the magistrate the next day in order to be remanded to judicial custody.

They had not allowed Moosa to make a call. They knew his influence and they had not taken a chance.

Moosa looked at Bhaskaran and talking without moving his lips, he said, "Memorise this number, and make a call. Say that Moosa needs you urgently. That is all you need to say. If they ask you who you are, say that you are my brother. Give them the location of this police station."

He had finished one cup. Reaching into the tray, he placed his empty cup, he took the remaining one and began drinking from it.

"Remember one more number, this is a very important one also. Will you get confused?"

"No, I have a good memory. Don't worry," Bhaskaran smiled at Moosa.

"Okay, this other number is a minister's number. Call him and tell him again that you are my brother and that I asked you to call me. Then tell him to come here. Give him also directions to the police station and tell him to come here before they take me to the court."

A thousand questions sprang to Bhaskaran's mind. Moosa sensing them in the youngster's eyes ruffled his wet hair and said,

"Don't worry. You just make these calls. I will come to see you at Mahim Irani Tea Shop. Do you have any money on you?"

"No, just bus fare and some change."

"Never mind here, take some," Moosa pulled out a few notes from his pocket and gave them to Bhaskaran, "Go and make those calls."

Taking the empty cups, he bent low and touched Moosa's feet and with tears filling up his eyes looked up at the man that he loved, "I am going to Mahim Church to pray for you today; come back to us, in good shape."

Moosa smiled a hint of a tear in his eye, the love for the youngster visible. He tousled Bhaskaran's hair again and propelled him towards the doorway.

Picking up the other empty cups from the others, he crossed the street and into the teashop and into a barrage of questions from the tea master to all the other onlookers.

He ducked them all, said something about having to go and eat something, and ran out of the shop.

He found an STD booth with a bored operator who was quite intently picking his ears with an old toothpick. Bhaskaran asked him if it was okay to make a couple of local calls.

"Okay, but it will cost you double."

Remembering that he was carrying a lot of money, he shook his head, walked into the small booth, and closing the door behind him.

Standing there, he scribbled the two numbers on the palm of his hand. He thought for a while, forming the sentences in his mind. Satisfied, he dialled the first number and on the second ring a voice answered.

"Hello, *kaun*?"

"I am Moosa's brother. They have arrested him and are holding him at the Ghatkopar Police Station. He sent word through someone asking me to call you and tell you this. Please speak to the necessary people and have him released."

"How do I know that this is not a joke?" The voice asked.

"I would not have your number and this is not a joke," Bhaskaran tried to sound older and very serious.

"Call me back in ten minutes." The voice said.

"Okay, I will call back." Hanging up, Bhaskaran dialled the second number and this time the phone rang a while. He realised that he was given only the numbers and not the names of the persons that he was asked to speak to. Moosa would have a reason for doing so, he told himself.

This time the phone kept ringing and after almost an eternity and several urges from Bhaskaran to pick up the phone, a sleepy voice answered the phone.

"Ha, *kaun*?"

He repeated the same thing once more and this time the man at the other end did not ask him to call back. He just said that he would do whatever was necessary.

Hanging up the phone, he walked to the operator and paid him ten rupees. The man opened his cash box put the money in and went back to digging his ears.

Walking in the rain, which was now a constant drizzle, he was on the lookout for another telephone booth. Seeing one in the distance, he ran towards it.

There were a few people ahead of him and he knew that he could wait.

In a few minutes, all the people ahead of him and someone who had come after him had made their calls. He picked up the receiver and dialled the first number.

It seemed that the phone had barely rung when the voice at the other end said, "It will be taken care of."

He hung up and walked back to the teashop, opposite the police station. This time he did not go right up to the teashop. His mind imagining that some constable would be right there, looking for him or the tea master wondering who the boy was might be looking for him. So he stood a few shops away under the awning of a textile shop, which still had not opened its shutters.

He had barely waited for about twenty minutes when three cars drew up. From one, a middle-aged man got off, and the moment the armed police guard noticed who he was, he stiffened and held his chest erect, bringing his 303 Lee Enfield Rifle up, in a salute.

The other two constables, whom Bhaskaran had seen inside with the inspector, came out and seeing the visitor saluted him.

Five minutes later, the visitor was back in his car and once he was comfortably seated in the back, the escort cars and the visitors' car disappeared into the drizzle and beyond.

Puzzled, Bhaskaran kept gazing at the entrance. He looked the way the cars had gone and by the time his gaze was back at the entrance of the police station, his eyes nearly popped out.

Standing at the entrance, with the two police constables flanking him was Moosa, stretching and yawning as if he had just come out of his house, pleasantly surprised at the rain and looking up at the grey sky. He said something to the constables, who both looked at him and smiled.

One of the constables looked around and spotting a cruising taxi hailed it. He said something to the driver and the man leaned back and opened the rear door.

Settling into the back of the Fiat taxi, Moosa gave him directions and it shot off from the police station as if it had stayed there for far too long.

Bhaskaran looked at the teashop where the master, the curious onlookers, and a few others were all standing in the rain, looking amused and confused at the happenings, and wondering what had just happened.

The tea master seemed rather disappointed. Then it struck Bhaskaran – this man was hoping that Moosa Bhai would be there for a while longer so that he would be able to sell as many cups of tea as would be possible.

"Arrey Bhai, I told you, Moosa Bhai has connections. I told you, that when Moosa Bhai calls, even Ministers come. That was whom you saw just now in the white Ambassador. The honourable Home Minister himself."

The others looked at the speaker, still wondering in amazement.

Bhaskaran took a train and went back home to Mahim. His mother seeing him drenched threw a towel at him and asked him to dry himself.

He felt that the whole incident was like a dream and he was waiting to see Moosa again.

Bhaskaran never realised that he had inadvertently played a big part in Moosa's life and that Moosa would never forget this day for as long as he lived.

It seemed to Bhaskaran that the hours of the clock were somehow stuck. He had glanced at the clock several times. Finally when the clock, which his father had got from his father on his twenty-first birthday struck five, he yelled to his mother that he was going to play cricket and before she could say anything, he was out of the front door, taking the stairs two at a time and out of the apartment complex.

He ran all the way across the corner to Mahim's most famous Irani Tea Shop, which was now thronging with people returning home or coming in from the Mahim Station – he looked around. He darted into the crowded shop and looked around. Seeing no one he knew, and slightly disappointed, he came out on the street and was lounging against the wall. One leg propped on the shop wall and leaning against it, he saw a taxi stop in front of the shop and Moosa in the back.

His joy knew no bounds. He ran the couple of paces to the taxi, yanked the door open, and rushed into the rear seat. Looking relaxed, wearing a cream shirt with some white Chinese looking letters running on side and a dark trouser, Moosa sat with a smile that was at once special and Bhaskaran knew, just for him.

"How are you, Moosa Bhai?" He exclaimed.

"How did you come to see me?" Moosa asked him.

"Well, I went to school this morning, saw the newspapers and came running to the police station."

"Okay, but how did you manage to get into the police station with the tea?" Moosa wanted to know.

"Oh that? I knew the teashop owner," Bhaskaran said with an impish grin.

"Yeah? I thought that teashop was owned by your father," Moosa said jokingly.

Moosa was holding Bhaskaran's hand in his like a father would hold his son's and Bhaskaran was turned around facing Moosa, talking excitedly a thousand questions racing in his mind, only a handful coming out.

Suddenly, he realised that he had Moosa's money with him and reaching into his hip pocket, he pulled out a small wad of wet notes.

Handing it over to Moosa he said, "You gave me an awful lot of money to make two phone calls."

Taking the money from Bhaskaran, Moosa looked at him fondly and said, "This and a lot more of this would not have got me to a phone. Allah brought you to me this morning. Otherwise, I would not be sitting here. You know they wanted to produce me in court before the Home Minister was even aware of the arrest. He knew that some arrests were made, but he was not told that I was also arrested. Only after you spoke to him did he know."

"So that was a real Minister whom I spoke to this morning," Bhaskaran asked in awe. This was indeed the first time that he had spoken to a Minister in his entire life.

"Yes, and he is also a very decent human being, my friend," Moosa said.

Bhaskaran smiled.

"You know, the police do not have a clue as to how I managed to send a word to the Minister. They are very upset. Thanks to you."

"Bhai, where should we go to?" The taxi driver asked.

"Dharawi. Where else?" Moosa said.

"I do not want you speaking about today to anyone, you understand?" Moosa told Bhaskaran, "I am sure that there will be a lot of curious people including my own people wondering how I managed to get out, and I do not want your name figured anywhere. Do you understand?"

Bhaskaran nodded.

"Does that mean I cannot see you anymore?" Bhaskaran asked.

"I will give you a number. Memorise it and call that number whenever you need me. We will meet somewhere. However, we will not be able to meet like this for a while now. At least until things are a bit quiet."

The car had pulled up outside the same building where Bhaskaran had met Moosa a few weeks ago.

Inside, there was food and some gifts. There was no one else there.

"Come, I want to have something to eat with you and then I want to give you something."

"But Moosa Bhai, it's very early to eat," Bhaskaran complained. He just wanted to talk to Moosa and ask him more about his world. Apparently, Moosa had other plans.

"Eat early today, it's not going to harm you," Moosa chided him.

Sitting there with Moosa, Bhaskaran felt very proud. This was a moment that he knew, very few people experienced. This very private moment with the great Moosa Bhai!

"Now I want to tell you something. I have connections in the university. I want you to study well now, concentrate on your studies, and top your exams. I want you to become the best university product that your family ever had. Then one day, when you are ready, I want you to go abroad, study some more. Study about how the *goras* run their companies so well. Then I want you to come back. I want you to start something here in India. And I want you to know that I am with you one hundred percent. I will give you all the support that you will ever need. Remember this one thing – the world is going to be your stage. Not Dharawi, not Mahim not Bombay not India, but the world, and I want you to be remembered for being this wonderful, excellent and successful executive from India. That is my dream for you. That is a part of my life, which I can never become. But which I want you to fulfil for me! And I know that I can trust you. I just want you to live it. Live your dreams; become your wildest imagination. Money is not going to be a criterion for you to give up on your dreams. I know that there is no competition in Bombay for me. It's only a matter of time before I control the whole of Bombay. But I know also that I cannot wear the mask of decency ever. The world will continue to remind me of the gutter from where I rose. Never mind that. You will not become another Moosa Bhai. I will not let you do that. You are going to become the master and the brain behind a business empire. A completely legit one. Do you understand me, Bhaskaran?"

Moosa looked like he was talking from somewhere deep beyond his being. His whole countenance was lit up, he was looking deep into Bhaskaran's eyes, poring into the young man's mind, touching a part of that young absorbing soul and creating all at once a moment of sheer beauty and absolute magic for the young boy.

Once more it seemed to Bhaskaran that the Angel of God had touched him, sending goose pimples running down the length of his body, his eyes brimming with tears of gratitude, hope and a lack of words to thank this man – whom so many feared as 'The Enemy'.

For the second time in the day, he felt himself lowering his head and this time he placed it on Moosa's feet, whispering to them, "I owe you my life."

Pulling him up by his shoulders, Moosa said, "Okay, now that I have told you what I have to tell you, I want you to eat with me. Eat well and then go home. Tell no one about it. The next time I see you I want to see how much forward you have worked your way to the goal that I have set before you."

With that, both of them sat down to one of the best meals that Bhaskaran had had in recent times. *Biriyani* from the famous Mohammed Ali Restaurant where even the rich stood in queue to buy their famous and indeed, very tasty, *Hyderabadi Biriyani*, onion *raitha,* boiled eggs fried in a batter to a golden brown delicious look and *Ras Malai* in clay pots.

Almost an hour later, when the taxi dropped him off at Mahim station, he was wondering what he was going to tell his mother about skipping dinner. He also had forgotten the wristwatch that Moosa had strapped on to his wrist. It was a gleaming new watch and he was worried what his mother would think. Slipping it off his wrist, he shoved it into his underwear. He would hide it somewhere in the flat; and sometime later, he would produce it and claim that he won it a prize for something. He would need to conjure up a believable story for them.

21

Kozhikode, A Few Years Later

The city was becoming smaller, Abubacker told himself. The number of cars on the road seemed to increase at a pace that was almost overwhelming. He was quite amused at this whole process. Ask someone for some money and all you would get was the entire gamut of excuses for not granting you your request for a loan. A look at the jewellery shops and the sari shops, revealed another story. You could not find an inch of space inside these huge shops to stand. People were buying. Property, gold, new vehicles, you name it – but there was this whole façade building exercise too.

Here only God was your banker, and you knew just how much money you had. No, not the government, they are not privy to such information, which even your wife did not know of. The government was only told what you deem is necessary for them to know. Nothing more, nothing less. Be that your annual taxes or the stamp duty on the purchase of a plot of land. The government usually did lose money.

So the charade of being a very simple-minded businessman or just another ordinary housewife, even though you might be very well off in order that your immediate circle of friends, relatives and well-wishers – and not necessarily in that order – did not ask you for undue favours was a game that was ceaselessly played.

In a larger context, perhaps the whole tapestry of Kerala was a story with a similarity to this mindset. You could look around you, you would find narrow lanes that have always been narrow, open sewers, creaking infrastructure and swanky houses that Non Resident Indians built with the money they were pumping into the state. They stood side by side the legacy of a bygone socialism hanging on as some mist shrouding one of the beautiful hills on the several mountain ranges of Kerala. Abubacker wondered if there was one industry that had sustained its growth and had contributed either to its own investors or to its immediate community.

He had heard some talk of how the Capitals of Socialism in the former USSR and indeed in China were crumbling. While he thought that the Chinese were smart – his kind of people he often mused – who embraced the opportunities and exposures that Capitalism offered – they just changed a few rules and continued to brand themselves as a Socialist driven economy and country.

It seemed to him a funny thought that on the one hand you could have a piece of statistic that every Malayali was proud of – a 100% literacy state and on the other hand – a state with minimum industrial growth. For him the rules of the game were simple. If he invested in a business proposition, he would like to see money making money. This, according to his auditor Shankaran Pillai, was called return on investment. Well, he had told Shankaran Pillai, you do not need a degree and a college education to understand that. You just needed common sense. Shankaran Pillai was wise enough not to argue uselessly with a client who was one of his best paymasters and a master survivor. Apart from that, Shankaran Pillai did agree with that rustic piece of argument that money has to make money.

Unfortunately, in Kerala, Abubacker thought, in comparison with the other cities and states in India – the will to succeed, the spirit of entrepreneurship were not really burning high here. If someone did venture in with enough capital, goodwill and love for the soil that he was born into – then in a couple of months this same institution or person, would become yet another disgruntled investor. Either the unions would kill his spirit or the errant power supply would or if either of these did not – the politics would.

On his several visits to meet Moosa in Jeddah and Dubai, he was surprised to see Malayalis from his own Kerala, who were very successful either in jobs or in enterprises of their own. He knew that a majority of them had to sell meagre and only belongings of either gold or land, in order to pay for a passage to these Middle East havens of opportunity and promise. He felt that they were successful here because there was no politics of any kind – just work and more work. There were incentives provided to enterprise here and there were no two ways about the way an entrepreneur would go if all the inputs that he needed is provided along with his own will to make it work.

It seemed that a new initiative like the new Nedumbassery Airport just outside Cochin, was the answer forward. Here, private investors parted with hard-earned money in collaboration with the state and Centre to produce an excellent facility. The building and its facility stands mute testament to the fact.

Change had to come, he thought. If progress was the mantra which Kerala needed, he knew that people would have to speak one language – that of enterprise. If people thought they deserved a better tomorrow for their children and for themselves, they needed to have one religion where the prayer was in progress. The government under the aegis of a visionary bureaucrat had created a slogan that marketed alongside the pristine natural beauty of Kerala that attracted hordes of tourists. They called it God's Own Country. It indeed was, it still is. Except that God in his Eternal Wisdom granted Kerala the riches that a Saudi Arabia did not have – natural beauty along with lush natural greenery, flora and fauna that the human eye might not behold in the most exotic locales of this world, usually. In His Eternal Wisdom, God also did not grant Kerala the financial wealth that He bestowed upon countries like Saudi Arabia.

No wonder, Abubacker thought wryly, they say God is Wise. He rarely gives everything to one entity.

In his own growing empire, Abubacker on Moosa's direct instruction ensured one aspect. Every one who worked for him directly or indirectly was inspired to grow. Human aspiration was encouraged without trampling on other's sentiments and emotions, without politics. Every day he constantly reminded himself of his own meteoric rise, of how he had become a part and parcel of the Kozhikode elite, an acceptable version of society and an example of enterprise growing alongside the will of wanting to create something, not just for oneself but also for one's society, country and family.

From gold running, Abubacker had graduated to money laundering and today he controlled the entire market for the major deals. Only the small fry – remittances of salaries from the working blue collar class from the Middle East, petty smuggling were left to the others. If he was not directly involved in a deal, then he provided the protection and these days it was not just muscle protection, but protection from prosecution at the highest levels.

When one of the major transport operators of lorries and buses which went on to cover the entire South of India went bankrupt and that organisation's entire infrastructure that was created painstakingly over a period of almost fifty years was about to collapse, he stepped in. Suddenly and dramatically, Shankaran Pillai appeared at the office of the Managing Director of BMD Transport with an offer to buy him out – lock, stock and barrel for an amount of money that made the Managing Director want to cringe.

"I cannot sell for such a paltry sum," he said indignantly.

"If you wait another week, the creditors will take away all that you have, and then what will you do?" Shankaran Pillai asked.

"I am talking to a few other people also," the BMD honcho said.

"You can talk to the Prime Minister of India, and even he will not be able to save you. We know everything there is to know; otherwise you think that Abubacker will send me here?" Shankaran Pillai asked, donning the role of a suave takeover banker that he never was, with almost dramatic perfection.

"Give me a couple of days, I will talk to my board, and if they agree, I will get back to you," BMD's Managing Director said.

"We know each and every member of your board and you can call each of them on the telephone while I wait outside. They will all agree. I can give you two hours, not two days. If you do not come back to me within two hours, we will still take over your company, not from you but from your creditors. It is entirely your choice. Forget your ego, forget your broken dreams, and accept this offer. Abubacker was quite emphatic that you do not lose your stature in this society of ours; he knows how your father built this company up brick by brick and he would not like to see you leave here a broken man," Shankaran Pillai said, standing up to pick up his briefcase.

A decision was indeed taken, not in two days, not in two hours, within fifteen minutes. The board decided to meet later in the day at the company headquarters near Velliangadi and by six in the evening, BMD had a new boss and a new lease on its life.

The next morning Abubacker had installed Shankaran Pillai as the acting MD and he asked Shankaran Pillai to communicate to every employee of BMD of the new turn of events and asking them to actively support the new management in its quest forward.

Within a short span of time, BMD had almost doubled its fleet capacity, its employees were smiling for the first time in a long time, and Shankaran Pillai assured Abubacker with facts and figures that he was actually seeing his money grow.

In Beypore, however, things were not so rosy for Syyed Muthalali, Abubacker's erstwhile boss.

22

Beypore

Abubacker had been visiting Syyed Muthalali from time to time. Although there was the initial awkwardness in their conversation, the love that the younger man had in his heart for the older always showed; and slowly, the older man relaxed in the knowledge in his heart that Abubacker would never ever insult or demean him.

Things were not looking good for Syyed Muthalali too. People called him Muthalali all right, but he could sense that the respect had gone out of the title. There was little for people to respect in a Muthalali who was not flashing the latest 'imported' car, or throwing huge parties or failing to gift liberally at weddings.

He continued to live in the same house that Abubacker once was a proud visitor. The warmth that used to engulf the house seemed to have gone; only Syyed Muthalali, his wife and his remaining daughter Saffiya were there. Gone were the hordes of servants, drivers and the usual hangers on – they hardly had a visitor to their house these days.

The paint was flaking outside and the gloom seemed to permeate even the walls of this household. Saffiya, though, seemed as chirpy and as vibrant as ever. She would call Abubacker almost every day and somewhere deep down, Abubacker still cherished the thought of marrying her. He did not have any timeframe to do that, and had no plans as to how he would broach the subject to Syyed Muthalali. He was happy in the knowledge that his relationship with Saffiya was growing rapidly. Especially now since she told him that all he would have to do is formally propose and she would speak to her parents and accept.

Syyed Muthalali had lost control of the last vestige of his empire – the *Dhow* making business – to a brother. Although the unwritten agreement was that he would remain at the helm, the brother had sidelined Syyed Muthalali until such time that no one in the small firm took any orders from Syyed Muthalali, no one asked him for advice. Sadly, the old man stopped going to the docks and the brother took complete control, the two families snapping even day-to-day contact.

One day, a *Dhow* that Syyed Muthalali's brother had made was returning for 'repairs' to Beypore. The Coast Guard stopped the vessel and boarded it to search. In its shallow hull, they found silver, 200 kilos of it. They seized the vessel and its crew and upon interrogation found that Syyed Muthalali's brother had masterminded the operation. And because the company was still Syyed Muthalali's on papers, they brought him in for questioning too.

Saffiya immediately called Abubacker and informed him of these new developments. He knew the Coast Guard officers personally and well. He called them and enquired of this case. They gave him a run down and told him that if someone did not do something quickly, Syyed Muthalali would be in deep trouble. For the time being, Syyed Muthalali had managed to cough up enough money to buy bail, but that was only breathing time and not a solution.

Abubacker had come to Beypore to visit Syyed Muthalali's house and to enquire from the old man. Protocol established over time and the uneasy alliance that they found themselves in today did not allow Abubacker to broach the subject immediately. They talked of Abubacker's business, how it was flourishing, and the old man's health. Syyed Muthalali never asked Abubacker if he had heard of the new problems that besieged him, did not ask if Abubacker could help and as time dragged on, Abubacker finally got up to say that he had to meet someone and left.

In a restaurant at the junction of Beypore, Abubacker got off his car and made a phone call to Syyed Muthalali's house. Usually Saffiya picked up the phone and this time was no different. Upon hearing his voice, she immediately asked him, "Did you speak to my father?"

"About everything else under the sun, except his current problems," Abubacker said.

"He is so proud about asking you to help him. I do not know what to do. The bail will lapse tomorrow and they will come with an arrest warrant. If that happens, he is as good as finished here," Saffiya was crying, he could sense.

"What is his brother saying about all this?" he enquired.

"Well, to get out of the mess, he has maintained in his statement that he was just a representative employed by his brother and that he had no way of knowing that the *dhow* contained contraband. The onus of proving that is untrue is on my father," Saffiya sobbed.

"Let me see what I can do and then I will call you later today around four in the evening. I will find a solution to this. You don't worry so much. When you have me, why are you so worried, Saffiya?" Abubacker asked as gently as he could.

"Abba is visibly disturbed by all this and he cannot take this strain. I can see him hurt and for the first time in his life he seems to be so alone, I cannot tell you how that hurts him. You know that there was a time when he could make one phone call and people would come to Beypore. These days are different," Saffiya said in an almost matter of fact tone.

Abubacker talked to her some more, comforting her and reassuring her. He then drove back to Kozhikode.

Calling Syyed Muthalali's brother from Kozhikode, he spoke clearly, demanding to know how the entire sordid tale unfolded. The menace was not so much in Abubacker's language, but in his tone. Instantly, the other man sensed it. He spoke to Abubacker not in the language that he had always used when Abubacker was a vassal at Syyed Muthalali's, but in a deference that was exclusively reserved for real Muthalalis.

"I am sending you a car just now. I want you to come here to my office," Abubacker said.

"But I have promised to go to the Coast Guard Commander's office just now and perhaps I can come after I see him?" asked Syyed Muthalali's brother.

"No, you come here first. If you are not in my car when I send it to you, you will never go to meet anyone, least of all the Commander. Understood?" Abubacker barked into the mouthpiece.

Within one hour, Syyed Muthalali's prodigal brother found himself seated in the lobby of Abubacker's office and deliberately asked to wait one more hour before Abubacker saw him.

Eventually he was shown into Abubacker's personal office. Not a muscle twitched on Abubacker's face that betrayed the slightest emotion – just a cold stare at the man who had betrayed his former boss and his own blood brother.

"I want you to do something and you will do it now," Abubacker ordered.

"What is it?"

"I want you to go out of my office with my man, who will take you to my lawyer. Meet him and then sign a document. This will ensure that you no longer control the *Dhow* making business. Syyed Muthalali, your brother will become the only owner. You will receive a substantial amount of money. I want you to pack your bags, your family and come here to Kozhikode. I have at my disposal a suitable house for you and your family. You can stay there for as long as you live. I do not ever want you to lift a finger against your brother. If you do, if you ever cross him or if you ever hurt him, I myself will kill you," Abubacker talked slowly, deliberately, each word a threat; the other man cowed down totally – not offering the least bit of resistance.

"I then want you to go to the Coast Guard Commander's office and give him a declaration that it was you and not your brother who masterminded this run. He will take necessary action against you. However, never mind him or his department. For this one case, I will use whatever resources are at my command to see you get off lightly, but I want you to understand that you will no longer be involved in any gold or silver runs. If I want, after I am convinced about your loyalty, I will give you a small territory to run. Otherwise, you will stay put in your house, offer your daily prayers, and live peacefully. If you object to this, you better tell me and tell me now," Abubacker continued, the fingers of both hands stretched creating a steeple of sorts, held in front of his face, only his eyes staring at the man in front of him. Any pitiful semblance of self-respect disappearing every passing moment, the man shrivelling in the presence of another more powerful man, who was completely reassured and knowing exactly what he was talking about.

Syyed Muthalali's brother did exactly as Abubacker had instructed him to. By the time the car dropped him off at his house in Beypore, his wife had packed everything, including their cooking vessels, clothes and the children were asked not to run out to play. Their immediate neighbours were informed quite hurriedly, that the family was shifting to their other house in Kozhikode for the convenience of the education of their children.

A large BMD lorry with several people to help load the luggage had arrived much before Syyed Muthalali's brother had arrived and was already loading all the furniture in.

When Saffiya opened her door to the insistent ringing of the doorbell, she took one step back in surprise. After years of a no-contact relationship, she was quite surprised to see her uncle and aunt standing at the front door, with the entire brood behind them.

"*Abba, Ammi*, see who is here?" she yelled back into the house.

"*Arra*, who is that, Saffiya?" her father asked as he stepped into the living room.

"*Maasha Allah, Maasha Allah*, what is this that I see here today?" Syyed Muthalali asked. Saffiya was surprised to see the genuine pleasure and the smile on her father's face.

"Why are you standing like strangers out there?" he asked.

"Come in, come in and make yourself comfortable," he invited.

But the couple and their children did not move. Syyed Muthalali's brother stepped forward, hugged his older brother, and said, "Forgive me; I have caused you terrible pain."

"Never mind that, where are you going? Why don't you sit down and have lunch with me and go?" the older brother offered.

"No, we have packed everything and the lorry has already left. I have come to hand over my house keys to you. Someone will come here to collect them. Please hand over these keys to him. I am leaving you now, and I will never come back to Beypore. Just don't hate me, please."

Syyed Muthalali was shocked at the change in his younger brother and looking at the man he only asked him, "Did you speak to Abubacker?"

"Yes, it was Abubacker who took care of everything. There are no charges and the case is closed. Nothing will be brought up against you or for that matter, me too."

Before he could say anything, Syyed Muthalali watched in silence as his younger brother left his house and his life, for the last time.

By the time Beypore knew of what had happened, Syyed Muthalali was back at his modest office and in control, once more of the *dhow* making business that his forefathers had established.

Within a week, a broker appeared at Syyed Muthalali's office and offered to buy his old cars in exchange for new ones. Yet another contractor also came by – he was instructed by his client BMD Transport to take measurements of the house and office of Syyed Muthalali in order for the contractor to submit a quotation to the BMD Administration for doing up the interiors and exteriors. The contractor explained to Saffiya, who was the only person at home that this was just a formality, and that he would begin work the following week.

In one swift move, Abubacker had given Syyed Muthalali his former stature and the old man knew that he had nothing but his heartfelt gratitude to give back Abubacker.

23

A Marriage Proposal

When the phone rang, Abubacker was fast asleep after lunch nap in his favourite office in Kallai on a hard wooden bench, which he preferred to the couch in his city office. This was a short siesta. About twenty minutes or so, then he would wake up, refresh himself and then donning a fresh shirt, and a fresh *mundu,* would go on working till almost midnight.

Grabbing the phone, he was instantly awake. Syyed Muthalali might have become old, but Abubacker never forgot his voice.

"I want to come and visit you, Abubacker. I have some good news for you," Syyed Muthalali said and Abubacker was surprised. For the first time since he'd broken off from Syyed Muthalali, the old man had broken the invisible wall between them and there was a touch of genuine camaraderie in his voice, a love that was always there but never on display.

"Muthalali, you can come anytime. You do not need to ask me at all. Why are you being so formal with me?" Abubacker asked.

"No, there are no formalities, Abubacker. You are a truly busy man today and if I have to come to see you all the way and if you are not in, then I will have to come again another day to see you. You see, this is my need and therefore it is imperative for me to see you," Syyed Muthalali explained.

"Muthalali, I can come to see you," Abubacker offered.

"No, that is not the way. My wife is also going to be coming and perhaps a few other relatives. So tell me what time would you prefer?" Syyed Muthalali persisted.

"How about this evening? Around five o'clock? I will wait for you at my house."

"Okay Abubacker, I will be there," Syyed Muthalali smiled and hung up the phone.

Turning around Syyed Muthalali saw a grinning Saffiya standing with tears brimming in her eyes, hardly believing what she had just heard. "Abba, how can I thank you?"

"Thank Him, Saffiya. It is His Will," Syyed Muthalali pointed heavenward with a smile.

Her mother pulled her towards the bedroom and told her, "Your father had spoken to me last night and I thought that he is making a good decision. He is a good boy. No one else would have helped your Abba, the way that boy did. Not only that, we have known him for such a long time. We know that he is a good human being. And we also know that he will always keep you happy."

Heart beating faster than it ever had, Saffiya could only cry into her mother's shoulders, the tears falling for the love that she had cherished and which she thought would die without ever blooming. For the hopes that she had secretly had of marrying a man who had become king in her heart long before the world crowned him one. For all the days when she had thought that she would have to marry someone else whom she never knew, whose children she would have to bear when she desperately wanted to have children from the man whom she knew she was born for.

She thought of what Abubacker had always taught her – If you can taste your dreams, they would become your life. She had clung on to hope, and when hope itself had faded against the harsh realities of life, she still hoped, and prayed and continued to hope.

Today, she knew, neither hope nor prayer had failed her. She would give Abubacker all the love and all the support that he never had in his entire life.

She did not know how – but she just knew that she would!

The car carrying Syyed Muthalali and select members of his family drove into the driveway of the former Managing Director of BMD Transport's Bungalow on a hill just by the side of the Commonwealth Tile Factory office in Kozhikode where Abubacker currently lived.

Abubacker personally was there to welcome Syyed Muthalali at the large verandah dotted with islands of cane furniture and palm trees in large Malabar pots, ancient ceiling fans on the high ceilings swaying lazily not with the electric power that is meant to drive them, but in the cool evening breeze.

"Salaam, Salaam," Abubacker said, arms outstretched and hugged the older man.

Standing one step behind Abubacker was an old man. Syyed Muthalali squinted trying to adjust his eyesight to the comparative darkness of the verandah from the still bright evening sun. "Who is this?" he said surprised. Abubacker had not mentioned anything to him about anyone living in the house with him, other than the servants and he was quite surprised to see this man, whom almost everyone in Beypore knew by sight. Kunhali, the erstwhile cleaner and live-in janitor of the Beypore mosque, his hair completely white now, but looking much healthier than he had ever looked in Beypore and smiling his usual smile.

"Salaam, Muthalali! I have been staying with Abubacker for some time now."

"But you never told me, Abubacker," Syyed Muthalali said.

"What is there to tell you, Muthalali? I had always promised Kunhali that I would look after him, *Inshallah*, and now that I am able to, I guess I just kept my word. And like me, the old man has no one now, so here we are, just two grown orphans living under the same roof," Abubacker said very modestly.

"I do not know what to say, Abubacker. Your heart is big and it is great," Syyed Muthalali said, leading his family into the living room of this wonderful, old house.

As soon as they had settled down, the servant appeared, carrying chilled tender coconut in cut glasses on a large bamboo tray.

Serving each visitor, he then offered the last two glasses to Kunhali and Abubacker.

Sipping their drinks, Syyed Muthalali looked at Abubacker and asked him, "Do you know why I am here, Abubacker?"

"I must say I have an inclination, but I cannot be sure. Therefore, I will wait for you to tell me, Muthalali," Abubacker said with a smile.

"We have come here to propose our daughter's hand in marriage with you, Abubacker," Syyed Muthalali said, "We are sure that you will look after her well and that she will be happy here with you. We look forward to welcoming you into our family as a new member."

Abubacker was speechless, and he looked down at his hands. Kunhali sensing the awkwardness in Abubacker told Syyed Muthalali, "You are wise, and you will never get a better man than Abubacker who will honour you, your family and look after Saffiya."

"So what do you now have to say, Abubacker?" Syyed Muthalali asked Abubacker.

"Muthalali, I have always been at your command. You tell me how we should go forward and we will have everything done as per your wishes. All I want to say is this. For your sake, I want this wedding remembered in Beypore as one of the best weddings that people would have seen in a long time. They should say that it's because it's Syyed Muthalali's class. If it was for my ego and for my sake, I would rather have married Saffiya in a very quiet ceremony and made no bones about it. However, it is not just I here. It is your honour… your reputation… and I want everyone here to know that Syyed Muthalali is not finished; he is still the Muthalali and what better a way than a wedding to express that. So do whatever you have to do, I will send Kunhali to you and I will take care of all the expenses. Between us Muthalali, there are no formalities. No issues of whose money, no egos here! You know me and I am here where I am only because of you. I cannot and will not forget that, Muthalali," Abubacker spoke from his heart.

No one spoke in the room. No one had seen such magnanimity, such unassuming humility. Saffiya's mother had tears in her eyes. These days not even a son did as much for a father and here he was a mere errand boy who had come so far and had not forgotten the paths that he had walked, totally assured of his own place, yet without a touch of arrogance. Deeper love than this Muthalali had never seen and tears in Syyed Muthalali's eyes was not something that Abubacker and Kunhali had ever seen.

They flowed today and they flowed freely as if some hidden reservoir had just given way, opening a cascade of unbridled passion, love, and all the unsaid words that seemed held back in the name of decorum, position, status, and indeed age. Syyed Muthalali came from a background where you did not state the obvious, whether that meant telling your wife that she was a good cook or that you loved her or telling one of his several employees that he was doing good job. One did not state the obvious. Abubacker was different. He told people exactly that. Even if they knew it, he believed that even a coolie likes a pat on the back when he did a good job; he believed that people like recognition and he was rarely wrong. His companies did well today because that was all that he did – go around, meet his people and exhorting them on, congratulating them, being their cheerleader and trailblazer – knowing that they would work better if they knew that he was a man who rewarded them with not just money, but also with kind words. From his own experiences, Abubacker knew that you could buy only so much with money, but you could buy the world with kindness and kind words. He knew the awesome power of Love.

Today, sitting in this house that Abubacker had inherited upon the purchase of BMD Transports, the only noise was Syyed Muthalali clearing his throat and when he spoke, all the eyes in that room were on him.

"It will be as you said, my son. Kunhali will come to Beypore tomorrow and I will discuss everything with him and the Imam at the mosque. After we have finalised everything, I will inform you and Kunhali can tell you everything in detail when he gets back here by this time, tomorrow evening."

Saying that, he stood up and walked towards Abubacker who also stood up. Hugging him, the older man said, "Truly you are a blessing for this old man. I thank God for having brought you to me."

The women who were silent until then, also stood up, all their eyes moist and Syyed Muthalali's wife looked at Abubacker and said, "My Saffiya is lucky and very fortunate to get a husband like you. I am so happy for her."

Abubacker smiled and asked them if they would mind staying a little longer as he had asked the cook to make something for the visitors to eat along with tea.

"There will be time for all that later, Abubacker. Now we have to go. Saffiya will be eagerly waiting for us at Beypore and if we don't leave now, your phone will start ringing," Syyed Muthalali said smiling.

"Okay, at least, carry them home?" Abubacker asked.

Without waiting for a response, he asked Kunhali to go to the kitchen and ask the cook to pack all the eatables that he had made for the visitors so that they could carry it back.

In a few minutes, the cook and the servant who had served them their cool drinks came carrying what seemed a large parcel.

"It looks like you have cooked for an army here," Syyed Muthalali joked.

They smiled back at him as they loaded the food into the car. Waving at Abubacker, the car descended the driveway and disappeared onto the main road.

24

The Nikaah

The Nikaah is a marriage ceremony. During this ceremony, there are present the bride's and groom's family and friends, the Imam from the mosque and it is a colourful affair. The women are all attired in their best finery, gold glinting in the sun, hands covered in tapestried *mailanji*, the artistry going beyond the ornate.

Essentially the Imam reads a few *suras* from the Holy *Quran* and then after a short prayer, he has the bride-to-be and the groom-to-be seated on either side, along with their families and he asks if she will take him to be her husband and vice-versa. In some instances, the women and the men are seated separately, as is the custom amongst the Arabs.

When they agree, he pronounces the confirmation of the marriage. After which both families congratulate each other, a prayer is offered and then lunch is served.

Usually the Muslim groom pays his bride a hefty dowry and in this case, there was nothing different. Abubacker had planned this to the last detail and he did not want any talk from anyone that he got Syyed Muthalali's daughter for free or in return for a favour.

Sitting to the right of Abubacker was Moosa who had come in from Bombay, along with a few of his friends. Kunhali was also there seated along with the groom's party. A large suitcase was noticed and many presumed quite rightly that this might be the dowry amount. A guessing game began right then by several people who wagered on how much it would contain, by the size of the suitcase and the stories that they had heard of both Abubacker and Moosa. The amount of money that it allegedly contained began to go up as the stories of these men and their achievements began to gain momentum.

Finally, just before lunch was served, one of the elders in the bride's party announced that the dowry that the groom was paying was in the region of around 1 Crore of rupees in cash, along with ten kilograms of gold in the form of ornaments for the bride, some of which she'd worn today. The best artisans had made the silk and gold sari that she wore from Kanchipuram. She was also being presented with a brand new car and complete trousseau for her new home.

The silence with which the announcement was heard was so pregnant with disbelief and sheer incredulity, that when a child blew on his toy trumpet quite by accident, almost everyone clapped.

The Imam, then, announced the wedding as solemnised.

The entertainment today was a Ghazal singer who'd come from Bombay and the food that was served was the best of the Malabar Muslim fare and there was not even a single guest who did not eat a soul-satisfying meal that day.

The guests who had daughters of marriageable age went back to their respective homes, wishing ruefully that it should have been their daughters there at the Nikaah instead of Saffiya.

Sitting around with some remaining guests was Kunhali talking to them, about how he had known Abubacker since he was a boy and how it filled him with such happiness to see his Abubacker so happy.

"For we do worship a very benevolent, very merciful and a very compassionate God. He knows and He Blesses accordingly," Kunhali told his small group of guests.

25

The Road to Madras

When the results were declared after a month of the gruelling examinations, Saraswathi was relieved beyond her wildest expectations. The unexpected had happened and she was sure that it was because of her constant efforts to push her son to do better at school.

She was not aware of Bhaskaran's friendship with Moosa and how close the two were. For Bhaskaran, that was a closely guarded secret and not even his own friends were actually aware of how close he was to Moosa. It suited him just perfectly.

He had topped not just the school but stood first in the State of Maharashtra. He accepted the congratulations of his teachers and the other students in the school. KRK Menon, his father's boss, personally came over to their flat in Mahim and gave him a gift – a brand new cricket bat along with an invitation to come to his house for a meal with his parents. His grandparents too claimed credit for his performance. Bhaskaran knew who was responsible for igniting the flame in his young heart to succeed. And in his mind, he knew that no one else could ever claim credit.

He had already been applying to various universities for admission and Moosa had told him that should he require his assistance, he would take him to the Bombay University Dean and secure him an admission. Bhaskaran wanted to be admitted on his own merit and he knew that it would not be difficult. He had also begun to play cricket for several local teams and was rated to be a good all-rounder.

He was keen on completing his B. Tech from IIT and so had joined private tuitions to train him for Joint Entrance Examination. Once he'd passed it, his IIT dream would be fulfilled.

One day the postman rang the door bell. He was carrying a thick brown manila envelope with something written on it.

Opening the envelope with trembling fingers, the letter informed him that he would have to write an examination the following month and if he succeeded in it, he would be granted a seat at the prestigious Institute.

He began to work hard. His brother and sister began to wonder how their older brother had managed to change. While earlier, his parents would chide him constantly for not studying; now they had to chide him to stop studying for a while. The only time that he got up from his mother's sewing table which also doubled up as his study when it was not in use, was either to sleep or to eat. Otherwise, he would go to the library to get some more reading material.

He was hell-bent on getting through the entrance examination and finally on the day that he was leaving Bombay, he called Moosa. Moosa was not available and the man who answered his phone told him to leave a number and that he would ask Moosa to call back. It was quite late when Moosa called and Bhaskaran thought how provident it was that Moosa had called then and not earlier. His parents had gone out for yet another party. He did not ask them where they went and what the occasion was.

They talked a while, and Moosa asked him when he was leaving. Moosa seemed distant and was it sadness that he detected in Moosa's voice? He was not too sure. They wished each other and Moosa told him that he would meet Bhaskaran when he got back from Madras.

The IIT Madras was a sprawling campus with beautiful avenues named after German cities in fond remembrance of grants and technological assistances that the German nation had contributed to the Institute. Deer, mongoose, and monkeys visible to the eye populated the woods in the campus. There were a couple of schools inside the campus and the atmosphere was at its sylvan best.

Bhaskaran liked it immensely and the bus that wound its way into the campus, he discovered were part of a fleet, all named after several Indian peaks. The local buses would only stop near the gates, and did not ply within the IIT Campus.

At the IIT buildings, he discovered that it was a virtual city. There were hostels for the students, living quarters for the faculty, with the classrooms being distributed carelessly over a wide area. The large banyan trees provided enough shade and from a cursory glance into some of the now empty classrooms, he found them to be quite cool.

He had reached the campus along with his paternal uncle who was a long time resident of Madras and the gentleman was kind enough to receive him at the railway station, accompany him to his modest house in Mylapore and then after a sumptuous breakfast, all the way to the IIT.

His uncle spoke Tamil like a native and therefore it was not difficult to get directions.

One of the peons told him that the exams were to begin in about an hour and directed him to another floor. Here, there was a big crowd of expectant faces and most of them were peering at a huge blackboard on which were neatly drawn columns, with figures written in chalk. Each number referred to a candidate's number and against that was the location of a candidate's classroom, also mentioned in numbers. Bhaskaran looked at his reference number, ran his fingers along the board, and then began to look up and down the corridor.

He finally found his classroom and took a seat at the rear. He kept his letter, as so many had before him, on his seat and walked out to meet his uncle.

His uncle said that he would wait and asked him to pray before he began writing his test.

At the strike of ten, a bell pealed, and all the aspirants who had come there that day, to attempt for a place in the current academic year for various disciplines, entered classrooms to write their tests.

Within two hours, the entire exercise was over and the rush to get buses back to the main gate began.

Bhaskaran and his uncle decided to walk back and slowly trudged back the long winding avenues, taking in the sounds of the crickets in the trees, the birds and the beauty of the deer feeding without a care in the world, the smell of ripe wood apple fruit hanging in the air, lingering on in his mind.

He would have to wait another month before he knew of his fate.

26

Back to Bombay

Back in Bombay with a lot of free time, he found himself spending a lot of time with Moosa and getting to know the man better.

Moosa had spread his operations to cover almost every aspect of business enterprise and it had now reached a stage where it was very difficult to draw a line between the legal businesses that he controlled and the illegal businesses.

One of his most recent forays was into the world of films. He would finance the production of movies and get leading stars to act in them. It was a heady experience for the upstart businessman to mingle with the cream of Bombay's film industry. In reality, these people cringed at the thought of dealing with a man like Moosa. They hated his guts; they hated the power that the man wielded. But they could do little else.

He had hired a young man, Mohan Singh, who was showing promise as a newcomer. He told him that all he wanted him to do was to teach him to dress well. There was this talk around town that this newcomer was a real snazzy dresser and Moosa had seen him at a couple of parties. He was quite impressed with the boy's taste. Mohan Singh hired Bombay city's best tailor Kachins to outfit Moosa.

Mohan Singh became not just a man who would teach Moosa about clothes and dressing sense. He spent long hours with Moosa teaching him everything about eating in good restaurants, ordering food and something that Moosa never had a chance to acquire in Dharawi – etiquette.

Mohan Singh was the youngest son of a failed business tycoon. His father sent him to some of the best boarding schools in India and ensured the best for his son. Unfortunately, Mohan Singh displayed a greater affinity to the members of the opposite sex – regardless of their age – than studies and the school soon expelled him when they caught him in a toilet with his female English teacher.

He shunted from one school to another, one incident to another and finally in an attempt to clear his High School exams, he failed gloriously.

He had already been dabbling in modelling assignments and it was at one of these that a popular director noticed his good looks and offered him a small role in a new movie.

In order to play safe with Bhaskaran's parents, Moosa introduced Mohan Singh to Bhaskaran who would drive every day to Mahim to pick up Bhaskaran in a brand new Fiat. It also helped that somewhere in the past, Mohan Singh had briefly played on the cricket team of a leading textile mill and therefore explaining Mohan Singh to his parents was not a major issue. It was also a known fact that some of the movies that had just released had a few prominent scenes of Mohan Singh and his parents were not averse to the fact that their son was a friend of a 'film hero'.

The two did get on famously. They were always playing practical pranks and Moosa had warned Mohan Singh not to take Bhaskaran along with him to any of his 'women' friends.

Mohan Singh needed no second reminder from Moosa.

From Mohan Singh both Moosa and Bhaskaran got an education on the fine nuances of a society that they were not originally privy to, but which now beckoned them with a plastic welcome. Both Moosa and Bhaskaran were quite happy with their 'coach' for the education, understanding that this was one investment that Moosa had made that would stand them in good stead in the future.

Mohan Singh was a good teacher. He taught them not just the art of using a fork and a knife, he also taught them how they could both behave like perfect gentlemen without ever being ridiculed as uncouth boors with money. Both of them lapped up everything that Mohan Singh taught them like two avaricious puppies lapping up the last drop of milk.

Eventually, out of gratitude for the obvious changes that were wrought in their physical make up and the phenomenal amount of time that he had spent with them, Moosa gave Mohan Singh the break of a lifetime when he cast him as his hero in his latest movie with the leading lady of the celluloid world, Madhu Shah.

The movie did well, was acclaimed all over India as one of the best love stories of all time and it was also not long before Mohan Singh was romantically linked with Madhu Shah. Of course, both of them denied it vehemently even when a scribe snapped them together in dark glasses in a hotel corridor walking hand in hand at night.

Sadly, Mohan Singh died when a deranged female fan of his ran a sword through him protesting against his affair with Madhu Shah.

Madhu Shah quietly retired from the hectic world of cinema to become a homemaker and migrated to the United States for ever.

Moosa gave Bhaskaran a fond farewell from Bombay when the word arrived that Bhaskaran had been accepted into the IIT Madras.

27

'Pankajam' Bala Govind

After Bhaskaran left for Madras to study there, Bala Govind was becoming increasingly involved in the hectic growth of KRK Menon's business. There were almost a dozen branches sprouting up all over India in a week.

KRK found himself leaning heavily on Bala Govind and trusting him with new initiatives. Travel was becoming commonplace for Bala Govind. He was one of the fastest rising meteors in the KRK Coterie and there was nothing much that KRK decided in which Bala Govind did not have a say.

His relatives in Kerala would write to him pleading for employment opportunities, classmates would write asking for favours. However, Bala Govind was not a man who helped anyone else but himself. He was riding a crest in his life that he had never experienced before. He was a member in most of the best clubs in Bombay, and was well known amongst the small but growing Malayali community in Bombay.

To match the social and professional profile of his stature within KRK's organisation, Bala Govind began to live a life of luxury that he could not really afford. Saraswathi complained but to no use.

KRK had graciously given Bala Govind a better flat in the upmarket Bandra area of Bombay and this only inflated Bala Govind's ego and his self-importance.

When his colleagues began to buy apartments and houses for themselves, he vainly argued that it was useless to do so as it was far cheaper to pay rent than to buy a house. Then again, why buy a matchbox in Bombay, he argued, when there was a palatial house that was his wife's ancestral property back in their native Kerala?

Of course, he never bothered to explain that that ancestral property was slowly falling apart without maintenance combined with abject neglect.

He had also begun to borrow heavily spending next month's salary today to fuel his rising expenditure and then borrowing some more to pay for the bills and the borrowings in the following months.

He then began to look forward to making money on the side whenever it was possible. He would claim for fictitious payments supposedly made to real estate brokers whose services, he explained, were necessary to find property for new offices to fuel the juggernaut that Pankajam had become.

KRK had also entrusted Bala Govind with a majority of the administration functions, including a whole lot of vendors, contractors, and suppliers. He chose the softest and most vulnerable of them and insisted on a cut for considering them.

Bala Govind pursued every possible avenue to make extra money to fuel his lavish life style. Finally, when KRK came to know, there was only one verdict. Dismissal!

For the rest of the family who were quite oblivious to Bala Govind's activities – legal or illegal – the loss of his job came as a blow. Inadvertently, they had been sucked into the social scenario; they were friends with the children and spouses of the who's who of Bombay society. They had unconsciously created for themselves a lifestyle, which suddenly became inaccessible to them. The first thing that they lost was the upmarket flat, the company provided car and chauffeur.

The high snob value school, which Bala Govind had chosen for his younger children were suddenly too expensive.

In desperation, he looked around for alternative employment. That is when he found out that Bombay although was supposedly this huge city with so many people, was in fact a single microcosm where news, especially bad news travelled so swiftly.

People had known through the vicious gossip grapevine of the reasons why Bala Govind was no longer with KRK's establishment. Finding alternate employment now became almost impossible.

He had lived his life on a day-to-day basis, enjoying today and facing tomorrow when it came. When the crunch came, one of the first things that had to go to sustain the family was some of the jewels that Saraswathi had. It was not much, but it managed to fetch some money.

The children moved to a lesser grade of a school, where the fees were not too much, and the people whose wards came to study here were the hardworking lower middle class. For the first time in what seemed a long time, Bala Govind's children were going to school in a bus.

Ironically, nothing of this affected Bhaskaran in Madras, whose entire educational expenses were underwritten by Moosa through one of his companies. His parents were blissfully unaware of this situation and welcomed one mouth less to feed and protect.

It was only when Bala Govind's brother in Madras went to meet Bhaskaran that he was made aware of the fact that his father had no longer a job with KRK and that he was finding the going very tough.

Bhaskaran thought of asking Moosa to help his father. But knowing his father, he knew that they would not get along with each other because each of them had different attitudes to life. Essentially Bala Govind was the type who helped no one, selfish to the core and did not say a kind word to anyone. Moosa was the typical opposite. The vicious streak in Moosa only surfaced when he was dealing with similar circumstances. He was a giver, a man who never hurt anyone just because he had the power to do so.

Bhaskaran remembered a conversation that he had had with Moosa a long time ago. He had asked Moosa why he was not able to leave behind his involvement in crime and in the illegal activities that the press bandied about and the government made some noises about. Moosa said something that Bhaskaran would never forget.

"I am the convenient avatar for many of these people for some of whom I carry out these various activities. Ministers who want to stash away huge amounts of ill-gotten wealth yet portraying to be protectors of the poor. Businesspersons need me to hide money that they have plundered from investors fully knowing the non-viability of their projects. They can conceive their various sins in their minds, but their images will not allow them to execute them. They are the people who gave birth to this phenomenon the world calls Moosa Bhai. Not my parents, not my blood that the press says, run rife with vile cruelty and terror. They and the people like them are the powers that created and will continue to create people like me. One day when they decide that I have grown too big for my own self and too big to dislodge them, they will promote another Moosa Bhai and finish this one off. But that, when the time comes, is a factor that He will decide. Not them or the likes of them."

No, he decided. He would have to wait for his father to come out of his own graveyard.

Bala Govind, in the meantime, had been in contact with an army mate of his who had also resigned his commission and was now in Madras.

He decided to move his family once more. Madras, he thought, might be better to him than Bombay was to him. Of course, even then, it was everything else including time, fate, destiny, and the Gods, except his own actions, which were to blame for these turn of events.

28

Raashid

Raashid looked out of the camp at the rising sun. It looked liked the true fireball that the books said that the sun really was. Here in the Sahara, life moved at a pace, which was incomparable to anywhere else, especially Bombay. All that one could do was work, if one had work.

Raashid was the youngest of Moosa's brothers. When he was about ten, his father had given Raashid off for adoption to a relative of theirs who were living in far away Nagpur. This couple, Altaf and Rubaina, had no children after a ten-year marriage and when the opportunity came to adopt a child, they thought it was a great idea.

So young Raashid was packed off to Nagpur and it was there that he lived for almost the next ten years. The nightmare of living with his father in the hell that Dharawi was to the mind of the young boy was fast receding as a nightmare that the young boy was learning to forget in the comparative luxury of his new parents' home. Although they were not exactly rich, they could afford three square meals a day, which he did not have in Dharawi. And then there was a regular school to go to, a better quality of children, and a life that not many youngsters in Dharawi get.

Unfortunately, life has this mean habit of lousing up even the happy moments of a child. Within a few years of his moving to his new home in Nagpur, his 'mother' conceived and had twins – a boy and a girl – healthy and whom the parents deemed as a Gift from Allah.

His mild-mannered 'father' ridiculed Raashid's instinctive fear that he would become an outcast as baseless. He always got him to believe that he, Raashid, was the first born of the family, even if he was not really born to them. These reassurances only managed to push the boys fear behind temporarily.

By the time the twins were three, he found himself becoming more of a servant in the family than the first-born son. He was confused in the beginning but when it became obvious that the couple had no intentions of giving him even a part of their love that they so willingly displayed for their own children, Raashid knew that it was just a matter of time before they sent him back or he ran away from Nagpur.

He did not want to go back to Dharawi. He contemplated going to work for someone as a servant, or better still, he thought brightly, why not work as a helper in a mechanic's shop? That way, in a couple of years, he could learn a trade and then go on to becoming a full-fledged mechanic himself. In a slightly better frame of mind, he volunteered to his 'father' that since he was not keen on studies, would he mind if he also took a job. While his 'father' was delighted at his son, more because of the fact that he longer would be required to pay the child's school fees, the uniform and other such expenses, he was happier at the prospect of an extra income, however slight the contribution was.

And so it was, that on the day that he was done with his 10th standard examinations, he found himself working for one of the largest lorry mechanics in their area – Shapoorji and Sons.

Shapoorji and Sons was a large lorry workshop. It was the biggest in Nagpur. They had a large yard, almost two acres on the outskirts of Nagpur city. To reach there, the boy had to wake up early in the morning, help his 'mother' in the kitchen and take a series of buses in order to be at work around nine.

On the first day at work, an entire army of mechanics warmly welcomed him and he felt truly honoured to be there. They were his kind of people. People who had come up in life with nothing, but the hope that tomorrow would be a better day! The smiles that they wore on their faces did not reflect the pains and agonies that they had all surely experienced on the path that brought them to this point in life. All of them, irrespective of their positions, were dressed in blue shirts and blue trousers.

By the second tea break at three in the afternoon, he had become 'great friends' with another boy whom everyone called Appu, who was older than he was, but a great chap, he thought.

Appu was the son of the foreman, Kesavan, at Shapoorji and Sons and therefore, there was a certain amount of fair treatment that Appu got that most of the new 'apprentices' never got. Raashid was shocked at mechanics using their knuckles liberally on the back of young apprentices' heads if they made a mistake on the job. When he asked Appu if that was fair, Appu laughed it away and said that even his father had been 'knuckled' a few times before he became a good mechanic.

By the end of that week, Raashid was happy that he had chosen this profession. This was something that he felt that he was born into. He loved the smell of the engines as he lay underneath massive chassis and felt the grease between his fingers. He loved the coarse life that these mechanics lived and hardly ever complained. They would all eat together in the backyard under the shade of an awesome banyan tree, after which the senior mechanics would doze for a while before the bell rang. They would then all troop back in, and in a short while, the grinding, banging, yelling and cursing would be heard heralding another session of work.

Only rarely was there a need to work overtime. A customer's lorry would require urgent servicing or some part would need to be replaced and some of the seniors would stay back until late at night in order to finish the work and leave early morning. Raashid took permission from his 'parents' to stay back at every given opportunity and they never complained. As long as he was bringing back some money, why would they complain?

In six months, he became known around the workshop as a reliable hand; he was always on time, never complained of the extra workload, and was always smiling. He had become every senior mechanic's favourite apprentice. He would joke with them, laugh with them and instinctively had picked up their style of talking including the cuss words that they used so lavishly embellishing each and every sentence that they ever uttered with classical embellishments that would make every mother, every sister and indeed any woman, cringe.

One day while they had just finished lunch, Appu made him a proposition. He said, "Raashid, would you like to stay here at the yard instead of commuting every day to work?"

He was speechless. He would have loved it. But he dare not cut his bridges with the only shelter that he had right now – his 'parents' home. He had nothing there, just a place to sleep and just an imaginary place to call home. There remained not an iota of love anymore. He knew that they were using him only for the meagre salary that he brought to them and all he wanted was a decent place to sleep in. When Appu asked him, he did not know what to say.

"Well, I have to ask my 'parents' about it, Appu."

"*Arrey yaar*, what is there to ask? I will ask my father to speak to your father and tell him that since we have got a lot of work, you will be required to stay back in the nights and that it would be difficult for you to commute every day like this," Appu reassured him.

"Okay, but where will I stay?" Raashid asked.

"You know the store room next to the boss's office? Remember that water cooler, well right next to that is a small room, which used to be meant for the security guard. But the boss caught him sleeping on the job one night and immediately had his quarters shifted to the one that they are presently using – right next to the gate," Appu offered as explanation.

"So when will your father be able to speak to my folks?" Raashid asked.

"What we can do is to come over to your place on Sunday and then after they speak you can come over on Sunday itself and start working here as usual from Monday. How about that?" Appu asked.

"Let me give them some hint today," Raashid said.

That night he nervously broached the subject with his 'father' who only asked him if they would pay extra for his working overtime. No mention of what will you eat, will you be okay, nothing. Raashid quickly reassured him of extra money and told his father that the Foreman would be coming on Sunday to meet him.

"No, don't worry. Please inform your Foreman that you have already spoken with me and that I have given you my go ahead. Otherwise, they will come here on Sunday and your mother will have to cook a meal for them and all that trouble for what? To take permission for you to stay in the workshop? Don't be ridiculous. It's perfectly alright with me and if you want, I will speak to him on the phone," Raashid's 'father' said.

The next morning, he packed his meagre belongings and he left his house, a place that he had come to with so much hope and a couple whom he thought were as good as God.

29

Towards A Life Beyond Engines

Life at the workshop was slowly revolving to become a new world for Raashid. He enjoyed the life very much. He was even getting to see a few movies with Appu. He spent the whole of Sunday at Appu's place and they just treated him like another member of the family. He could not have found a more loving family and they never pried about his 'parents' and about his previous life. They just accepted him for what he was.

He was able to strip an entire lorry engine by himself and he was proud of it. It would take some more time before he would be called a junior mechanic, but he was more than willing to wait for his turn. It took approximately two to three years by the time an apprentice graduated to a junior mechanic.

Under Kesavan's constant supervision, he became better each day. Slowly, he felt himself being drawn closer to the father-son duo and opened up his heart and soul to them.

He could talk to Appu about anything under the sun and it was to him that he decided to confide about his past, his life in Dharawi about his father. He told Appu how his real father suddenly disappeared after a fight with his eldest brother Moosa. He told Appu about how Moosa was becoming a *dada* in Dharawi and of the cars that would come to Dharawi to seek him. Appu's ears prickled when he heard about Moosa.

"Are you telling me that the famous Moosa Bhai is your brother?" Appu asked incredulously.

"I don't know if it's the same person," Raashid said.

"*Arrey yaar*, there is only one Moosa Bhai from Dharawi and if that is your brother then we have to do something."

Excitedly he went to seek his father and pulling him out of a discussion that his father was having with other mechanics about the current gossip in Maharashtra politics, he told him what Raashid had just said.

Kesavan was flabbergasted. He looked at Raashid and said, "Why didn't you tell me before?"

"I did not think that it was very important." Raashid said.

"Not important? If Moosa Bhai knew that his brother was being treated in such a lousy manner, he would have come back that very instant to fetch you," Kesavan said, still sounding very incredulous.

"I am sure that he must have thought that you were being well looked after and that is why he has not come to fetch you," Kesavan explained.

"Moosa Bhai has certain business interests here in Nagpur and some of the lorries that we service belong to him. I am going to contact someone here and ask him to pass on a message," Kesavan said.

"No sir, don't do that. I do not want to go away from here and leave you, Appu, the others here and your family. You have all been so good to me," Raashid said, almost in tears.

"Listen Raashid, if you are indeed Moosa Bhai's brother and if he wants you to be here, he would not have any objection. But I am sure that the man does not know what fate has befallen you," Kesavan said softly to the boy, "So let me send a message and if he comes here, we'll see what is to be next done next. Okay?"

Seeing that Kesavan had already made up his mind, Raashid mutely agreed.

Kesavan went straight to the public phone in the main workshop for the use of all the employees of Shapoorji and Sons and made a call.

By the next morning, a car was waiting outside the gates of Shapoorji and Sons. Moosa Bhai was waiting in the car, the driver said.

The Nepali security guard did not even know who Moosa Bhai was and asked the driver to inform his boss that the Foreman would arrive in the next ten or fifteen minutes and he would have to wait until such time.

The first to come to work was Raashid as he was staying just above the workshop. He did see a parked car at the gate, but did not bother to ask the Nepali as he had seen several cars waiting, several times in the past. This one, he presumed, must be someone who had come to meet either Kesavan sir or pay a bill. Anyway, he thought, it was not my problem. Let them come.

He was busy inside the workshop when he heard Kesavan yell his name.

He sensed urgency in the call and he ran out.

"Where have you been?" Kesavan asked pulling Raashid's hand towards the office building.

"Why, what is the matter?" Raashid asked, quite perplexed by now.

"Moosa Bhai has been waiting for almost an hour here," Kesavan said.

"Moosa Bhai?" repeated Raashid dumbly.

"Yes, he has been waiting here and how come you did not see him?" Kesavan asked as if it was the most normal thing for Raashid to have done.

"I did not think that it was him at all, Kesavan sir?" Raashid said.

By then they had reached the main office building and there, sitting in the reception, reading an old newspaper, a cigarette just lit dangling in his mouth, sat Moosa Bhai.

He turned around when he heard footsteps. Taking the cigarette out of his mouth and slowly placing the newspaper on the small table, he stood up.

"Raashid?" he asked.

The boy did not say anything. He just stood and stared at this tall, dapper dressed man. This was his brother, he was sure.

"Yes," he managed to stammer.

"Do you remember me?" Moosa asked.

"Not really," Raashid said.

But Moosa remembered. He remembered the young boy who was forever crying, a boy who did not have enough to eat probably because he was the youngest and therefore the weakest. He remembered the day when his father's relatives had visited with gifts of fruits and some clothes for the youngster and how they had left with him.

He remembered how his mother had explained to him that his brother would now have a good life and how he was lucky to escape their combined hell.

Slowly life had thrown up other and more challenging priorities and the memory of his brother had slowly receded in his mind, always reassured by his mother's statement that his brother was being taken care of somewhere by someone.

He looked once more at his brother and said, "I have come to take you back with me, Raashid."

"Where to?" Raashid asked.

"Go with him, Raashid. He will look after you much better than your life here," Kesavan said. By then, the whole workshop had gathered outside the small office reception and was looking at this curious scene between two long lost brothers.

Raashid was confused, his mind not working. He did not know what to do. One part of him wanted to embrace his older brother, not for the life that was ahead of him but for having got back into his life a part of which he always believed would never come back. The other part wanted to reject him.

Blood, they say, is thicker than water. Raashid looked up at Moosa and said, "Moosa Bhai, I will come with you, but on one condition. Promise me that you will never ask me to go away from your life, ever again."

Even the most hardened of mechanics outside the office felt a pull in their hearts. They knew what it meant to have someone love you, they also knew the pain of loneliness, and they all knew Raashid well by now to wish him well. It was almost as if they were willing him to leave this small world that the boy had come to love, leave each and every one of them and walk forward into a new life. They would have loved someone to walk into their lives one fine morning and push away the struggles of toiling so hard to make a decent living, almost as if by magic. And when it was happening in front of their eyes to one of their own, there was no jealousy, no envy – just a feeling of absolute relief, a sense of joy and above all a great sense of release!

Then it happened. They watched as the older brother hugged his younger brother and saw something that not many people witness and live to talk about – Moosa crying. Tears flowed onto Raashid's head, almost as if they were baptising him into a new life that the younger brother never dreamt of.

"Let me talk to your boss and let us leave here," Moosa said.

"Don't wait for the old man, he will come much later. I will tell him and collect Raashid's pay," Kesavan said.

"No, don't bother about the pay. You can take it," Moosa said.

"No Moosa Bhai, Kesavan sir has been very kind to me. He and his family gave me the only love that I have ever known. They have been very good to me," Raashid explained perhaps seeing the pained look on Kesavan's face when Moosa asked him to take Raashid's pay.

"You should take the money, Moosa Bhai, and fling it on that insensitive moron's face that your parents gave this fine young man to adopt," Kesavan said almost venomously.

"Where do they live?" Moosa enquired.

"I will take you to them, Moosa Bhai," Appu volunteered.

Moosa turned around to look at the source of this new voice and instantly, Raashid said, "Moosa Bhai, this is the other brother that I have, Appu. He is Kesavan sir's son."

Moosa smiled at him and said, "No, I think that will be fine. I think Raashid should know the way."

Stepping outside the small room, he faced the entire group and told them of how grateful he was that they had all made his young brother's life so enjoyable and how thankful that they had all treated him so well.

They were uncomfortable with such praises. Shifting feet and grumpy noises of throats cleared greeted Moosa's message and all they could do was smile at this man.

"If there is anything that any of you might want, not just now, but anytime in the future, please do not hesitate to let me know. For what you have done, I will never forget to help you – whichever way I can," Moosa said, his voice choked with emotion.

He held Raashid's hand and led him out of the workshop. Turning around, Raashid saw Kesavan, Appu and the others and suddenly freeing his hand, he ran back towards Appu, hugging him; no words came forth despite his need to tell Appu a thousand things. Letting go of him, he moved to Kesavan – his mentor and his guru – who hugged him and said, "God Bless you, my son. Come to see us whenever you can." The others milled around him and he thought of all the times that he had joked with them, played pranks on them, teased them and shared their meagre lunches.

When a hand fell on his shoulder, he turned around to see Moosa who said, "One day, we will come back. I am sure you would like to see your friends again."

He left Shapoorji and Sons behind him, carrying with him only the memories of carefree laughter and the smell of engines.

30

Repayment

Altaf who immediately recognised Raashid opened the door but he did not recognise Moosa.

"What are you doing here on a weekday?" asked Altaf.

"I am going to be leaving Nagpur," Raashid said.

Not comprehending, he looked at the other man and asked him, "Are you from the workshop?"

"No, I am Moosa. Raashid's brother!"

Altaf's eyes lit up in recognition. He immediately called to his wife and stepping aside, he said, "Why are you standing outside, why don't you come in?"

Moosa and Raashid stepped inside.

They did not sit. Moosa explained that he had come to tell Altaf that he was taking Raashid back with him to Bombay.

There was an awkward silence and then Moosa took out a bundle of notes, held it in front of Altaf, and said, "This is all you wanted, isn't it? Money? Here, take it." With that, he flung the notes on Altaf's face. He just stood there trembling. Rubaina had her hands across her face as if recovering from a slap.

Moosa took a step forward and grabbing Altaf by the shirtfront he asked him, "Are you a man or a *hijada*?"

"Moosa, please let me explain. We looked after your brother very well, ask him. I am not a rich man and when I was blessed with two children, I had no other option but to send him to work." Altaf pleaded.

There was no mercy in Moosa eye's. He pushed back Altaf and looked contemptuously at Rubaina, "You are a woman. What happened to your heart? Do you have a heart at all?"

She looked down at the floor, not daring to say anything in reply.

When Altaf touched his hand, he angrily shook it off and almost in reflexive action, slapped him with the full of his palm. It was a hard slap, backed with the frustration of having lost his brother to this hardened couple, the knowledge that whatever he did for his brother in the future, the scars that would remain in the young boy's mind were there to permanently haunt him.

Altaf reeled back and fell to the floor, holding his cheek and his ear, shocked with the insult and the sting that he could feel from one ear to another.

"That was for treating a human being so badly. That was for promising a child something that you could never give him. That was for all the tears that my brother must have shed. And for the times when he must have prayed asking desperately if there was God above to see his misery."

Rubaina, seeing her husband down, rushed forward. Kneeling on the floor beside him, she asked Moosa, "How dare you hit my husband?"

He raised his hand, "Thank your stars that I never hit women. You are a curse on womanhood that would never hesitate to sell your own daughter into prostitution if that suited your convenience."

Turning around, holding his brother's hand in his, Moosa walked out of their lives.

31

The Road to the Sahara Desert

Back in Bombay, he spent enormous time with Raashid. His mother had died a few years earlier. His sister had been married off to a doctor who was now in Saudi Arabia. The other brother had died from a drug overdose. He hardly had any contacts with his sister who welcomed the anonymity of Saudi Arabia and had settled down very well as the wife of a doctor.

He spoke of his business with Raashid and told him that he could take his time and settle into the business.

As days passed, Raashid found that he did not have the natural flair for business that his brother possessed and that he was not made of similar stuff. Although life was very comfortable, he did not feel too comfortable. He wanted to make something of his own life. He wanted to be his own man.

He spoke to Moosa and expressed his desire to go abroad and work somewhere and earn some money. Moosa did not argue. Only if you have lived in a family, grown roots of flesh and blood, had developed feelings for each other, can you grow on them. You cannot graft a family, Moosa thought.

He asked Raashid what he wanted to do and Raashid told him in a matter of fact tone that since he now had a trade, he would like to go and work as a mechanic.

Moosa made a few calls, within a few days, a passport arranged, and in exactly three months of having come to Bombay from Nagpur, Raashid was on his way to the airport to board his first flight to an unknown place, and a new chapter in life.

He had never heard of Libya. Did not know where it was. Someone would come to pick him up at the Tripoli airport, was all that he was told by the agent who had arranged all the papers for him.

Moosa did not hate his brother for leaving him. He knew that Raashid would have to understand the meaning of brotherhood by himself rather than be taught about it. He knew that he had found his brother and that one-day he would come back. This was not the day.

Standing outside Juhu International Terminal, he gave his brother some money and said, "These are American Dollars, tuck them inside your pocket. I am sending a man with you and he will see you through the customs and security. Use the money if you have to and when you reach Tripoli, try to call me from somewhere and let me know that you have reached safely."

The brothers hugged. Each knowing how difficult this was and each knowing that they had to let go to find each other, they had done that once, and they knew that they were never going to lose each other again.

The moment Raashid went through the glass doors of the airport building, Moosa turned around and got into the car.

32

Bala Govind in Madras

The family arrived in Madras and everything about Madras was different to their life in Bombay. There was lesser traffic and people did not seem to have the urgency that was part of the lives of people in Bombay.

Bala Govind put them up in a small hotel quite close to the Marina Beach, which a friendly waiter told them was the second longest beach in the world.

His army friend, Ram Mohan, had started a small business of ice cream. When he started it, he just wanted something that would sustain himself and his small family. In a very short span of time, Madras was swearing by the new product and there was a tremendous demand.

Ram Mohan knew that he would need to expand but did not know how. When Bala Govind had called him, he welcomed the opportunity thinking that Bala Govind having gained the experience of handling an expansion drive at Pankajam would be able to do something similar in Madras.

After a detailed discussion, where Ram Mohan explained to Bala Govind what he would be able to pay him and what he thought Bala Govind could do, Bala Govind agreed to work for Ram Mohan.

The family would continue to live in the small hotel until they found some suitable accommodation. Ram Mohan provided Bala Govind a car that he could use and soon Bala Govind settled into the new job, relieved that he was soon putting behind an experience that he and the family were keen to forget.

Within a week, they found a very decent flat, quite close to Bala Govind's brothers house in Mylapore. Ramakrishna Nagar was not the best of addresses in Madras, but it was clean, quiet and quite close to the school that Bala Govind was able to find for his two younger children to go to.

After they had met the owners and had decided on the rent, they paid the advance and moved in. The family was fast expending their last resources. Ram Mohan sensing this, advanced some money to Bala Govind and brushing aside the collective gratitude of both Bala Govind and Saraswathi, helped them settle down to a new life.

Bhaskaran continued to stay in the hostel and would visit them during the weekends. He was studying well and he was confident of becoming one of the select few who would be able to apply to a good American University for further studies.

"*Moneh*, I won't be able to pay for your tuitions, if you decide to go abroad to study." Bala Govind told his son.

"No *Acha*, don't worry about that. The Chairman of that company in Bombay which is sponsoring my studies had written to me stating that I could pursue my studies abroad and that I would not have to worry about the financial aspects," Bhaskaran reassured his father.

"Well, I hope that everything works out well," Bala Govind said.

His younger brother and sister soon settled themselves into their new school; they began to make new friends, and life seemed to settle into another routine.

Bala Govind was eager to prove himself and he literally threw himself into his new job. Ram Mohan was happy to see his friends' boundless energy and was supportive. The two families became close and in Latha, Ram Mohan's wife, Saraswathi found a good friend and a confidante.

Her parents who had moved in with them in Bombay continued to live with them. They were all cramped in the flat, but it was not half as bad as the ones that they were used to in Mahim and Bandra. Bala Govind told Saraswathi, that it was only a matter of time before they could move into a better house. She, the optimistic sucker of all that he told her, smiled actually visualising a new house!

The ice cream business, which they decided to call Iced Cream, began to expand. Soon all the neighbouring towns around Madras began to retail Iced Cream, children pestered parents for Iced Cream, and soon they began to get enquiries to go into other cities in the state.

Some things do not change at all, and Bala Govind, or was it just his character, did not. He was seething within himself at the injustice of having to live in a small flat, at the amount of hard work that he had to put in while Ram Mohan had moved into a larger house and was obviously living better. He and his family soon found that he had an infamous temper, which could rage out of control at the slightest provocation.

The people who worked at Iced Cream were testimony to the man's temper. He would scream at the top of his voice at the slightest provocation. They would tiptoe around his office for fear of being pulled up for some imaginary infraction.

His contributions at work dipped considerably, but were not immediately noticed because the business was growing on its own. Money was pouring in and they had a large market share of the ice cream business. They had established a quality which none of the others in the market were able to deliver. This combined with a very smart marketing campaign attracted more business.

Smartly he told Ram Mohan that it was only due to his brainpower that Iced Cream was where it was and Ram Mohan gullibly believed it. In fact, he could not care less, he had made more than he ever dreamt that he could in a lifetime and whatever else was coming in every day, was just a bonus.

He offered a hefty raise to Bala Govind who smilingly accepted it. Ram Mohan provided them a new house in a better area and once more the family moved there. This one had a lawn in the front, the children no longer needed to share their bedrooms with their grandparents, and overall their quality of life increased.

Secretly, Bala Govind was fuming. He felt that Ram Mohan should not have offered him just a hike but should have made him a partner. Furious at the oversight, he took out his frustrations on his wife. She would get a mouthful for just about everything. The food was bad at home, the kids were not getting the best grades, and her parents were intruding on his privacy and even the dogs, which they now had, took the brunt of his anger. He would entice the dogs with endearing words and some titbits, and when they came close wagging their tales, he would slap them.

It was then that he took to drinking. At first, it was just a peg or two, then it became more. On Sundays, he would begin drinking in the morning and continue till the evening and drop off into a drunken sleep from which he would awaken only the next morning.

The staff began noticing these small changes. They kept quiet, but some of the people in the finance department were making merry. They were blatantly stealing money. Cash, which came in for sales made, would be written off as credit and they became bolder when they would sell entire consignments without entering it into the records.

Still, Iced Cream was making money – enough to carry on without causing any major hiccups. As long as no one complained, there seemed to be no reason not to go on with what each was doing.

Bala Govind became a member of a nearby club that the new rich of Madras frequented. The old rich had their own hangouts – The Boat Club, The Madras Club and the Gymkhana Club. This one, the Queens Club, was also old, but was never managed well, until now. A new management went on an aggressive membership campaign and provided better services and facilities.

He told Ram Mohan that it was necessary to frequent the club, as this would only enhance their business further and get Ram Mohan to agree to pay for some of the entertainment expenses. Not that it really mattered. Bala Govind okayed all the Iced Cream bills and Ram Mohan did not have any reason to object as long he received his money for all his expenses.

The members of the Queens Club were floored by the magnanimity of Mr Bala Govind of Iced Cream. He would offer to pay for their liquor, he would host an impromptu party, and they had never seen nicer man than him.

The children began to drift slowly, but surely. Bala Govind's youngest daughter Veena, who was performing very well in her school in Bombay, seemed to have lost all interest in her studies. His second son Ram Kumar seemed to have developed a passion for badminton and was perpetually excusing himself to play in different matches or go off to some coaching camp or the other.

Bhaskaran became aware of all this when he visited his family. His exams were on and most of his classmates had decided to go home to study. He thought it was a good idea to spend some time with his family, and he came to stay there for a few days. Within three days, he regretted his decision.

His mother was looking haggard, tired, and harassed. His grandfather was bedridden and his grandmother seemed to have aged overnight. He only saw his brother on the third day and the chap seemed to have grown suddenly. He was thin and lean and his friends called him Rudy after Rudy Hartono, the famous Indonesian Badminton Champion. They exchanged a few pleasantries and that was that. Somewhere in the middle of finding their own identities, Bhaskaran realised that they had all grown apart. He realised that this was no longer a family that bonded together with a common love for each other. This was just a group of people only staying together because they had no other choice.

He was quite sure that if his father had the temerity and the gumption, he would have gladly walked out of the family. They seemed to be a burden to him. The way he treated them, talked to them, and abused them! He was living out his best fantasy and he did not need the constant reminders of his responsibilities as a father, a husband and indeed – the head of the family. Somehow, he never spoke to Bhaskaran that way – there seemed to be a fear factor there and Bhaskaran did not know where that came from.

Then there was Veena. She had discovered her femininity, growing up to become a beautiful young girl, far different from the noisy, nosy pest that he always fondly remembered her as. She was shy now, very introverted and would not make friends very easily. He remembered the time when he and she would go around to their friends' houses in Bombay and ask for short eats complaining of a sudden bout of hunger! He remembered sneaking into the kitchen when their mother and grandparents were fast asleep in the afternoons, to check out the 'larder' – a small kitchen cabinet that doubled as a safe house for the biscuits and other goodies that were edible. It had a close-knit wire mesh around it and this prevented the ants and flies getting to the food.

Now she was almost gawky. He thought that she was spending far too much time gazing into stupid romantic novels that she devoured voraciously.

She used to learn to dance classical Bharatanatyam, but Bala Govind had tired of it. Funny, Bhaskaran thought, his father had never once encouraged any one of them to pursue any one thing that the children were passionate about, persevere in it and excel in. He wondered if he was not doing so in order to save himself the expense or just that he did not care. He never would know the truth.

He had a couple of years more to go and he was keen on finishing on the top of his class to earn his scholarship. Packing up his books and his clothes, he told his parents that one of his professors was conducting a series of special classes and that he would have to go.

Only Veena and his mother seemed sad to see him go. Veena asked him if he did not like staying at home; he just smiled at her and tousled her long black hair.

"Take care of yourself, kiddo," he said, before closing the door.

33

Rome Airport

The flight from Bombay to Rome was both the first and the longest that Raashid had taken.

There was not a direct flight to Tripoli from Bombay and so he was now in Rome, waiting for another transit flight to Tripoli. An Alitalia ground staff told him, in a mime of words and writings that he would have to spend around five hours at Rome's Leonardo da Vinci airport. His flight to Tripoli, she explained, was at six o' clock in the evening, tapping her watch and indicating six on her fingers. He was quite thrilled at the prospect of spending such a long time here at that airport.

He was given a couple of coupons, which, he was told, could be given at the restaurant overlooking the runway for a meal, coffee and tea.

Raashid would have laughed if someone had told him of this airport in Nagpur. There were people all over the place. He did not know if they were coming or going. He had never ever seen so many *goras* in one place. That made him a little nervous. He found a few passengers who spoke in Hindi and walked over to them. They too were on their way to Libya and were in the airport for the past two days as their baggage had gone missing.

He saw couples walk hand in hand… and he had always thought that only happened in the movies. Suddenly, he saw another couple, kissing. He stood rooted to the ground as if struck by lightning. Allah! He thought – what am I seeing here?

Without warning, the man turned around to face him and stared right back at the young man and asked him, "What are you staring at, you moron?"

Raashid did not understand what was said, but he understood the tone and blushing slightly, he walked away. That experience indelibly printed in his mind causing him to shake his head, more in disbelief than in amusement.

He found that the airport was filled with policemen who were a lot better dressed and armed than the ones that he had seen back home.

Walking on, he was stunned by the myriad of artefacts displayed in the windows of the shopping area. They seemed to entice him inside, looking lost and bewildered at this massive array of fine things that even the best shops in Bombay would not have.

Walking past a counter, he was asked by a lady who looked a lot like Simi Garewal, the beautiful Hindi movie actress, if he wanted anything. Not understanding her, he moved closer to her counter, more attracted to her personality and her beauty than anything else.

She whipped out a bottle of perfume and reaching for his hand sprayed the contents on his wrist and asked him to smell it.

The aroma was mystical and reminded him of Moosa Bhai. Moosa Bhai had this love for perfumes and his dressing table was full of these bottles, he remembered nostalgically.

She asked him something and again he did not understand her, just shook his head, and picking up his small handbag, sauntered on.

Another counter attracted his attention. Here he found cigarettes that he had only seen in some old foreign magazines that lay around in Shapoorji and Sons. Not just packets, cartons of it along with some of the most elegant lighters, in gold and various other hues. He used to watch Moosa Bhai light his 555 cigarettes with a lighter and wondered what pleasure his brother derived from smoking so many of them. Tobacco in pouches, pipes, and other smoking artefacts littered the display shelf. In one corner, he was pleasantly surprised to see a whole rack full of *beedis*. So, he thought, even the *goras* smoke *beedis*!

There were men at this counter who seemed to be buying cigarettes and even a woman who was smoking a cigarette attached to a long pipe. He had never seen a cigarette holder and watched in admiration as she inhaled on her cigarette, watching her hold the cigarette in her beautiful fingers, the long nails painted in red.

Suddenly the man at the counter looked at him and asked him in Hindi, "Do you want to buy something?"

Caught off guard because the man had spoken to him in Hindi, he smiled.

"I did not realise that you were an Indian," He said.

"I am a Pakistani, not an Indian. Anyway, do you want to buy something?"

"How much for these cigarettes?" he asked as bravely as possible.

"Which one do you want?" the man asked.

"How about the 555's?" Raashid countered.

"They will cost you six American dollars a carton." the sales clerk explained.

In the aircraft, he had pulled out the bunch of notes that Moosa Bhai had given him at the airport and after carefully looking at the denominations, he realised that he had close to a hundred American dollars. He had no idea how much that translated into Indian Rupees or any other currency.

He pulled out the wad of notes from his pocket, prised out a ten-dollar note, and handed it over to the sales clerk.

The man suddenly became very interested. He had seen a whole lot of Indian workers on their way to Libya and they all seemed so impoverished; but this one, he was sure, was different. The young man was wearing a good pair of shoes, a good pair of jeans a nice t-shirt, and a leather jacket. Probably comes from a good family, the man thought.

Handing over the carton, he also gave Raashid a plastic lighter and magnanimously told him that the lighter was a compliment. Leaning over the counter, he asked Raashid, "Do you want to change some of those dollars? I can get you very good rates."

The man did not realise for an instant that he was talking to a very street-smart kid who could size up a person in a flash, and who really knew how to look after himself.

Raashid looked up at the Pakistani, gave him his best smile, and said, "No thanks." The man knew from the smile that there was no point in repeating the offer.

Moving away from the tobacco counter, he suddenly realised he was quite hungry. He decided to find some food and remembered that the ground staff had given him some coupons with which he could get something to eat.

He went back to the group of Indian workers who had lost their baggage and asked them if they knew which restaurant to go to with the coupons.

They sniggered at him and one of them who seemed to be the know-it-all of the group, said, "Arrey Bhai, you cannot get any *daal chawal* there. The foods that they give you to eat there even our dogs back home won't eat!"

"That's okay. But which is the restaurant?" Raashid persisted.

They pointed to the one on the extreme right and thanking them, he walked away.

Entering the restaurant, he found a vacant table and sat down. A little later, he realised that there would be no waiters serving him. He noticed a couple that had come in after him, went to a table placed their belongings there and came back to the counter. Picking up a tray, they walked the length of the counter sizing up the fare.

They then went back and filled their plates with all that they seemed to like.

Slowly he slipped out of his table, walked to the counter and picking up a tray for himself, he too walked the length of the counter. He could not recognise any of the food that was on display. All that he recognised was chicken. This was not tandoori chicken or even chicken curry. It seemed to be just boiled and it did not look very tasty. Although he was not very fussy about food, he had no clue as to what to eat. Some stuff looked like a whole bunch of string hopelessly intertwined with each other and he was not sure how to eat it.

The chicken was the safest bet and he saw some salad, which he also thought, was safe.

Picking up a few pieces of chicken and some salad – he did not even know what the vegetables were – he caught site of some bread on the corner. This did not look like the normal bread. It was brown, coarse and was more round in shape than the square Modern Bread slices that he was used to seeing.

"Never mind," he told himself, "You have to eat and you have to eat something."

Sitting at his table, he looked around, it was then he saw the entire stretch of runway. Planes seemed to be landing every minute and planes seemed to be taking off every minute. Fascinated he kept watching. Taking his eyes off, he looked around the room once more and found that all the people in the restaurant were using forks. This seemed to be another problem until he saw another man, wrap the chicken in the paper napkins and holding them gingerly almost as if they would fly away, eating them.

He opted for that choice and did exactly as the other man did. In between, as if he was engrossed with the planes taking off, he picked up a piece of the salad and crunched on it, looking from the corner of his eyes to survey the room. He was looking for anyone who might give him a disdainful look because he was using his hands. He need not have bothered – everyone had their plates and minds full and just needed to get some food into their stomachs.

Satisfied that he no longer was hungry, he walked out of the cafeteria not knowing what next to do, when he suddenly remembered the cigarettes.

He sat down on a chair quite close to an ashtray, opened the carton, took out a packet, and very casually took out a cigarette. Searching for the lighter that he got with the carton, he found it in his jacket pocket.

He lit it and just as he had seen Moosa Bhai and a few others, he took a deep drag and immediately bent double coughing his lungs out.

He looked around expecting to see derisive laughter. Again, no one seemed to have noticed.

He looked at the cigarette and once more decided to take a drag. This time he took a more tentative drag, and slowly inhaled the smoke. Although his eyes smarted and he felt the bile rising – he did not choke on the smoke.

By the time it was six in the evening and he had walked back to the counter where the Alitalia ground staff person had asked him to come back to report for the flight to Tripoli, he had smoked more cigarettes and enjoyed everyone of it.

34

Tripoli, Libya

When the flight from Rome reached Tripoli, it was very late at night. The airport was deserted but was brightly lit and he followed the crowd of people who got off the aircraft and went to the conveyor belts to collect their baggage. From here, they went into the large hall where they all stood in queues waiting for the immigration and custom checks.

Some of the Indians were carrying foodstuff in their baggage and the Libyan Customs officers demanded to know what it was that they were carrying. As they stood in a queue, sleepy, tired and completely dumb to the questions the Customs Officer asked gutturally in broken English and Arabia and Hindi, what they were carrying. One of the smartest, figured out what was being asked. He gestured they were edible stuff that they were carrying. So the Libyan Customs Officer asked him to eat whatever it was that he was carrying. He was carrying some dry tamarind, he just pulled off some and shoved it into his mouth, grimacing at the sour taste as he chewed on it. Convinced that it was edible stuff that this man was carrying, the Customs Officer moved down the queue, eyeing each of them closely.

The man standing in front of Raashid looked back and said, "What if he asks me to eat what I am carrying?"

"What are you carrying?" Raashid asked him.

"Chilli pickles," the man said worried.

"Well, just pray that he does not ask you to eat it. If he does, your ass is going to be hell," Raashid said with a smile.

After almost two hours, they were done with immigration and customs and once again, he followed the passengers as they walked out of the hall. He did not know whom to talk to and whom not to. The Libyans spoke in a language that he had never before heard and he remembered what the agent who had processed his papers in Bombay had told him. That the Libyans speak Arabic, yes, that is right, he told himself. So, this is what Arabic sounds like?

He found some more Indians, or were they Pakistanis? Approaching them, he asked them if they could help him. They asked him what he wanted and he said that he was to wait near the arrival door for someone to pick him up. They asked him for which company he had come to work and he said, Brega Petroleum Corporation. He had memorised the name a thousand times and he would never ever forget it.

They looked at him in a rather weird manner. And for once, he thought, he was stumped. He did not understand the looks and he did not know why they looked at him in such a fashion.

A *sardar* in the group looked at him and said, "Where in Brega are you going to be working?"

"I don't know, I was just asked to meet someone at Tripoli Airport and that this person would take me to meet the concerned authorities in this company," Raashid said.

"This company? You said this company? Arrey yaar, thank your lucky stars that you enter the country and you enter into one of the best paying companies here. People like us are dying to work for Brega, where they pay good salaries. You understand?" the *sardar* asked him.

"I am sorry, I did not know," Raashid said, quite chastised by the education that this *sardar* just gave him. Moosa Bhai had got him a visa into what these people claimed was a great company.

"Come out with us. We are also going out. Let's see if we can find your man, usually there are people waiting with placards, and then they take you to the camps. Perhaps you will be taken to the office tomorrow morning," smiled the *sardar*.

As he had said, there was indeed someone waiting from Brega Petroleum. He was a tall black man. Raashid thought this must be a giant. He was taller than any man he had ever seen and it quite intimidated him.

He caught the man's eye and said, "Brega?"

The man smiled and stuck an awesome palm in front of Raashid quickly pushed aside any doubts.

"Jaffer, ya khooya, ismi Jaffer. Ahlan wah sahlan," the man went on. The only thing that Raashid understood was the word Jaffer and he thought that the man was telling him his name.

Taking the huge palm in his own, he shook it and said, "Raashid Abdul Latif." That was the name that was mentioned on his passport and that was the name that he would use. He never knew where the 'Abdul Latif' came from, and since no explanation was forthcoming from either Moosa Bhai or the agent who had arranged the visa, he did not bother to ask.

The driver kept talking to him and finally in desperation Raashid looked up at him said in a smattering of English, "No speak Arabic."

This seemed to satisfy Jaffer and he was quiet all the way to the camp.

He was shown a small room with a toilet and then Jaffer left.

The next morning, he got up hearing a lot of commotion. The camp was alive and he got ready.

Getting dressed and carrying his passport, he looked at the pack of cigarettes and decided not to carry it, as he was not sure how people would view him smoking.

His bags were already packed and locked. He walked out, closing the door behind him.

Behind this room seemed to be a sprawling camp. He could see an endless sea of cabins, all white, all parked in neat rows. There were paths to walk. He walked on, not really knowing where to go.

He passed a huge swimming pool and looking at it he realised that there were three of them, all lined up side by side. He did not understand the reason for three pools.

Further down, he saw basketball courts, tennis courts and there to the right he saw a huge mosque and at this time, there were a few people who were coming out. Next to it was a white block with glass windows and he read the word 'hospital' written in Hindi. He realised that it was the same word that was written in more than a dozen languages. Common sense told him that in this camp, there were more than a dozen nationalities.

He was amazed at the size of this camp. As he turned around to find someone to ask for directions to the camp office, he found a group of Indians. They were walking towards another building and he ran to catch up with them. He asked them breathlessly in Hindi, "Can you help me?"

They looked at him curiously and asked him what he wanted.

"I just arrived last night. Could you show me the camp office? I need to go and show them my passport."

"Have you had anything to eat?" One of them asked him.

"No, nothing. I just woke up, had a bath, and came out of the room," Raashid said.

"Okay! Come in and have some breakfast, and then we will take you to the office. The office opens only at 9 and we have more than half an hour," the man said.

He had never seen a bigger eating hall. Several food counters on either sides and the middle was full of people eating breakfast.

Another man who was in the group that he came in with said, "There are many nationalities of people here and there are different kinds of foods available. Anyone can eat anything. You can also eat whatever you want. We prefer to eat bread and eggs in the morning, but if you like, there are *rotis* available too."

"No, I'll just have bread too," Raashid said.

He nibbled through breakfast, taking in the enormity of this awesome place and wondering how many people this huge company might employ.

The office was staffed by Chinese looking people, whom he later was told were Filipinos and one took his passport, checked a list and then asked him if he spoke English. He shook his head in negative and the man turned around and yelled, "Daya Singh, please come here."

A portly, cheerful looking Indian came into the room. "Arrey Ronnie, why are you always screaming, *yaar*?" Daya Singh asked the man who had just yelled.

"I think that you need a woman very badly and I suggest that you speak to your boss and ask for emergency leave to go back home," Daya Singh whispered conspiratorially.

"That's all that you can think of Daya Singh. Women, women, and women! And you think that everyone else is also so desperate as you are," Ronnie chided him.

"Anyway, why did you call me?" Daya Singh asked, suddenly all business and bluster.

"This is Raashid Abdul Latif. He has just arrived from India. My list says that he is to be sent to Kufra. The agent could have routed his ticket through Benghazi instead of sending him here. However, never mind that. Since he is already here, you tell him that he will have to stay here for a few days, complete his medical formalities and then we will finish his paperwork and then send him to his new location," Ronnie explained to Daya Singh, a pencil twirling in his manicured almost lady-like fingers.

Daya Singh turned around and introduced himself to Raashid in the typical manner that most people from the sub-continent usually do. "Where are you from?"

"India," Said Raashid.

"*Achha, apna aadmi hai, kya*?" Daya Singh smiled, extending his hand.

"Where in India do you come from? Please don't tell me that you are from Kerala. This place is overflowing with them, *yaar*. I think that they are now exporting Malayalis from India," Daya Singh said.

"No, I am from Bombay and not a Malayali," Raashid said.

"What is your profession?" Daya Singh asked.

"Oh! I am a diesel mechanic," Raashid said.

"Well, this is a surprise. I thought from your dress and your manner that you must be some high funda supervisor," Daya Singh, once more giving Raashid a thorough look.

"Let me tell you what Ronnie told me. You should be working in Kufra. They had requested for a diesel mechanic there at the airbase. He thinks that you should have been sent to the Brega office in Benghazi and then sent onward to Kufra from there, but since you were sent here, we will have to process you and send your passport to the immigration department here for your work permit, bank accounts etc," Daya Singh explained patiently.

He took him to the car pool and saw Jaffer, the tall man who had picked up Raashid from the airport.

"Jaffer!" Daya Singh called out.

Jaffer turned and spotted them. He waved.

"Daya, kaif halek," he greeted.

"Jaffer, this is Raashid Abdul Latif. He just came in last night," Daya Singh said.

Jaffer smiled at Raashid and once again stuck his hands out to the young man. This time Raashid smiled and took the giants hand in his own.

"I know Daya, I picked him up from the airport," Jaffer said still holding Raashid's hand in his.

"Oh! So you two have already met? Anyway, Raashid meet Jaffer Bushara, the future President of the Sudan," Daya Singh joked with his usual warm smile.

"Ya, Raashid. That is me. And did Daya tell you that his dream is to make enough money here and go back to India and become a politician?" Jaffer asked in a smattering of broken English and Hindi.

Raashid smiled at them, understanding the easy intimacy that seemed to flow between these ordinary men. Between the Indians, Pakistani's, Bangladeshi's, Filipinos, Turks and the many other nationalities here the *lingua franca* was a pidgin mix of Hindi, English, Arabic and any other language that you could throw in.

"Take him to the hospital and take him to Dr. Bhattacharya. Tell him that this is a new employee and ask him to run the usual tests. You can either drop him off and go to the office and pick up all the letters from the post office or wait with Raashid and then go to the office. Choice is yours," Daya Singh told Jaffer.

The drive in a white Toyota Land Cruiser was beautiful for Raashid. He was getting to like everything about Libya; the roads were superb, the cars were fast and there was order everywhere.

He saw huge portraits of a man in different uniforms and Jaffer explained that they were of the man who ruled Libya since 1969 after a coup in which he overthrew the ruler of Libya, King Idris.

"What's his name, Jaffer?" Raashid asked excitedly.

"He is Colonel Muammar Al Gaddafi. The leader of the Socialist People's Libyan Arab Jamoharriya. That is what he has renamed Libya."

He saw young boys and girls in army uniforms and Jaffer said that here in Libya, a military service was mandatory for all Libyan citizens.

They reached the hospital and Jaffer parked the car and went to look for Dr Bhattacharya.

They found him, a small bird-like man whom Raashid immediately took a liking to.

He was talking throughout to Raashid, asking him of any illness that he might have had in the past and asking him for any allergies – and he just went on and on, it seemed to Raashid the man was trying to be reassuring, almost telling him that he need not worry, without actually saying so.

Then he took him for the various tests and x-rays and by the time the whole process was over it was almost noon.

Jaffer was hanging around chatting up with anyone who even remotely looked Sudanese and occasionally Raashid could hear his booming laughter accompanied by this rather loud clap, which was typical of Jaffer.

Dr Bhattacharya asked them to come back the next morning for the results and his report. Shaking hands with him, they left for the Brega office.

In the administration department, Raashid met more Indians who were equally nice to him and he felt happy of being part of a fraternity and all that he could think of was that he was here because of his brother. Even with this awesome distance between them could not somehow dilute the tremendous feeling of gratitude that he felt just then for his brother. He would call Moosa Bhai today from the post office as one of the Indians he had met had instructed him to.

Two days later, he boarded another aircraft – this time a Libyan Airways Boeing, which was going to Benghazi. Jaffer and Daya Singh came to the airport to see him off and each of them gave him a hug and wished him luck. Never had he seen such human warmth ever and was glad to experience such new phenomena in his life.

Daya Singh had told him that from Benghazi he would have to collect his baggage and check into another flight – his last one that would leave for Kufra at around ten in the morning. He also told him that he would be put up at the Kufra Hilton for a couple of days before they arranged suitable accommodation for him.

He could hardly believe his ears. He had heard of the word Hilton. Someone had told him once that the Hilton Hotels were spread across the world and that even the Hotel Taj in Bombay was a poor cousin to the Hilton. He could only imagine what that meant. Moosa had taken him for dinner several times to the Taj and he was struck by the absolute grandeur of the place. Now he was going to be staying in the Hilton. He could not believe his ears.

35

Kufra, An Oasis in the Sahara

When the plane stopped at the terminal building and as the doors opened, the controlled atmosphere inside the aircraft suddenly became very warm.

There were not many people in the aircraft and as the handful of passengers piled out onto the tarmac to walk towards the terminal building, Raashid felt the intensity of the heat.

Hot, was what Bombay was. This was heat at its purest best. There did not seem to be a single tree in the vicinity. He could see waves of heat rising up in a shimmer from the tarmac and he pulled off the leather jacket that he was wearing.

Even then, there was not much comfort. He could feel a rivulet of sweat begin to spring from the nape of his neck and travel to his waste along his spine. Other than that, he felt something strange. Here in Kufra there wasn't the stifling humidity that Bombay was famous for. He would learn later that the humidity in Kufra was 0% and that temperatures could rise up to 72 degrees Celsius and could drop below zero at nights.

Here in Kufra, there was no conveyor belt to carry the luggage, just a trailer on which the luggage was brought from the aircraft and the passengers collected it themselves and walked back to the terminal.

At the exit, he recognised a Brega Petroleum placard and walked towards it. This time he had no problems as he had in Tripoli. Here was an Indian waiting for him.

Arjan Singh was a strapping *sardar*, he was a driver who had brought in an oil truck from Tripoli. The Brega Kufra office manager asked him to go to the airport and pick up someone who was going to be working with them in Kufra. Arjan Singh who was famous for never saying no to anyone – simply smiled, picked up the offered keys and drove to the airport.

It seemed to Raashid that he had known this affable man all his life.

The drive to Kufra was a short ride and all that he could see on either side of the road was sand and more sand. Camels were everywhere and as they neared town, date palms lined either side of the road.

He met the office manager at Kufra who told him to rest for the day and that he would have to stay in the hotel for a couple of days before they could fix up his accommodation in the camp. He was sorry, he said, about this small accommodation problem, but the camp was full and he would have to juggle something, somewhere.

Not that he did mind. He was thinking of his last conversation with Daya Singh in Tripoli when Daya Singh had told him that he would have to stay for a few days in the Kufra Hilton.

He was looking forward to his day of rest in a truly world class hotel.

When Arjan Singh pulled up the car in front of an almost ramshackle building, he thought the man might have stopped to talk to someone he knew.

He was quite surprised when Arjan Singh asked him to get down from the car with his bags.

"Is this where I will be staying?" Raashid asked.

"Yes, for a day or two, I think," Arjan Singh said.

Seeing the surprise on his face, Arjan Singh asked Raashid, "Did Daya Singh mention anything about the Kufra Hilton?"

Raashid could only nod.

Arjan Singh loudly laughed. Clapping Raashid on his back, he said, "Well, my friend, this is indeed the Kufra Hilton. I will now introduce you to meet the proud owner and Managing Director, Mohammed Nashem."

Mohammed Nashem turned out to be a Libyan who was the chief cook, dishwasher, coffeemaker, cashier, and owner of this august establishment.

Despite his disappointment, Raashid could only smile and promised himself that next time he met Daya Singh, he would personally strangle him.

The room at the Kufra Hilton reminded him of his tiny room at Shapoorji and Sons at Nagpur. It was almost a carbon copy of the room and probably dirtier.

He preferred to sleep on the floor. But during the nights, it got very cold and he had to use a blanket in the night to keep himself warm. It really was cold.

In the morning, he just had to shove his head out of the window and yell, Mohammed, *chai*. Within minutes, Mohammed would come up the stairs, carrying thick Arabic tea in a kettle, which certainly had seen better days, and a thimble-shaped small glass.

By seven in the morning, Arjan Singh was back in a pickup truck to pick him up and drive him to the Kufra Air Base where he joined that day, as the Brega Petroleum's Diesel Mechanic. The company's truck workshop was situated there and it was here that Raashid would begin working.

Working here in the desert was not difficult; they began early and finished work at half past two in the afternoon. With nothing else to do, he would work until six along with the chief mechanic – a Greek wizard who had been working on diesel engines for almost twenty years. "Wow," thought Raashid, "That is almost my entire lifetime!"

The Greek, Christos, who could only speak Greek and bits of Arabic, English, and now Hindi, did not think of his handicap with language really a handicap. He talked to the Indians workers in the base and had conversations ranging from politics to the weather here and the wonderful time that the Greeks always had back home.

For Raashid the major problem was that he was not really a diesel mechanic and secondly he was not at all familiar with the vehicles that were being serviced here. Mercedes Benz, Mann, Volvo, Fiat, and a few other makes were part of the fleet of trucks in Brega Petroleum.

Christos spotted that immediately and putting a hand on the young man's shoulder, he said, "*Maalish*, don't worry. Stick with me and by the time your contract is done, you will be better than me."

Raashid was relieved and even more so when the camp administration allotted him a cabin almost next door to Christos'.

Little did he realise that from Christos, he not only would learn to become a great mechanic but he would also learn the fine art of distilling *grubba*, the hooch that almost everybody seemed to be making and consuming in the camp. For most people in the camp, *grubba* was the only relief from the monotony that soon sets into camp life.

And it seemed to him that the biggest bootlegger in the entire camp was Christos. His distillery was an entire 40′ container and on its door was written in Arabic – DO NOT ENTER, POISON INSIDE. Here Christos made *grubba* for himself, those who were close to him and those who chose to could buy from him the best hooch that money could buy this side of the Sahara Desert.

36

Bombay, The Dawn of a New Era

Business had never been better. There seemed to be a general recovery in not just the economy but in the minds of people too. Foreign companies were investing in India like never before and the mood was upbeat.

By a series of sheer cunning and careful manoeuvres, Moosa had now taken over most of the underworld. There were a couple of other loosely run outfits, but they were not a patch on his empire and truly, it was an empire. He had a finger into every pie that one could possibly conceive of – Real Estate and Property Development, Finance, Movies, Transport, Cargo, Food and Beverages, Hotels and Resorts, Liquor – the list was endless.

The more he grew the lesser people that he dealt with. He hired the best minds in these various industries that money could buy. He would deal only with them, he would encourage them to perform better and better, the employees of such companies hardly knew Moosa as the owner – but the hired professionals were seen as the owners. Here too, the rules were very simple, just like his other underworld businesses. Perform and you were the king of whatever you saw – fail and you were doomed. He encouraged his managers to higher levels of lifestyles and ambition – but warned them of the consequences of stealing.

It never bothered him one bit that some of his managers were from the best Business and Engineering schools. He would get a layman's brief and it amazed even them at the speed at which he would grasp the matter presented before him.

In any case, they would show no disrespect to him because of his lack of education. They had absolute freedom to act and as long as they did not compromise the businesses, in which they were involved in – Moosa hardly interfered. For that one aspect they respected him tremendously. They also loved him and would do their best for him because they were paid stupendous salaries, the best homes were provided to them, memberships to the swankiest clubs, and healthcare at the Breach Candy Hospital and holidays at the finest destinations across the world. To top all of these were the fat bonuses that he so willingly gave them when they achieved their own goals.

Each of them he'd taught to become less of employees and more of entrepreneurs. He taught them that they'd never fail if they mentored their employees, taught them ownership and taught them to take their responsibilities as seriously as their religion. So it was not surprising that most of Moosa's operations were highly profitable, very high on innovation, very low on absenteeism, high on productivity and almost nil on attrition. People came to work! That was visibly evident. They came to work with enthusiasm, their complete self and left for home satisfied that they had contributed from within.

Every January in every single organisation that he owned, there was a ritual. Each and every employee from the top to down was asked to write down his dream to achieve for the year. That could be anything – but it had to be realistic and it had to be achieved. So you could write, for example, "To Own a Dream Car", or "Send Son to Yale" – but you'd also have to achieve it by the end of the year.

All of his employees had to undergo this ritual. Write down what you earned, then you wrote down your dreams and then you measured what you could achieve of your dreams on your pay.

Then you had to make a call as to how you're going to achieve your dreams. You have to presume that you are not going to win the lottery; you're not going to land a windfall amount of money – that the only source of money that you were going to get is what you were going to make at work. So you could think of making more for your organisation, you could get innovative, you could pitch for a new account – any way that would help you get the funding for your dream.

What Moosa wanted to achieve with this ritual was to focus each and every employee on his or her annual target, both personal and financial, then give that person whatever support was required to help him or her achieve that target. This way, he believed, his organisations could save cost on 'supervising' people, ensuring that people were satisfied with what they did and he sincerely hoped that by working for him they would be satisfied with what they had achieved.

He was now beginning to feel that this was the time to venture abroad. He was happy to hear from Raashid. In the past two years, that the boy had left for Libya, he was doing very well, mastering something that he was passionate about, and enjoying it.

A couple of times, Raashid had requested Moosa to send some money for the families of some of his colleagues and before an hour, the money had been delivered to the utter satisfaction of Raashid's colleagues.

He had asked Raashid to take some more interest in such operations, as the rules in Libya did not permit one hundred percent repatriation of salaries that expatriates earned.

Slowly Raashid was increasing the flow and these days anyone in Brega who wanted to send money to India would contact Raashid. The boy was turning around more than a hundred thousand dollars a month! Moosa wondered in amazement.

He wanted Raashid to take the initiative and tell him that he was ready to get into business than him pushing his younger brother into something that he was not willing to get into.

The phenomenal growth of his businesses left Moosa with hardly any time to even think of starting a family. Yet, sometimes when he came back into the swank house that he now lived in on the Worli sea face which he had purchased a few years ago, he did wish that someone would be there at home, other than his cook and his servants, to welcome him and to talk with.

These thoughts were just wishful thoughts, he would tell himself. He had no time to dedicate to a wife, a family. There were too many things happening just now. Many of the businesses that he controlled were actually those that he fronted, but actually belonged to the several Ministers whose money he handled as investments and which helped purchase these businesses.

Moosa's empire was vast, complicated, and intricate. The sheer professionalism with which he managed them was almost legendary. It was surprising that many of his organisations were voted 'Best Places to Work' and it was with great surprise that Corporate India watched the way in which his enterprises ran so smoothly and profitably.

✪

37

Madras

Bala Govind's personal hell was becoming increasingly complicated. He had built a monumental hatred for Ram Mohan that had begun to manifest itself into every vestige of their relationship. Ironically, Ram Mohan never knew of these imaginary elements, which for now, only existed in Bala Govind's mind.

Ram Mohan moved into a spacious, indeed, palatial bungalow right in the heart of Madras. On the day of the housewarming, the entire cream of Madras was present, congratulating this ex-Army officer turned successful entrepreneur. It was Bala Govind's responsibility of organising the whole event and he did it with practised ease and a venomous heart.

He felt that where Ram Mohan was today was all because of him and thus he felt cheated. Cheated for the lack of recognition, cheated out of a partnership and cheated out of wealth which he truly believed was more his than anyone else's, including Ram Mohan.

When a few people asked him why he was not looking his best, he put it down to the tension of ensuring a hassle-free event. Unable to vent his frustration, he had picked on Saraswathi and her parents just that morning.

His in-laws were becoming older and his father-in-law especially was sicker than ever before. He had wanted to speak to

Bala Govind, especially because it had seemed days, indeed months to the old man's mind, that he had a chat with his ever-busy son-in-law. Saraswathi asked Bala Govind, if it would be convenient for him to speak to her father just before he left for Ram Mohan's house.

"Why, what's the matter?" Bala Govind demanded, adjusting his tie in the dressing table mirror.

"*Acha* has been wanting to see you for a few days. Nothing special, I just think that he wants to see you and spend a few moments with you," Saraswathi replied mildly. She too, was going for the housewarming, later. The car would drop off Bala Govind first, and then return to pick up Saraswathi and perhaps the kids.

Possessed by his own demons, he did not even remember last time that he had actually spent time with his children. Bhaskaran would occasionally come, spending more and more time on studies. His final year at IIT was fast ending and he gave it everything that he had, ensuring that he got himself that coveted scholarship. The other two children, busy with their own lives, did not really mind that their father hardly spent any quality time with them – it seemed to him that if at all he did, he spent it all in abject criticism and showing absolutely no appreciation for even the smallest of achievements.

"I do not have the time to hold his hand and listen to his tales. He is being looked after, isn't he? You are taking him to the doctors, whenever required. Isn't he getting his food on time? What more is there for him to worry about?" Bala Govind asked Saraswathi.

"It's not to complain, just that he has not seen you for a while and he just wanted to have a chat with you," Saraswathi tried to explain.

"Maybe he wants me to know that his will has been drawn and that I am the sole beneficiary," Bala Govind leered, using the comb for the hundredth time to comb in place that imaginary hair that had somehow managed to swing out of place, since the last time he had combed it.

"Is that all you can think about? Money and wealth? Don't people matter to you?" Saraswathi asked, fed up with his attitude and his growing arrogance. She had been noticing that Bala Govind would only respect those with money. The people who were not wealthy enough, his attitude seemed to imply, deserved no respect.

"What you will never understand is that there are people who love you for what you are and not what you will or might become," she tried to tell him.

He waved his hand at her, ridiculing her suggestion. "When you possess money and power, you will get love, loved ones; and if you do not, you just suffer, perhaps in silence or in open derision," he said.

"I am sorry that you seem to think so, because in our case as a family, none of us ever see you as this wealthy, successful man and none of us ever behave with the ulterior motive that we might get a lot of special attention from you or perhaps, gifts – if we behave well with you," she said defiantly.

Surprised at her tone, he stopped fixing the cufflink on his shirt and turning to face her, he asked, "So what do you, your parents and your children think of me? A hero to the world and a zero to the family, isn't it? I know what you all think of me. I understand the veiled comparisons that you make of me with other men; don't think that I am a fool, Saraswathi."

She looked at him, this man whom she had learned to love and support, now a total stranger in front of her.

"You have no clue. You have no idea what we think of you, do you? You have raised your own expectations from the world and you therefore think that we, your own family, have higher expectations from you and you are feeling guilty that you cannot meet them and thus you take it out on us. Well, let me tell you something Mr Pompous Business Executive, and you listen to me well. We all think of you as someone who is doing his best to make things work for himself and his family. We do not expect you to be able to give us gifts of gold and expensive clothes. We just want you to be happy, to live within our own means. We just want a normal, peaceful, happy life for all of us and that includes you. We wish that there were nights when you could have dinner with us, we wish that you would be able to spend more time with us, share in the ordinary jokes that makes us laugh, talk to us and share your sorrow, your joys and your hopes. Instead, you live life as if you are forever on a roller coaster. You only see your own importance, your convenience, and your priorities. Nothing else matters to you. Not me, the children, or anyone else," she seethed.

That was not the end. All the bitterness of dashed hopes, aborted dreams and the small optimism of one day living in their own house in Madras seemed to vent today. She was livid with anger and the sheer hopelessness of trying to make this man see some reality.

"I have seen you talk to your friends, have seen you treat people. I have noticed the way that you make plans which you will never be able to see to fruition. And I want to ask you – are you working your way towards your dreams? No. You are not. You just have some fancy get-rich-quick dreams that somebody brings along to your notice. For all the high flung talk and the philosophising, this image that you are trying to create of yourself as some hotshot, smart business executive, I am surprised how naïve you are and how easily you get carried away. You should listen to what people have to say about you when you are not too busy shooting your mouth off bad mouthing someone who just happened to be your latest target simply because you are not, in your own mind, as good as he is. Simply because you are not wealthy enough as that person is! You cannot stand it that Ram Mohan is spending such a phenomenal amount of money on a house and to top that this lavish housewarming ceremony. Yet, you do not have the gumption to shout and swear at him like you do at the kids and me," she said.

Bala Govind just stood there staring at this very docile, meek woman who had never raised her voice against him all these years. His mind told him to slap her, to push her against the wall, or slam her head against it.

Sometimes truth is so powerful that you cannot even move in its presence.

The tears that ran down her cheek were not shed for herself in self-sympathy. It ran down her face, tracing all the broken paths that she had taken along with this man, silently and without complains. She did not crave for recognition or for that matter even gratitude, but when he thought that he was fighting this lone battle for survival without ever realising that he had the support of his family, it really hurt. And today she could not care. This was the pinnacle of her elasticity. She could take it no more.

"You ask yourself why KRK then or Ram Mohan now has not helped you. You feel that you are not being rewarded suitably. Do you have the slightest idea that there are better men than you out there who will do whatever you are doing, perhaps only better, for half the cost that you are being paid? What have you done for KRK and Ram Mohan that you have to crib so much, and feel robbed as you do? You just did a job. Is there something that you have gone out of your way to do for them? No, not at all. The problem was and is that you do not realise that there was a job to do; they needed someone, and they were willing to pay a cost. Nothing more and nothing else; therefore, it's not their fault that you emotionalised the whole notion of an ordinary employment and without giving of yourself completely to the job without doing anything extraordinary, you began to make expectations within your heart that they never felt obliged to meet. Whose fault is that? Yours or theirs?" she shouted.

"Ask yourself, don't tell me – but ask yourself – is there anything, just about anything that you have gone out of your way to do for someone without asking him or her for either payment or gratitude? Have you done anything for anyone that you felt you ought to do? Just as one human being to another? No, the truth is that you have never done anything. How can you believe that you deserve the best when you have never done your best for anyone? Not to your employers, not to your family, not to your friends, your society, your environment and least of all those people who have served you – your peons, your staff, your drivers. How can you be so foolish to expect good to come to you when you have not done anyone any good, ever? How? How stupid can you ever become?" She sobbed, her heart broken for this man steeped in arrogance and self-importance who never saw the true treasures that he was blessed with – a great family.

Bala Govind stood mesmerised, his mouth open, his jaw hanging, not believing a word that was just said by his wife.

Glancing at his watch, he suddenly realised that he was running late. Without a second glance at his broken-hearted wife, he walked out of the room.

38

Family Regained

Out of the six scholarships that were awarded, one was awarded to Bhaskaran, to the prestigious Massachusetts Institute of Technology in Boston, in the United States. His professors were proud of him and his friends were equally envious. When he called Moosa, even before he called home to inform his parents, Moosa was delighted.

"Moosa Bhai, this is Bhaskaran calling from Madras," he said excitedly. It had been a while since he had spoken to Moosa and although Moosa had made a few trips to Madras to spend a full day with Bhaskaran, he had not called him in the last six months since he wanted him to study.

"How are you, my dear friend?" Moosa asked him. Bhaskaran could almost hear the smile in his voice.

"Moosa Bhai, I am a gold medallist and have earned a scholarship to one of the best Institutions in the United States," Bhaskaran told him.

"*Arrey Raja, jiyo meri jaan*, I knew that you will succeed. I am so happy for you," Moosa said.

"So what is next? Why don't you come to Bombay and spend a few days with me before you go to America?" Moosa asked him.

"I can do that. Let me first see what I have to do here before I go. I will call you in the next couple of days and then I will come to visit you," Bhaskaran said. He had to go home and spend a couple of days with his family.

His parents were happy to see their son doing so well, and his father said that they should all make a trip to Kerala, so that his grandparents could visit Parappuram and then they would all go to pray at the Sri Krishna Temple in Guruvayoor.

He was thrilled at the idea. It had been a long time since he went to Kozhikode. God, he thought, it must have changed so much.

He was amazed at the change in his father. No longer did his father spend long hours at work and then dash home for a shower and change, but he spent time at home, with his mother, his sister and brother and spent long hours with his grandfather, teaching the old man to play chess and now being regularly beaten by the old man.

The atmosphere at home was lighter. No longer was there that palpable tension that always seemed ready to burst.

"I wonder what really changed here," thought Bhaskaran and seeing Veena one day, it suddenly dawned on him.

Everyone here was smiling more often than he could ever remember. For the first time in a long long time, he could actually see this entity, which he called home behaving, acting, and actually living as a family.

He was happy that his mother was finally looking radiant, happy and at peace with herself. His brother whom even his father now called Rudy had become the youngest State Champion in Badminton. Veena had begun taking classes in classical dance and had won several awards. People were flocking to their doors from the cinema world – but his father shooed them all off. Bhaskaran was surprised at his gesture. Under old circumstances, his father would have welcomed them more interested in what kind of money they were offering than knowing anything else. Today, he thought, family did matter to his father quite sincerely.

39

Moosa Meets Bhaskaran

When the Indian Airlines Boeing 737 touched down at the airport, Bhaskaran was eagerly waiting to get off the aircraft. He wanted to meet Moosa and he knew that Moosa might also be eagerly waiting for him. He had told him that he would send a car to pick him up from the airport and Bhaskaran wondered if he would remember the man who brought the car to the airport. Before leaving for Madras, he would proudly tell Moosa that he remembered all the people by their first names that Moosa had introduced him to in his organisation.

There was a surprise waiting for him. None other than Moosa was waiting for him. Moosa was looking very elegant and looked every bit the dapper businessman that he was these days.

He was waiting inside the arrival lounge. As soon as they saw each other, Bhaskaran ran to him. Although Bhaskaran was almost as tall and quite well built, Moosa lifted him easily off his feet in a bear hug, and twirled him around almost as he would twirl a small child.

"It is so good to see you, my dear friend," Moosa breathed into Bhaskaran's neck.

The younger man too was very happy to see his mentor and the reason for his successes. No one had quite fuelled Bhaskaran's mind with so much ambitious drive than this one man who was holding him just now.

"Come, let's collect your luggage and then we are going to have a good time," Moosa told him.

"No Moosa Bhai, I have nothing else. Just this small bag with me."

"But, I thought you are going to spend a few days with me, aren't you Bhaskaran?" Moosa asked, almost disappointed.

"Of course, I am going to be here with you for at least a week. If I need anything else, you can always buy me new clothes, Moosa Bhai," Bhaskaran looked at Moosa and smiled mischievously.

Moosa only smiled back and throwing his hand on Bhaskaran's shoulders, pulled him closer and said, "But of course, why didn't I think of that?"

Moosa's Mercedes Benz was there, parked in the special area which was reserved for Ministers and other VIP's. While the chauffeur took Bhaskaran's bags, the two settled in the back seat.

"Welcome back to Bombay," Moosa smiled once again at Bhaskaran.

"Let's go home, Murali," Moosa told the chauffeur.

Moosa showed him around his house, which Bhaskaran had never seen before. It was spacious, well designed and suited the austerity with which the man lived. There was nothing pretentious about the house. Settling down in Moosa's comfortable den after a really splendid meal, they talked of the old days, Moosa explaining to Bhaskaran his involvement in newer things and newer arenas and how he was having to learn so fast that even he was astounded that he could grasp so many things so quickly.

When he told Bhaskaran that instead of pretending to be someone who knew everything, he accepted easily the fact that he could never be master of all. Bhaskaran was amazed to learn that in Moosa's empire, people whom he had hired to run these businesses took most of the decisions. Moosa simply got the right people, gave them the tools that they required, and then stood back, encouraging them on.

He was amazed to learn that companies which Moosa had acquired, which were sick and had severe labour-related issues were all improving. No more labour problems, and that even those owners who had sold these establishments were surprised at the performances that they now witnessed.

"People are the key, Bhaskaran. Unless you look after people, unless you realise that the true capital of any business is the human capital, no business will survive. As days go by, we are going to witness killer competition and survival is going to be tough. It is therefore vital that all the products that we produce have the clear stamp of quality. For if we believe that no customer that we transact with will lose by transacting with us, then without a doubt every transaction that we indulge in will be a profitable one. There are fools who pretend that today is what counts. So they indulge in malpractices, they sell inferior goods, but how long can one go on cheating? And the irony is, whom are they so intent on cheating? They are cheating themselves, their future generations and the trust that their customers are placing in them and their products," Moosa would tell Bhaskaran.

For the younger man, this was a revelation of sorts. A few years ago such business philosophy coming from this man sitting across him would not have sounded hollow. But today, listening to Moosa, Bhaskaran knew that there was no falsehood here. Here was a man who knew what he was talking about, a man who knew exactly what he had to do stay on top. Time had metamorphosed the Moosa Bhai from Dharawi with this suave and dapper man who now spoke such fabulous business philosophy. Bhaskaran had heard of few business heads who had such a great heart, such honesty about them. He realised then, that Moosa's heart and soul had not been replaced by greed and avariciousness and that is what stood him in good stead today.

"You know, it's amusing to hear of the stories that I hear around here from various people who are in business. While one has labour-related issues, the other has problems because his best people are being poached by the competition. To handle the labour issues, they hire the best minds in Human Relations and they believe that with the academic excellence that their new man has combined with some experience, their problems will soon be a speck on the horizon. They are wrong. They don't realise that when they hand over the responsibility to someone for managing this critical human capital of their organisation, they would need to find a man who can drive even the worst pessimist to excel. They would need to find a man who can lead by example, a man who can find the strength in his heart to give and not stop to look for the gratitude that sometimes people look for when they give. I have always believed that the man who is usually called the Head of Human Relations should be a man who is a visionary, a great human being worthy of the position and a man who can drive others forward. He has to be a man who can visualise that the human capital that he holds together is an asset that has to evolve, much like the financial capital of the organisation."

"If the human capital of any organisation is not cared for and nurtured, the balance sheet would also reflect poorly. My companies are healthy, thriving, and prosperous for both the employees and the investors. That is not because of me, it is because of the people who work in these organisations who have been encouraged to perform beyond their wildest imaginations and who have been more than amply rewarded for it. Look at my balance sheets and it will reflect the health of my companies. So remember this Bhaskaran, if you want your company to be profitable and healthy, your people have to feel that they are in an environment that improves the quality of their own lives and therefore they aspire higher. When they aspire higher, they produce better. This is so simple that many people make such a big hue and cry about it as if this were rocket science," Moosa explained to Bhaskaran the subtle nuances of managing people, productivity and profits.

"As for the problems of their people being poached by the competition? Well, I do not blame those people who are going to the competition. After all, Bhaskaran, what does one aspire for in this life? *Roti, Kapada aur Makaan*! Isn't it always that or something close to that? These people who are losing their talent should realise why they are losing good people. Sometimes it is not just the money that is the pull factor. Just recently I was told that a plastic tycoon lost the head of his R&D, a scientist, to a Multi-national that has just set up its brand new factory here in Bombay. I found out that the plastic tycoon never said a kind word to the man, never told him that he was doing a good job. You know, it was only after the man left to join the Multi-national company did this tycoon realise that it was the scientist who had actually made him. However, by then it was too late," Moosa said with a shrug of his shoulders.

"You know, if I were in that tycoon's position, I would have given the scientist the best house in Bombay, given him those things in life that not even the richest have at their disposal. Given his family something that they would never forget, and more than all that – I would have got to know the man better. Despite all this, if I still lost a man – I am sure that the man's family would not allow him to move. *Arrey yaar*, we are in India – we still have some semblance of a family culture. I do not think that the family is any different from one's company. Just that while one is a small entity, the other is a larger one," Moosa said very earnestly to Bhaskaran.

Without Moosa precisely saying so, Bhaskaran knew that Moosa was practising a form of management that many of his classmates were talking, which was prevalent in a few companies in India, and in a larger extent in the West.

He admired this rustic man so much, for his love, for his wisdom and for practising something that Father Dominic used to say that Jesus always said, "Treat others just as you would have others treat you."

He was soon to learn that in Moosa's entire array of businesses there was not a day lost in a strike, not a person had resigned, not a single person had been poached by the competition. If someone did want to leave, say to the Middle East where there were better prospects – Moosa ensured that there were no hurdles in the man's path. He also told that person – "Go and try your luck, if things don't work out the way you want it to, come back here. We are family. Understand?" Few people left. And those who left came back, bringing back horror stories of poor work conditions and a life without the comfort of family and friends.

On the day that he was about to leave for Madras, Moosa took him out and the first thing they bought was a huge suitcase, then going from shop to shop he bought his young ward shoes, trousers, jeans, belts – everything that Bhaskaran might need. In the end, they laughed at the thought of buying another suitcase, so they stopped.

At the airport, both of them were quiet. Moosa smoking a cigarette and finally as they were about to leave, took Bhaskaran's hand and said, "When you reach Boston, open a bank account and call me. Give me the account number. I want to deposit some money for your expenses. Don't tax your father. He has to look after your sister and brother. I will send you all the money that you will need. I have heard stories of young people like you going to study and working in supermarkets and restaurants. You will do nothing like that. Okay?"

Bhaskaran could only nod dumbly. This man, with no relation to him, kept doing so much for him that he did not know how he was ever going to repay him. Not that he had a doubt in his mind that he would ever have to repay Moosa, but sometimes 'thank you' is such an inadequate word, he thought.

He hugged Moosa tightly, knowing that if he said anything, the tears that he held back in check would never be quelled.

40

Benghazi, Libya – 1985

Raashid Abdul Latif – almost any Indian in Libya who had sent money through the '*kozhal*' system knew of Raashid Abdul Latif.

Not only was the man so very reliable, he was also known for his generosity of heart.

They have a saying in the Sahara – Nothing tames a man like the way Sahara does. It teaches you to be patient, it teaches you to be kind, it teaches you everything that you want it to teach. It's like someone gives you a book, called the 'Book of Life' – and it's up to you entirely, to flip through these pages at your fingertips and learn from the wisdom that is contained in the book. The Sahara is just that way. You see nothing on the surface, if you give it a very cursory glance. Look a little more carefully and you see life – plenty of it. From small deer to foxes, rabbits, deadly scorpions, some of the most beautiful looking flowers on cactuses that you have ever seen, dates, and above all – the awesome presence of God.

You could be an atheist, you could be Hindu, Muslim, or a Christian – anything under the sun. If you did spend a few days in the Sahara in those typical desert conditions, you would look up, and there would be one word that escapes your lips – 'God', you would catch yourself saying. If you stay there for a few weeks, you would be surprised at the calmness that you could sense inside yourself.

There is the silence that you would never hear anywhere. You can sit on a massive sand dune and when the sun has almost set, but it's still quite bright – the pre-twilight kind of light that has a different hue, a different feel, with a different kind of wind blowing here in the Sahara. It envelops you and you would believe that the sound of your heart beating is the loudest sound that you had ever heard. You catch yourself listening to your own breath, and you would be surprised that you had never tracked your breath from the moment you breathed in until it reached your lungs, deep inside you. You suddenly feel alive, and when you do, that is that very special smile that lights up your eyes, reaching down to your lips and when that remains with you, people seeing you look at your visage and say that you do look different.

Raashid had spent several weekends on the sand dunes, far away from camp, far away from anyone who mattered, all by himself, sometimes with Christos – their four-wheel drive vehicle parked a distance away. Once they made the mistake of parking the vehicle close by. Within a few minutes, they found that even vehicles have odours. This one, the smell of burnt oil, diesel, and rubber left an indelible impression. It was an amazing experience but something, which they would never forget.

In the night, the desert came alive with rabbits, foxes, and a whole plethora of animal life that made the landscape so different. They would use high power strobe lights that would pierce the darkness like some powerful finger freezing the animals in their tracks as if some giant wave had caught them and froze them almost in some theatrical mime. Their eyes, gleaming in the light and the only moving objects in that moment suspended in time, as if desperately seeking for a way out of the triangular beam of light that had appeared magically out of the darkness.

And when the dark sky began to be replaced with streaks of deep blue, dark red and the whiteness of the rising sun, the desert would begin to resemble its unfathomable façade, only the footprints in the sand giving away the secret lives that had scurried on its surface, just a few hours ago.

A little later, when the sheer artistry of nature that far outshone the works of some of the best artist on canvas became the white blankness that is the desert sky and when the wind blew, carrying specks of sand which would gently wipe the tracks away, the camouflage was complete. It was almost as if even the forces of nature were hand in glove in the preservation of these small animals, embracing them in a cloak of absolute secrecy which a few were privy to.

He had befriended the nomadic Bedouin. They were the only people who roamed these sands. Tribes of them, each with their plethora of camels, horses, women, children, and almost all of them dressed in an undistinguishable black. From a distance, if you saw a caravan, it looked like a line of ants scurrying towards food.

He wondered how they could be dressed like this in such penetrating heat that broke even the most hardened of men. They traversed this landscape trading in camels, hunting in the night and travelling. Kufra attracted many Bedouin because of the fact that here was a place, supposedly the hottest place on this planet, yet with a depository of water that was almost amazing. It was discovered that the water deposits below Kufra was about 200 times the amount of water that flowed into the sea through the River Nile. Pristine, cool, and very fresh water that was any day better than the best-bottled water that money could ever buy.

Once after a good meal of *khous khous* and lamb, which was always served on a large platter – the men eating separately from the women – the men sitting around the platter and using their hands ate from the platter. Then relaxing on goatskins with camel saddles used as props for spines that had taken on an almost elastic characteristic after such a heavenly meal, sipping bittersweet Arabic tea and talking of things far away – Bombay, Nagpur, India for Raashid, and the cities of North Africa that the Bedouin had travelled to, they talked of many things.

He asked Mohammed, a man who was probably very old but who did not know exactly how old he was, how they lived in such conditions, especially the heat.

"Never fight anything that you cannot change, Raashid." The old man said sipping some more tea.

Looking up at Raashid he said, "Take this climate, where most people cannot live in. You know it's hot, you know that sometimes there is not even a rustle of the wind blowing to disturb the smallest fleck of sand. Sometimes you are in the middle of a sandstorm that looks as if the whole world is covered in sand. Your hair is full of sand, your nose is full of sand the food that you have is full of sand. Nothing is spared. But we don't fight it. We know, like everything in life this too will pass. Once you learn to master that you will never fret, you will never fume. Just tell yourself – This too will pass. Suddenly you will realise, you will accept the fact that yes, it's hot, but you don't worry about it, because you cannot control it. You cannot change it. You will not ruin an otherwise perfect day worrying about something and wishing you were elsewhere, just because you are foolish to even think of the heat, the sun and the sand. They are here to stay, you are not. You are just a traveller who is here for a time. All of us are. We move on, like the sand on the surface of the desert. So, do not fight those things that you cannot change. Its futile and useless, and above all a sheer waste of time." The old man smiled shaking his head. "But what you can do to overcome the heat and the prevalent conditions is to change your mind. Don't fight what you cannot conquer. Accept it – say to your self – yes there is nothing I can do – the wind will blow, yet, it will die down. Change your mind Raashid and you can change everything else." The old man said.

He'd remember that piece of advice for a long time – Change your mind and you can change anything.

Raashid could speak Arabic fluently now. He thought it was a beautiful language rich and full of character; it had a certain music to it and if you could understand it – well, nothing like it.

Mohammed told him that during his travels he had met Muammar Al Gaddafi who spent a considerable amount of his spare time in the desert almost all by himself. No wonder, thought Raashid, that the Libyan leader was a man who was considered a master survivor, a man whom many hated, many loved, Gaddafi was a man who knew himself well. It was Mohammed's studied opinion that Gaddafi wrote the *Green Book*, the handbook on Libyan Governance, in the desert. While some critics shot it down as a non-practical doctrine, others praised it for its socialist theme.

Raashid, now living in Libya after having lived in India, wished that someone like Gaddafi would govern India for the sheer discipline that he brought into daily life.

At work Raashid was no longer the young hesitant man who had arrived here a few years ago. He was one of the best mechanics and Christos was proud of him.

He was busy, in either the workshop or receiving requests to send money to families of people working here. Earlier, he used to process only the requests for people who were working in Brega, but then the Indian population of Libya was not restricted just to Brega. There were doctors, engineers, nurses, cooks, painters, plumbers – you name them and they were here.

The restriction to repatriate just 60% of one's earnings was a damper. Actually, it made sense – after all the deductions that were mandatory, after one's own living expenses, one did not have 100% of one's salary to repatriate. One could only repatriate so much and that would probably work out to around 60% if one were careful. The Indian population had just one priority. They were here to save money. Not to splurge on good living, but to save, and that is precisely what most of them did.

Some of them did not repatriate money every month, they would save enough money and send the maximum amount that they could every quarter. And if someone was offering them something slightly more than the official bank rate, delivered at your doorstep – nothing better than that.

With the flood of people coming to him, he knew that it was a matter of time before he moved either out of Kufra or out of Libya. The authorities were not going to be very happy to see his activities flourish. All it would take was a phone call and all this would end.

Fortunately, the Personnel Department in Brega came to his rescue. They transferred him out of Kufra to Benghazi on the Mediterranean coast.

He loved Benghazi. The city was filled with a friendly population. Soon he began to understand that Benghazi was a city whose population understood English, whereas Tripoli was a population that was more inclined to Italian. This had to do more with history than with personal preferences. General Montgomery had been here on his march towards Tobruk and El Alamein on the Egyptian border where he masterminded the defeat of the German's under Erwin Rommel the German General popularly called the Desert Fox.

Here in Benghazi communication facilities were better than at Kufra. The city was more cosmopolitan than Kufra was. Here there were people from all over the North African coast, Sudan, Chad, Ghana and a from India, Pakistan, Sri Lanka. There were Germans, Swedes, Russians, Bulgarians, British and a few Americans.

He loved the expatriate community from Europe. They lived life to the fullest unlike most of the Indians and Pakistani community. These *goras* were diving in the Mediterranean on the weekends if it was not parties at the huge sprawling housing complex on the way to Benghazi airport. All that was required was one introduction into this circuit and he took to it like a fish does to water.

Another added advantage and an acceptability factor into the group was his expertise in making *grubba.* He had toiled long and hard under Christos' careful eye until he had mastered it.

The hooch was made quite indigenously using two oil barrels that were cleaned out thoroughly. One would have its top cut open and re-fitted with clasps that would hold it in place. The other would have a coil of copper pipe that would begin in the other drum and end at the bottom of the other, completing a crude, but effective, distilling cycle.

Placed on a huge gas stove, the drum with the removable top would be filled with water almost 160 litres, sugar added along with seasonal fruits or dates. Finally, a little yeast to ferment the liquid, the drum sealed with a cement of wheat paste which when hardens, nature takes over.

In a few days, if you put your ears to the side of the drum, you could hear the sound of gurgling. In about a week's time, depending on the weather, with the other drum with the copper tubing connected and with water running to cool the copper tubing, the gas stove lit, the process was ready to begin.

In approximately four to five hours, a good harvest would yield about 40 litres of excellent booze.

Raashid's quality was excellent because he used a charcoal filter in order to filter out any impurities in the liquid and instead of a smoky liquid that was the normal colour, his product, in a mineral water bottle, looked exactly like plain water.

But, all this came to a standstill when the Americans attacked Libya and Raashid found himself looking at the prospect of leaving Libya.

Very sadly, after enjoying what he rated as the best years of his life, he left Libya with a host of memories and a whole lot of friends, more than he ever had in his entire life.

41

Vartaa – A Malayalam Newspaper

With Moosa's constant support, the business in Kerala was growing rapidly. Abubacker now also had a newspaper, which they had bought. *Vartaa* was an old Malayalam daily, which had become sick after protracted labour problems. Despite knowing of the militant labour problems, Abubacker bought it. Many people advised him against such a move. He knew what needed to be done and he moved fast.

Shankaran Pillai, his trusted financial advisor now a full time director on his board, and Abubacker made the management of *Vartaa* a deal that they quickly accepted. They were sure that this was a mad man who was about to see his money go down the drain.

Within hours of concluding the deal along with an express warning to all the erstwhile management not to breathe a word of the deal to anyone, including their wives, Abubacker got a list of all the employees, beginning with the leaders of the unions. There were two unions at *Vartaa*. Neither had done anything worthwhile that had increased anyone's standard of living here at *Vartaa*. Perpetually squabbling, they hindered the management's every attempt at progress, shot down their appeal for increased work hours to drive up profitability and in the end the suffocation tactics worked – they killed the company and it now had a new owner… a man who would prove too much for their own match, someone who would change their entire concept of work, unions and indeed, their very lifestyles.

He drove alone, to meet with Prakash Puthanpally, the leader of the more militant of the two unions at *Vartaa*. Prakash was highly educated and had come into politics at his alma mater, Calicut University where he was elected President twice. It was here that mild-mannered Prakash became a firebrand revolutionary and a fantastic orator.

Passing out with a distinction in Malayalam Literature and known for his hard-hitting writing, he was one of the lucky few who got a job immediately upon graduation. Inducted into *Vartaa* as a junior correspondent, he soon became one of the fledgling union's most vociferous proponents.

He used his oratorical skills and political leanings to the maximum effect and created in the minds of the employees an image of someone who was not afraid to fight for their rights. They felt that Prakash was someone who could represent their demands at the highest levels without batting an eyelid.

Effectively squashing the voice of the moderates in the union, he got the union population to dream of higher wages, better work conditions and utopian theories without urging them to further productivity. They threw in their support and it was only a matter of time before he was elected president of the union, which had now become so dreaded that even the management stopped talking about productivity but began thinking of survival.

Work stoppages became the order of the day for the slightest and most whimsical demands. Prakash himself spent more time at work on union-related matters and eventually, all his time was dedicated to the union. He still drew his salary from the newspaper, but someone else did his job whom he had 'persuaded' the management to appoint.

It was to this man's doorstep that Abubacker found his way. Ringing on the doorbell, he heard footsteps hurrying to the door.

"Is this the house of Prakash Puthanpally?" Abubacker asked the man who opened the door.

"Yes, I am Prakash," the man said, slightly confused and not recognising the visitor.

"My name is Abubacker. Abubacker Muthalali is how I am generally known in these parts."

"Oh! Yes, I have heard of you. BMD Transports and a whole lot of other businesses, isn't it?" Prakash asked, stressing on the word 'other'.

"Yes! The very same person," smiled back Abubacker.

"What brings you here?" Prakash asked.

"I need to talk to you and I would prefer talking to you without any disturbance. Can you spare me some time or would you prefer going some place else?" Abubacker asked him.

"We can talk here. My wife has gone to her parents along with my children and there is only a maid who might disturb us when she gets here," Prakash said.

"That should be fine. I came here to talk to you about a proposition. I want you to think about it carefully and then let me know," Abubacker said.

"Come inside, we can sit down and have a talk," Prakash said, showing the way in without giving a reply.

Inside the house, there were just a few old chairs and a creaky old fan on the ceiling, which turned slowly, almost as if in protest.

"I would like to buy the newspaper that you are currently working in," Abubacker told Prakash.

Startled at the suddenness of the statement, Prakash could only shake his head and say, "I don't understand. Have the management decided to sell it you in the first place?"

"That is only at the last stage. First, I have to get the blessings of people like you. What good would it do to me if I buy the company and then realise that I have a union leader to deal with?" Abubacker asked.

"Oh no! You are putting me on a high pedestal. I am just an ordinary man who is keen on ensuring a fair deal for the workers," Prakash said, uncomfortably.

"Listen, let's not waste each other's time and let's not play. I know about you, your union, and what you have done for each member of your union. Let's not fool each other with such niceties and begin a charade," Abubacker said a steely edge to his voice.

"Okay! What do you want from me?" Prakash asked.

"I want you to speak to your union tomorrow and tell them that there is an imminent plan of an outsider purchasing the newspaper. I want you to tell them that they should cooperate with the new management and make the newspaper a success," Abubacker said.

"On what considerations?"

"No considerations for the moment. The newspaper is financially sick and cannot sustain a wage increase right now. The other major Malayalam daily has made huge incursions into *Vartaa*'s traditional readership and to get back lost ground, the quality of the newspaper has to improve. For quality to improve, the staff have to put in their best. If they have to put in their best, you will have to tell them to cooperate," Abubacker said, holding up his hand to stop Prakash, who obviously had something different to say.

"I haven't finished. You know about BMD and my 'other' businesses. You also know that BMD does not have a union. We are probably the only large company in Kerala without a union. We feel that there is no need for a union to exist when there is a transparency in the management. We feel that a union is unnecessary when the management does take care of its employees, bearing in mind their welfare and improvement, sharing wealth created. You also might know that the majority of the employees of my companies are homeowners and that we ensure that their children get the best possible education. You know of the medical benefits that they get. Therefore, when we asked them if they thought a union was necessary which lived upon contributions that they made from their salaries, they vetoed the idea. They are free to discuss any issues with the management and all my managers are accessible to them at any point of time. My companies are doing well because my people are doing well. That is what drives my companies forward, not unions and their representatives," Abubacker said, not taking his eyes off Prakash's who could not look back at this man sitting in front of him.

"That's all fine. But without any considerations, we cannot guarantee you all that you ask. We are in the middle of some wage negotiations and most probably we should get what we have asked for. You must consider granting us that. Then you will have to align the same policies that your other group companies have. You should have a uniform policy. You cannot have *Vartaa* becoming a part and parcel of your organisation without the employees of *Vartaa* not benefiting," Prakash said, getting into his groove, beginning on a spiel.

Abubacker cut him short again with the wave of a hand.

"Let me tell you something, my friend. The employees in my companies have earned what they enjoy. They were given all these benefits not because they sit around all day holding placards and shouting themselves hoarse with slogans. Understand? They work, and they earn. And if you think that you can sit there and demand for those things that you or your union members do not deserve, you better come up with another plan. That is not going to work with me. Let me tell you something more. I will buy *Vartaa* and if you care to work, please do. I will order the new management to go all out and get back the goodwill of those readers and well-wishers who have contributed to *Vartaa*'s growth. If you or your union members do not cooperate, I will close down the establishment. I can wait for the next ten years but I would like to see how long you, your union members or your respective families will go hungry," Abubacker said, gesturing with his hands, sitting on the edge of the chair.

"Abubacker Muthalali, are you threatening me?" Prakash asked, with a hint of an arrogant smile.

Smiling, Abubacker said, "You know that the paths that I have walked and you have walked are totally different. Irrespective of what you experienced in your life and what I have experienced in my lifetime, we meet now. You, my friend, at this point in time of your life are the sum total of your entire experience. The same goes for me too. You never would have bargained that you would ever deal with a man like me. You probably wouldn't even talk to someone like me who has no education, no family to talk of, nothing. I am from the gutter of this society, Prakash. You have had the luxury of your father sending you to school, to college and you have not had to really know what hunger is all about. Yet today, we talk. You invite me into your house, ask me to sit down and you talk to me like an equal. Why? Because you have heard of my wealth, my power, you have heard of this aura that is now sitting in front of you. You are satiating a curiosity in your mind and when you ask me a stupid question like you just did, whether I am threatening you, you are just answering your own curiosity. You are attempting to answer your own doubts, your own inferiority complex. You feel that the whole world is out to cheat you. To take away what is rightfully yours! Do you really trust anyone Prakash? Forget the management of *Vartaa*; do you trust your own wife?" Abubacker asked, absolutely honestly, speaking as if to a child.

Prakash was not certain how to proceed. The man was unfathomable. He could not read Abubacker. He did not detect any fear. For the first time, he was not sure on how to react. The man was breaking him down psychologically and there was very little in defence that he could do.

He kept quiet. Trying to get his mind straight, trying to think of what to say.

"So I will repeat what I said. Speak to your union members and tell them that a new management is about to take over the newspaper. Tell them that they will have to cooperate with the new management and help transform *Vartaa* to a vibrant, profitable entity. There will be no financial considerations, no hikes, nothing for now. I will give you my word, that if they work hard and ensure profitability, I will personally ensure that they get all what they desire and more," Abubacker told Prakash.

"They will want a guarantee, Abubacker Muthalali," Prakash persisted.

"You will want a guarantee, Prakash, not them. You will want this nice little agreement so that you can wave it under their noses and proclaim a victory that you can conveniently conjure up in an imaginary battle with the new management of *Vartaa*, to further your own selfish interests and to further your own self-worth," Abubacker shot back brutally.

"No agreements, Prakash. Nothing. Either you talk to them or I will ensure that they work. If I do that, you will neither be union leader nor an employee of *Vartaa*, when we begin to run the newspaper," Abubacker said with a smile on his face.

"I don't like your threats," Prakash tried to sound defiant.

"Stop throwing tantrums like a child. You, better than anyone else in this city, should know that I never threaten people. Threats are used by impotent people on others who are more impotent; I do not threaten, I promise. I promise only what I can do. I never threaten people, Prakash, and I am not threatening you either. I am being reasonable asking you to speak to your people. If you do not, believe me when I tell you, you will suffer the most consequences. I will ensure that you will never be employed in another company in Kerala, I will ensure that you will never get near a red flag in your entire life. You have not met anyone in your life like me. Take me on if you have the balls. If you do not, just do as I ask you to. I am not asking you to cheat anyone. I am just asking you to do something that I can easily do myself. I do not want to stamp on you and grind you out. I would like you to live, enjoy life with your family and become prosperous instead of staying in a miserable house like this. I know why your wife has gone to her parents. That is because you have not been paid her any allowance in two months, there is no money to pay for the children's school fees, no money to buy food. Is this what you want to see every day for the rest of your life?" asked Abubacker standing up, ready to leave this man and that suffocating house.

"Abubacker Muthalali, please sit down. I would like to have some time in order to speak to the members. I will call for an emergency meeting..."

Abubacker cut him short, "Twenty-four hours! That is all you have. If you have not spoken to them within twenty-four hours, I will act. Then, don't bother calling me or begging me. I will take *Vartaa* with or without your help. It's your choice."

Taking a business card from his pocket, he threw it on the chair next to Prakash and left.

Four hours later, sitting in Shankaran Pillai's office at BMD Towers, Mavoor Road, the phone rang. It was Prakash. The union would offer an unconditional support to the new management. Abubacker never spoke a word after he had said hello into the mouthpiece.

Lighting a cigarette, he told Shankaran Pillai, one down one more to go.

Immediately afterwards, he visited the other union leader and this was much easier than the visit to Prakash Puthanpally. The second union leader was amazed to see Abubacker and in complete awe of the man, who had come to see him; he agreed to do what Prakash's union had just done.

Abubacker spoke to Moosa that night to tell him that he had just completed the deal of *Vartaa*. Moosa smiled at the other end.

Vartaa never saw another day of strikes or work stoppage. It never had a union since, nor did anyone think that they need one.

Prakash Puthanpally became one of the best editors at *Vartaa* and won several coveted awards for both himself and the newspaper. He neither held a union position for the rest of his life, nor was he a member of any union.

According to a recent survey, more than two-thirds of the newspaper reading population of Kerala voted *Vartaa* as the newspaper of their choice.

42

Abubacker – The Family Grows

Abubacker had two children from Saffiya. The eldest, a boy he named Moosa, after his mentor and the younger, and a girl he named Ayesha. They continued to live on the hill in the lovely tiled house. Kunhali had died of a heart attack and these days Saffiya managed the household.

Abubacker found it practical to follow Moosa's example. He left the day-to-day management of his business to Shankaran Pillai and his team of professional managers. Abubacker spent his time in looking for new opportunities and enhancing his existing ones.

He was finding more time to spend with his children and Saffiya and his in-laws with whom he was becoming more attached to now. Syyed Muthalali's yard in Beypore was fully booked with orders and here too Abubacker encouraged Syyed Muthalali to adopt the measures that were becoming the hallmark of Abubacker's businesses. Union-less establishments that provided a great environment for human development and which encouraged hopes and aspiration!

He was passionate about wanting to start a school, a hospital, and a health spa, all rolled into one. This would be a blend of traditional Ayurvedic medicine and modern hotel facilities. Although, there did exist the famous Kottakal Arya Vaidya Sala, he had heard from several sources that the facilities inside were not the best. Certainly, the treatment that they provided was the best, but to attract foreigners with dollars to spend, he knew that the lodging facilities would also have to be the best. He wanted to develop something that would not be too expensive, yet a facility, which could boast of hygiene, good physicians, and a memorable experience for the guests that they would not be able to forget easily.

Students could enrol here for an education into the ancient science that Ayurveda was, and simultaneously work with renowned physicians. He did not want to take a fat fee from the aspiring students. This was going to become an institution that would be set up to propagate the merits of Ayurveda and his way giving back to the people of this great place called Kerala, a part of what he had earned here.

A site was located just outside Kozhikode, located very close to the airport. It was a beautiful coconut grove and had over a thousand coconut trees. A natural pond was situated in one corner and it was from here that water was pumped out to water the trees. Abubacker fell in love with the property the moment he set his eyes on it. Walking through the grove in the mid-afternoon sun, he was surprised at the natural canopy under these magnificent trees. There was hardly a spot on the ground where the sun did not shine through and the breeze that blew through, did not provide a sense of quiet and tranquillity, which he was sure, would be an important aspect to the spa.

One of the best architects, who had put up several resorts all over India, was commissioned for the project and soon a beautiful shape emerged. Abubacker instructed the architect that he would have to design the buildings without destroying too many trees. He wanted to preserve as much of the natural beauty as was possible.

Immediately he set about hiring one of the best Ayurvedic physicians and a man who had managed the Beach Hotel for several years. Both of these men would coordinate with the architects and later with the builders in order to ensure that what evolved would go on to become a paradise for Ayurvedic treatment in an ambience that it had never before been marketed in.

Twenty months after the idea began as a seed in his mind, Abubacker was once again inviting Moosa to Kozhikode to throw open their piece de resistance – The Maveli Lodge.

As people began to frequent this wonderful facility and as more and more people from abroad began to arrive for treatment and rejuvenation, Ayurveda itself began to receive and this made Abubacker happy. That was his objective, and he had succeeded to achieve it.

43

Boston

When Bhaskaran arrived in Boston, he had no difficulty finding the sprawling MIT campus.

Within a few days, he had already settled in and as Moosa had instructed him, he called Bombay to let him know of the bank account number that he received when he opened his savings account with Citibank.

He went around the campus familiarising himself with the various departments, the administration, and the lovely hostel facilities for the students.

MIT attracted some of the best minds in the universe and he could see a whole lot of nationalities represented here. There were a large number of Indians at MIT but the Chinese too were here, in equally large numbers.

Talking to some of the students, both freshmen and seniors, he was struck by the intensity that they displayed. It seemed to him that they were all aware of their own good fortune to be a part of this august institution and the stories that were heard around campus of the students, who had graduated from here to several great organisations, were phenomenal and legendary.

MIT was a springboard that not many people got in their lives. He was grateful to be here and once again silently vowed to himself that he would excel. The day he left IIT Madras, one of his favourite professors and a great human being, Prof Ashok Jhunjhunwala had told him, "You have done us proud here, continue the good work at MIT too and keep in touch."

He found his accommodation to be adequate and comfortable. His roommate was another Indian, Shrikanth Mishra. Shrikanth was the son of a businessman in India and had had joined MIT, graduating from BITS, Pilani.

Although roommates, they had chosen different disciplines and hardly saw each other except in their room.

On the second week at Boston, he was surprised to see a post-it stuck to his door with a message, "Citibank Branch manager asked you to please contact him urgently." It was not signed and there was no number.

Scratching his head, wondering what the problem was, he went to meet the Branch Manager. Charles Griffith was a Citibank lifer and had been with the branch all his working years. He had been posted to this particular branch and had been here for almost two years. In all that time, he had never seen a phenomenon like the one he had just witnessed. A student who had just enrolled at MIT, and who had just opened his savings account had received a bank transfer from another bank in New York. One hundred thousand dollars had been deposited to the new account and he thought to himself, that this must be someone who has a really rich father. One hundred thousand dollars? He never saw one hundred thousand dollars in a year!

Just then, a knock at his door made him look up from the transaction record that he held in his hand.

He waved for the person to come in.

"I am Bhaskaran, I was told that you wanted to see me?"

"Charles Griffith, I am the manager of this branch."

They shook hands and Charles Griffith showed Bhaskaran a deposit receipt that he offered to the younger man.

"This is for you to keep. Your account is credited with the amount and you can draw from it at any time. You do have the ATM card with you and you can use it anywhere in the United States."

Bhaskaran was stunned. One hundred thousand dollars! He did not know why Moosa had sent him so much money. He knew that it was not a mistake. Moosa would have a reason. He would have to call him, just as soon as he was able to leave the bank.

Thanking the manager, Bhaskaran shook hands once again and left.

Charles Griffith was still shaking his head.

"And they say India is a poor third world country."

Leaving the bank, Bhaskaran found a pay phone and using a prepaid card, which he had bought earlier, dialled Moosa's direct number in Bombay.

Two rings later and he heard Moosa's deep baritone.

"Moosa Bhai, this is Bhaskaran. I just got a call from the bank manager at Citibank here, and I just met him. He says that I have received one hundred thousand dollars in cash and that it's been credited to my account. Did you send me this money, Moosa Bhai?"

"Yes, I did send you the money. And no, there is no mistake. I do not want you to find work in order to earn pocket money for yourself. Live well, dress well, eat well and buy yourself a car. I am told that in America if you do not have a car, you are handicapped. Don't buy the cheapest car that you can lay your hands on, buy a good one. You enjoy yourself and study well. If you need more, don't hesitate to let me know. I want you to forget about everything other than studying well – that is why I sent you this money."

Bhaskaran was speechless. He did not know how in the world he would repay this debt of gratitude that he felt welling up in his heart for this man sitting halfway across the world.

"Hello, are you there?" Moosa asked.

"Moosa Bhai, how can I thank you?"

"*Arrey Raja*, since when do we thank each other?"

"But still, I don't think that even my roommate Shrikanth Mishra's father has sent such a huge sum of money for his own son. I don't know what to say, Moosa Bhai."

"*Arrey Raja*, I don't know your roommate Shrikanth Mishra and I don't know his father. You mean a lot to me. That is all there is to it. Nothing more. You want to repay me? Well, call me up like this one day and tell me that you topped your class. That is all that you can do for me. Okay, *Raja*?" Moosa always used that special tone when he spoke to Bhaskaran. Almost like a father talking to a special son.

"Moosa Bhai, thank you. I will do my best here. I will call you every Sunday, okay?"

"Don't worry about calling me. You can call me whenever you want. You take care of yourself. God Bless you."

Bhaskaran hung up the phone and deep in thought went back to his room.

Two days later with the help of Mr Charles Griffith, who was still under the presumption that this was indeed the son of some Indian Maharaja, he purchased a brand new car. A Ford Mondeo, which was a very popular car in the US, he also bought for Mr Charles Griffith a hand-painted silk tie, which he knew Mr Griffith would never buy for himself, along with two very elegant cufflinks made of sterling silver.

Mr Griffith was astounded at such generosity and was feeling rather embarrassed, but still convinced that such generosity did come naturally for the sons of Indian Maharajas.

Bhaskaran travelled around Boston, taking in the beauty of the city with so much of history behind it. As his confidence grew in his own driving abilities, he explored beyond Boston and whenever time permitted, he would discover a beauty of the land and the resilience of its people that had made it a super power in the modern world. America, it seemed to him, had opened her arms to him and he simply loved this great nation.

If only, he mused, India could become such a country. He believed in the potential that India had, it was only that his beloved homeland had not woken up to its own potential. India, he felt, needed an able leader who would set the course and steer her on to becoming a truly great nation.

44

Moosa and Raashid

Upon his return to Bombay, Raashid began to spend a lot of time with his brother. For the first time, he began to develop a love for business and he knew that his brother was waiting for him to make up his mind.

He wanted to be involved in the money laundering business, which was growing phenomenally. He had discovered that it took a lot of imagination, intelligence, and indeed some clever manoeuvrings to pull off such deals, without the authorities breathing down their necks.

Moosa now focused more on the legit side of his business. He was tired of the brushes with the law, the enforcement agencies and was more than willing for his brother to take over the business.

"I have been doing this for such a long time. I now want to get out of this racket slowly. But I cannot get out suddenly. I have obligations to keep. There are other people whose money is involved and these are no ordinary people, Raashid," Moosa explained to his younger brother.

"These are powerful people, some are politicians, some are businessmen, actors; I cannot get out of it. What I would like you to do is to manage this entire operation. To be able do so smoothly and without any problems, I want you to move to the

Middle East. Set up shop there and be based out of there. We can arrange all the formalities quite easily. Once you are there, I want you to quickly establish yourself. What you need here is a distribution network, which I already have in place; I want you to control this network from there. They will report to you. If you feel that you need more people to handle this, then I leave that to you to decide." Moosa said.

"I would like to be based out of Jeddah, Moosa Bhai," Raashid said. He chose Jeddah because of the tales that he had heard about Jeddah from Christos. Christos had worked for some company there and from the impression that he had, he liked to go there. The other choice was Dubai. Dubai was a better place to live in than Jeddah, Christos had told him. But Dubai was a very tiny place in comparison with Jeddah and indeed, when you compared the Emirates with Saudi Arabia, it was like comparing grapes to apples.

Surprised at the choice of a location that his brother had chosen, Moosa smiled.

He saw the changes in Raashid and he did not press him for an explanation. The boy he had seen off a few years ago to Libya had returned a man. There was more confidence in him, as if the exposure to living abroad and that too on his own had opened up small windows in his younger brother's head, throwing light into the darkest recesses of his mind and expanding the horizons of his thought.

"Speak to Salaam Bhai. Remember him? He was the same chap who got you your visa to work in Libya. Well, he is a big time travel agent now and he has several connections in the Middle East which you can ask him to explore for you."

They worked out the modalities of the operations and by the end of the day, almost all the bank accounts, some in Bombay, some elsewhere in the world were all transferred to Raashid. He would begin to work immediately, but before that, he wanted to make a quick trip to Nagpur.

45

Nagpur

Shapoorji and Sons had not changed one bit. The only thing that seemed to bem different was the Nepali security guard. The previous one had left back for Nepal and had appointed a relative in his stead.

He had flown from Bombay to Nagpur and a car was waiting for him with a driver.

He went straight from the airport to the workshop, his thoughts racing back in time when as a young boy, he had first begun to work there, little realising that he would come back one day, a survivor and a winner, to a place that still held a cherished place in his memory.

He got down from the car and asked the Nepali if Kesavan Sir was around. The man gave him a once over and reaching under a makeshift counter, brought up a phone.

He punched a number in and while the phone rang, he gave Raashid another once over. He could not quite place this young man; he had never seen him before.

"Allo? There is someone here looking for Kesavan Saab. I don't know his name, will you please come here?" he said into the phone.

Without seeming to wait for a response from the other end, he put the phone down.

Looking up at Raashid, he said, "Someone is coming from the workshop. He will take you in."

A young boy came out through the gates and called him.

"*Arrey Saab*, you wanted to see Kesavan Saab?"

When Raashid nodded, the boy gestured for him to come in.

A flood of memories came to Raashid. The workshop too had not changed one bit, how can time preserve something like a workshop perpetually, he wondered to himself.

He was shown to the reception. Here too nothing seemed to have changed. He did not remember too well, but he thoughts that even the worn out cushion covers were still the same. The only change here seemed to be a fat receptionist, who was looking very bored and reading a magazine.

When he coughed, she looked up.

"Yes?" she asked, wondering who this young man was.

"I am here to see Kesavan Sir or his son Appu," Raashid explained.

"Are they expecting you here?" she asked.

So there were some changes, he thought to himself. When he used to work here, there was no receptionist and visitors could walk into the workshop looking for the people whom they had come to meet.

"Go up the stairs and turn left. Kesavan Sir is in the first office your right," she said, pointing to the stairs.

He walked up the staircase and as directed he turned left and knocked on the door of three cabins. This too was a change. When he worked here, there was only one cabin and the accountant and storekeepers' desks took up the other space.

He knocked at the door and when the voice inside asked him to enter, he turned the handle and pushed the door in. The cool draft of air that hit him hid the surprise on his face.

There sitting at the table at which the 'old man' Shapoorji used to sit, was his old guru, Kesavan.

"Raashid! Welcome back!" Kesavan came around and hugged the boy whom he grown to love.

"I am glad you have not forgotten me, Kesavan Sir. I thought you must have forgotten me by now and that I would have to re-introduce myself to you," Raashid said, smiling at the old man.

Kesavan had indeed aged. His once dark hair was now almost white. He had also put on weight. Although he still wore the same uniform, minus the grease and the baggy knees and the piece of waste cloth that was permanently lodged in his shirt pocket, he looked different.

"So Kesavan Sir, when did you get promoted?" Raashid asked.

"I will tell you all that later. Let's go home now; I am sure that my wife and Appu will be glad to see you. Then we can come back here and meet your old friends, okay?" Kesavan said.

They went to Kesavan's house in Raashid's car. Sitting at the back with the old man, Raashid noticed that the car was heading to the same old flat that he had spent several weekends with Appu.

"You still stay in the same place, sir?" Raashid asked just to make sure.

"Yes, I still live there. Appu has married and he has moved to another flat, which is also close by."

"Appu has married? I never even knew," Raashid said, surprised.

"We got a good alliance for him and everything happened so fast afterwards. The girl's parents are also from Nagpur and have been here for a long time. They are originally from Kerala, just like us," Kesavan explained.

As the car came to a halt, he got out, eagerly waiting to see his old friend and Kesavan's wife.

"Meenu, see who has come," he yelled from downstairs. The old man's voice had not lost any of its timbre and prowess, Raashid thought to himself.

By the time they climbed up the two flights of stairs, Kesavan's wife at the door.

"Raashid, it's so good to see you," she smiled that welcome smile of hers.

She held his hands, and asked him if Moosa Bhai had come.

"No, I came alone, just to see you all," Raashid explained.

"Come, I have lunch ready. We were not expecting you, otherwise I would have made your favourite fish curry. But there is *sambhar* and *papaddoms* with a cabbage side dish. You used to like my *sambhar*, remember Raashid?" She asked.

"*Amma*, your *sambhar* is the best in the world. I can vouch for that," Raashid said, taking his shoes off at the doorway.

Kesavan had gone inside his bedroom and now returned with a massive photo album.

"Here are the snaps from Appu's wedding. Go through them while Meenu sets up the table. *Acha*, do you want some beer?" Kesavan asked Raashid suddenly taking the younger man by surprise.

"*Arrey*, don't worry, if you want you can have a bottle here," Kesavan smiled at Raashid, seeing the startled look on the younger man's face.

"Well, if you had some good non-vegetarian short eats, I would have loved to have one, but not now. *Sambhar* and beer don't go too well with each other." Raashid joked.

The old man laughed loudly. He went to the corner of the room and sitting on the narrow divan he dialled a number on the phone.

"Appu, can you come home now? Someone has come to see you."

"Are you at home now? Who has come to meet me at this hour?" Appu asked.

"You come here, I will ask him to wait and if Asha is not doing anything bring her along," Kesavan said.

Putting the phone down, he looked at Raashid and said, "Asha is Appu's wife. You will see her now when they come here."

Glancing through the album, he saw Appu decked up in the traditional *mundu* and Asha in a beautiful red sari. The wedding seemed to have been a grand ceremony and he saw many people whom he had not seen before.

"Relatives of ours who had come from Kerala," Kesavan said looking at the photographs from over Raashid's shoulders at the pictures.

There was a group photograph with all the mechanics of Shapoorji and Sons along with the bride and groom. All of them were smiling captured for posterity by the camera.

When he turned the page over, he saw another photograph that made him sit up.

There, standing next to Appu and Asha with Kesavan and his wife was Moosa Bhai.

"He came for the wedding, Raashid. He gave us all the money that we required to conduct the wedding in such a fashion," Kesavan said.

"You know after you left for Libya, Moosa Bhai came back to see me. He was very keen on doing something for me. I said that he owes me nothing and that if it had been anyone else, not just you, I would have treated him exactly in the same manner. But he would not listen. He tried to press a huge bundle of notes into my hand. I did not accept that either. Then he stopped trying to give me money. He asked me to introduce him to the old man. So the next morning I spoke with the old man and

Moosa Bhai came to meet him. Neither did I know what Moosa Bhai wanted to see the old man for and nor was I told. I did not press for any explanations. They were inside the office for about an hour. Then they came out and the old man called me in. The old man handed over the entire key bunch to Shapoorji and Sons to me telling me that from that day forth, I was the new owner of the establishment."

Kesavan took a deep breath and continued, "I could not believe my ears. I just looked at Moosa Bhai who was smiling at me. The next day, I called for a meeting with all the senior mechanics. I gave them fifty percent of the ownership and retained fifty percent for Appu and myself. Moosa Bhai was happy that I had done so and asked to visit the bank. I took him to our local branch and there, once again, he sat down with the manager. Twenty minutes later, the manager came out of his cabin with Moosa Bhai and congratulated me. I thought it was because I had now become the new joint owner of Shapoorji and Sons. But it was not that. Moosa Bhai had told the bank manager that he was depositing 10 lakhs of cash into the account and that it was a payment in advance for the annual maintenance of his entire fleet of lorries. I know, Moosa Bhai knows and God knows that even if we service his entire fleet for the next five years, the bill would not come to 10 lakhs. When he left for Bombay that evening, he thanked me for looking after you and told me to call him whenever I needed anything," Kesavan explained to Raashid, his hand thrown around Raashid's shoulder.

Raashid could not believe his ears. He had heard of Moosa's acts of charity, but he thought that this one beat them all. And the best part of the whole thing was that he never once mentioned any of this to Raashid. No boasts, no gloating – nothing.

"When this alliance was suggested for Appu, there was a slight problem. You know Appu has not even finished his tenth standard. Whereas Asha is a convent educated girl, a Commerce Graduate and her father has a decent job in the Government. Her mother is the headmistress of one of the schools here and they are much better off than we are, socially and financially. They liked us, but wanted some good references. I did not know whom to ask. So I called up Moosa Bhai and he asked the Managing Director of one of his group companies to speak to Mr Nair, Asha's father. That was it. Nothing more was said, nothing more was asked. They have been married for over two years now, and seem to be quite happy with each other," Kesavan continued bringing Raashid up-to-date on the events that had transpired since his departure from Nagpur.

Raashid was spellbound. His brother, he knew had touched the lives of these decent folk as nothing else had before.

"You know Raashid, there are many people who tell us that we should not have any association with Moosa Bhai and that we should be wary of his connections. They do not know whom they are talking about, your brother is truly a messenger of God, a *Farishta* who came into our lives and changed it for ever," Kesavan said.

Yes, Raashid thought, Moosa Bhai was indeed a *Farishta*.

When Kesavan's wife announced that lunch was ready, he stood up and just then the doorbell rang.

Kesavan went to open it and for a moment there seemed to be no one, then the old man was pushed aside and Appu ran in, yelling, "Raashid, my brother."

They hugged and thumped each other's backs, rocking each other as if afraid to let each other go.

Then Appu stepped back and looking at Raashid said, "I am so glad you were able to come to visit us. Come you must meet my wife." Pulling his wrist, Appu took him to where Kesavan was standing with his daughter-in-law.

"Asha, meet my best friend Raashid and Raashid this is your *bhabhi*, Asha," Appu said his smile growing wider, touching his eyes.

"Namaste *bhabhi*," Raashid said, hands folded, very respectfully.

"Don't be silly, you can call me Asha. I have heard stories and stories about you and I was looking forward to meeting you. I did meet your brother at our wedding. I am glad you could come to visit us," Asha said, putting aside any formality and treating him as one of the family.

"Have you had lunch or were you waiting for me?" Appu asked Raashid, still smiling at his friend.

"No, I was just about to eat, when you rang the doorbell," Raashid said.

"Come then, let's eat like old times. God! How I missed you!" he told Raashid, hugging him again.

"God," Raashid prayed, "let this love always grow stronger, let nothing come between us."

He felt so happy to be back here and all the anxiety that with Asha around there might not be much of a freedom to talk to Kesavan and Appu and his mother were all blown away by Asha's down-to-earth behaviour.

When they finished the meal, they moved back to the living area and he asked Kesavan, "Sir, why don't you move to a larger apartment?"

"For what Raashid? Appu has a nice flat, and we are only two of us here. These days to get hired help is so difficult and I want to retire in couple of years, after which I am not sure if I will continue to live here or go back to Kerala. This is enough, my son. I don't need anymore luxuries in life," Kesavan said. From the look on his face, Raashid knew that the old man was earnest and not saying so for his sake.

He had to fly back to Bombay that evening and after another round of prolonged goodbyes, he left them, happy in the knowledge that the people who showed him some happiness were also happy, and indeed, comfortable in life.

46

Iced Cream Blooms

Iced Cream was doing phenomenal business. Bala Govind, recently promoted as partner, had seen a turnaround to his life after that morning's showdown with Saraswathi. He had brought about a radical change in his own life. No longer was he the perpetually scheming disgruntled senior executive, he was proving to be a valuable resource not only to Ram Mohan's organisation but also to his family.

His in-laws had both passed away. Veena had become a first-rate Bharatanatyam dancer and was performing on stage as a professional. 'Rudy' was still playing badminton, for the State and it was rumoured that he would represent the country soon.

Ram Mohan came calling on them on Vishu day. He said, that he wanted to give them both a gift on this auspicious day, which was the Malayalam new year's day. On this day, it was customary for elder people to give a token cash gift to younger ones who would need to prostrate at the elders' feet to seek their blessings.

Since it was also the Tamil New Year's day, it was a declared holiday. Ram Mohan invited Bala Govind and his family over to his house for the traditional Vishu lunch. Just as he was about to leave, he turned around and walking back into the flat.

"I almost forgot. This is actually the reason why I came here, I could have asked Latha to speak to Saraswathi to invite you people over," he said, digging into his *kurta* pocket for a small package, neatly gift wrapped with a red satin ribbon.

"What is this?" asked Saraswathi to whom he had handed over the small package.

"Well, open it," Ram Mohan said.

She gently pulled the knot loose and carefully opened the package. Inside was a box, the one that you usually packed a jewel in.

She opened the box and inside it was a key. She picked it up and with a look of surprise, she asked Ram Mohan, "What is this?"

"What does it look like to you?" he asked, smiling at her.

"It's a key, of course."

"It's not just any other key. It's the key to your new home."

"What? Where is the house?" she asked very shocked.

"Three houses away from mine. It was built for someone who is in the US, but after it was built, the owners decided that they would not be coming back just now and wanted to dispose it. Someone approached me and asked me if I was interested. I went to have a look just for the heck of it along with Latha. Both of us liked it very much and then we decided that since you have been living in and out of flats and rented accommodation, it's high time you got yourself a good house. I think you will like it," Ram Mohan said.

"I don't know what to say," Saraswathi said, wishing desperately that this were not a dream that she would soon wake up from.

"Does my husband know about this?" Saraswathi asked Ram Mohan.

"No, only Latha and I know. I think that you should see the house when you come over for lunch today," saying so, he left.

She needed a glass of water and so rushed into the kitchen. She sat down and once more looked at the key. Her dream of a lifetime had just come true.

She waited impatiently for her husband to come back along with her children. They had been gone for such a long time, she thought. They must have been held up at the new Ayyapan temple, she told herself.

It was almost another hour before Bala Govind arrived home with his children. Saraswathi was waiting for them at the doorway and even before he could sit, she was showing him the key, excitedly repeating what Ram Mohan had just told her.

Bala Govind, too, could not believe this. This was too good to be true, he told himself. Rushing to the phone, he dialled Ram Mohan's number at home and when he answered the phone, he came straight to the point.

"What's this new surprise?" he asked.

"Won't you wish me? Today is Vishu, my friend," Ram Mohan said.

"Sure, Happy Vishu to you and Latha! Now tell me, you seem to have taken the breath out of all of us with such a present," Bala Govind told him.

"I have been wanting to do something like this for you for a long time. At first I thought I would get you all a good flat. Then I told myself that you deserve something better. I was waiting for the right kind of house. Then I saw this one. I thought it would fit your description of your dream house very well. You remember, you wanted a house with a lawn in the front and all that? Well, you might have forgotten it, but I remembered. It's been done up very well and all you would need to do is move in, if you like the place," Ram Mohan explained.

"All that is fine, but how am I going to repay you?" Bala Govind asked.

"Repay? Repay what, my friend? I am what I am today because you worked hard. I can never forget that. You know it and I know it, that my contribution to the success of Iced Cream was and is very limited. It is you who keeps it running, it is you that has been the driving force behind it and I figure that it's I who need to repay you and not vice-versa, my friend." Ram Mohan said.

"But…" began Bala Govind.

"There are no ifs and buts, okay? And that is an order. Come over for lunch and let's go and see the house together. If you like the house, then check with your astrologer for a good date. Have your housewarming done and move in. Simple, isn't it?" Ram Mohan asked Bala Govind.

They went to Ram Mohan's house and chatted about the prospect of becoming neighbours. Then all of them went to the new house and what they saw, floored them all.

It was a huge house, three bedrooms, a study and a den, a kitchen, which was as big as their present living room, a pantry, a laundry, and a separate *puja* room. There was a room at the rear of the house with a small toilet and bath, which could be used for the live-in servant, if they decided to have one. In the side, with an entrance into the house, was a garage that could probably take two cars. There was even a kennel right behind the garage.

The best part of the house was the lawn that was almost like a green carpet. There was also another garden full of flowering plants and a small pond with fishes in them. Someone had thought this whole thing out quite well, Bala Govind thought, stunned at the size of the house and at the magnanimity of the man whom he had once branded a selfish man.

He turned around as he felt a hand on his shoulder, turning around, he saw it was Ram Mohan.

"So, did you like the house?"

"Like it? I just love it."

"Then move in. All the paperwork has been done. I have asked my lawyers to draw up the agreements and check the documents of the property. As you would have noticed, everything has been done up with regards to the interiors. If you think that it's to your liking, then all you need to do is have the registration done and then move in on a an auspicious date of your choice."

He remembered what Saraswathi had told him, once a long time ago. "You have to give in order to get." Since then he had poured his heart out into his job, asking for nothing in return and today, he felt, someone was giving him back for all that he had done.

❂

47

Aditi

Moosa had met Aditi Sharma at a wedding. The woman was quietly sitting all by herself and he noticed that she seemed distant and lost in her thoughts.

He spent some time with the family of the groom. They insisted that he have lunch with them before he left. Not able to get away, he knew that he would have to have lunch.

Slipping away to the foyer of the huge wedding hall to smoke a cigarette, he found Aditi standing alone by a stack of plastic chairs, staring out of the window, gazing at the shimmering waves of the Arabian Sea.

He was caught in two minds. He was not sure if he should speak to her. He had not been introduced to her and if he tried to strike a conversation with her, she might either talk to him or she might not. She might also mistake his intention as someone trying to chat with her for some ulterior motive.

He would walk past her onto the verandah and would smoke his cigarette. If she glanced at him, he would say hello. Deciding, he moved forward, the heels of his shoes clicking on the polished marble flooring.

Hearing the footsteps, she turned around and seeing who it was, smiled at him.

"Hello, I am Moosa. I am afraid we haven't met," Moosa said, extending his hand.

"Yes," she said taking his proffered hand, "You are right, we haven't been introduced. I am Aditi Sharma. The man who is getting married today is my brother."

Her grip was limp. He let go off her hand and stood awkwardly, not knowing what else to say.

"So! What brings you up here?" she asked him.

"Came to smoke a cigarette, I am afraid I am terribly addicted to the darned thing," Moosa smiled ruefully, glancing at the cigarette packet and the gold lighter in his hand.

"Well, all of us have our weaknesses," she said.

"Do you smoke?" he asked her.

"No, I didn't mean that. All of us do have weaknesses, don't we?" she said.

"Oh, okay. I understand. What is your weakness?" he asked.

"I love chocolates, ice creams, but not necessarily in that order," she smiled for the first time.

He smiled back, looking at her face. There seemed to be a profound sadness about her and he couldn't place his finger on it. Wonder what was hurting her so much, he thought.

"Who do you know here?" she asked him. The change in the subject sudden and direct.

"Well, your brother and I are friends," he said simply without elaborating on the fact that her brother headed one of the companies that he owned.

"What do you do, Aditi?" Moosa asked, this time changing the subject himself.

"Oh, I dabble in a bit of interior designing and all that. I just started doing something. I used to work for a large multi-national corporation before, but I don't work there anymore. I just started taking up interior designing because I felt that I had something creative in me," she explained.

"That's nice," Moosa said politely.

"What do you do, Mr Moosa?" Aditi asked in her quiet manner.

"First, there is no mister before my name. Just call me Moosa. Second, I have a few businesses. I don't do much, there are good people taking care of those businesses and I just sort of travel around and generally have a good time," Moosa told her.

"You seem to be enjoying what you do, isn't it?" she asked, still refraining from using his name, almost as if she was awkward about saying it.

"Oh, it's alright," he said, shrugging his shoulders.

"Do you mind if I smoke here, would that bother you?" he asked her, once more showing her the packet of cigarettes.

"No, please go ahead. You came here to smoke," she said smiling at him, "not to talk with me, right?"

The smile did not reach her eyes; it just lingered around her face fleetingly and vanished.

"What is it that is bothering this woman?" Moosa wondered again.

Lighting up his cigarette and taking a deep drag, he loudly drew the smoke deep into his lungs.

"You really love to smoke, don't you?" she asked him noticing how he dragged on his cigarette.

"I love everything that I do, Aditi," he told her earnestly. She looked at him again, noticing the way he pronounced her name, with a certain softness. Was she imagining things? She shook her head.

He continued, "I try never to do anything that I am not passionate about. And unfortunately that includes cigarettes." He smiled at her.

"How many cigarettes do you smoke in a day?" she asked him, once more Moosa caught by her directness.

"Not much," he said vaguely.

"How many?" She persisted.

"Fifty to sixty cigarettes," he said lamely, amused by this woman in his presence, a stranger who somehow had him captivated. He did not know how, or why. He just wanted to enjoy the moment.

"That's too much," she said, shaking her head, "Way too much!"

"Well, my doctor thinks so too," his smile turning to a sheepish grin when she smiled back at him.

"Well, I think I better go back downstairs before someone starts a search party looking for me," she said, glancing at her watch.

He reached into pocket and took out his cardholder. Taking one out, he handed over one to her and told her, "Give me a call sometime. I might have some work for you."

"I am not a professional designer; let me warn you right now," she said, lifting her arms up in surrender.

"We'll know about that when the decorators execute your design. I will reserve my comments till such time," he said.

"It's been nice talking to you," she said, once more offering her hand, shaking his in a better grip than the first one.

"My pleasure Aditi, it's been a great pleasure to meet you," Moosa almost bowed over her hand.

She withdrew her hand, shy and almost blushing. The man was a romantic and he knew how to treat women, she thought. Was that out of practice or was it just that he was a thorough gentleman, she wondered.

They went downstairs and disappeared into the crowd.

Three days later, she called him. He gave her directions to get to his office and promptly at four that same evening they met.

48

Emotional Battery

Aditi used to work with the multinational PR agency, Plethoria. She was one of the youngest PR directors that the company had and they were proud of her achievements. She was a master strategist and her clients swore by her. Some of the biggest companies in India used Plethoria and that was primarily because of Aditi. Her clients simply adored the gutsy woman who could manipulate the press, conjure up a brilliant image, and create a brand almost by sheer magic.

It seemed that nothing could stop her. That was until she met the deadly Sanjay Bhatnagar. Sanjay used to work for a company that had just set up shop in India called PML Solutions. PML was an Atlanta-based software development companies that had just come to India to set up a state of the art, software development centre and Sanjay headed the initiative in India. Young and cocky, he was a big draw at the many discotheques in town and was seen at almost all the trendy parties.

A mutual friend introduced him to her at a press conference and she immediately felt attracted to Sanjay. Before long, he was dating her and the two made a very attractive couple and were seen regularly together.

It seemed to her that she had finally found a man whom she was confident would not mind her working even after they married, was himself quite successful and very very ambitious.

She would catch herself dreaming of setting up a home with Sanjay, raising a family and slowly fell deeper and deeper in love with him, giving of herself totally and completely to the man who seemed to possess her senses, her body, and her mind.

Although she worked in a very modern environment, there was something very conventional about Aditi. Perhaps it was the upbringing that she had from her very conservative parents or perhaps it was India – whatever it was, she never had any serious boyfriends before she met Sanjay.

He never had any qualms about pre-marital sex and convinced her that once the curiosity of sexuality was out of the way, their relationship would bloom. She never argued, she loved him and she surrendered herself to him.

Since his organisation PML was just getting started up, his workload was not too hectic. However, she had clients who wanted to discuss their problems even late into the night. Calling him up just before she left for home, she would hear the sarcasm in his voice.

"Another late night at work, is it?" she could almost see his sneer.

"Yeah, sweetie! This client had to see the write-ups that we have prepared and they are being released to the press tomorrow. They wanted to make sure that everything that they had mentioned in their inputs to us was covered. So we did a dry run," she would patiently explain.

"As if there are no others in that office of yours. Do you have to go to meet clients and prepare with them for dry runs?" he would continue in that irritating tone of his.

"Well, there are others too. I head the team and you know that."

"What is the name of that chap whom you said was your client?" he enquired, in a different tone, the sarcasm gone now.

"Prakash Wakankar," She said.

"Are you sure that you do not have anything else going on with this person?" his voice to go back to that same, sarcastic tone.

"What do you mean, Sanjay?"

"Oh, come on! I do hear stories of how you PR people have to 'soften' clients with special favours in order to get business in," he said.

"What do you think I am?" She retorted feeling angry and insulted.

Almost instantly softening his tone, he cried into the phone. Worried she asked him if he was okay. He said that he would die if he had to share her with someone else.

"How stupid can you be?" she asked him gently.

"Promise me that you are just mine?" he snivelled.

"Come on Sanjay, what is happening with you?"

"Promise me," he insisted.

"Of course, I promise. You know that very well," she said.

He must have been upset, she thought. Anyway, she would spend the entire weekend with him and make up.

Things became more difficult for her. He had a side of his personality, which was not on display until then. He was extremely possessive, following her to her clients' offices, making threatening and anonymous phone calls to male client representatives, and hanging around in hotel lobbies whenever she had told him that she had a press meet.

He would yell at her at the slightest provocation and slowly, very slowly began to dismantle the famous confidence that she was famous for in Plethoria.

Psychologically he was dismantling her, breaking her, and making her into a blustering, hesitating shadow of her former self. She desperately wanted him to be happy for her and in her attempts at trying to please him, she gave up more and more of her freedom and curtailed her late nights at work.

Her bosses were seeing the signs and wondered what had happened. They tried talking to her, but she would not accept that anything was wrong or different with herself. She worked hard, but they knew that something was missing. This was not Aditi at her best.

Whenever she gave a little more of herself to him, he would get back to his gregarious old self, making her feel as though she were the most important person in his life. Everything would seem all right for the moment.

She was always a very smart dresser. In the manner of her dressing, he found a new weapon. When she wore a stunning outfit, he would not even acknowledge it, remaining silent throughout the drive to her office. Just before getting off, she would ask him, if he did not notice the smart suit that she had specially worn for the very important meeting with a new client.

"You look like one of those cheap sluts," he would say almost cruelly.

Shocked at his outburst, she would stand there staring at him in sheer disbelief as he pulled away, the tyres squealing in protest.

Glancing at her watch, she would realise that she had set out early from home so that she could spend some time in the morning with Sanjay before she got to work. Now that that had not worked, she looked at herself.

Maybe, she told herself, the skirt was a bit too short. Sanjay was right; maybe this is not the right outfit for such an occasion.

Hailing a taxi, she would drive back home to the amazement of her parents. She would say that she felt uncomfortable in the suit and that she wanted to change.

Changing into a drab, nondescript sari, she would take another taxi back to her office.

Without a doubt, the press conference would go badly, with Aditi bungling on her speech, and unable to answer the pointed questions that the *Times of India* reporter asked her.

Losing patience with the man for asking too many questions, she would say something silly causing a total silence that was almost eerie. The scribes could not believe what they had just heard. Most of them would leave the press meet without waiting for lunch. The client could not believe what they had just witnessed and immediately got onto her bosses at Plethoria.

It was not long after that incident that she got a curtly worded fax informing her that her services were no longer required by them and would she please submit a resignation immediately.

Sadly, she quit the job that she was once very proud of. Sanjay when he was told that she no longer had a job seemed almost ecstatic. He hugged her and told her that it was not a problem at all and that he loved her very much. He seemed happy that she had given up her job for him. He spent time with her, buying her gifts and taking her out for long drives.

It seemed to her that whatever the problem that Sanjay had with her was all over and that he was back to the same old self that she had once loved so much.

Her brother did not see it that way. He was very close to his sister and saw her crumbling almost in front of his eyes. He could not help her, as she had built an impregnable wall between herself and the rest of her family. She would not tell them of her problems, knowing that she would be criticised, and knowing that they would not understand how she felt about Sanjay.

When she had first met Sanjay, she had spoken to her brother about him and happily told him how she had found someone as smart as he was. He was happy for her and now, almost a year later, she seemed to be very melancholic, withdrawn and silent at home.

He spent time with her and got her to tell him everything. When he learnt of her state of mind, it disturbed him deeply. There was not much he could do, he knew. He warned her about seeing Sanjay and said that if she continued, she would have to probably seek psychiatric help.

It was not long before she learnt from other friends who were also sympathetic to her condition that Sanjay was now seen at some parties with another girl.

Her brother told her that she should let go of Sanjay. Almost at a breaking point, she confronted Sanjay who pleaded ignorance and told her that her friends were lying.

Speaking to a few close friends in Delhi, her parents arranged for her to take a vacation. She did not come back to Bombay for almost eight weeks. When she came back, she seemed to be in a better frame of mind, determined to continue her life, without Sanjay Bhatnagar.

A few months later, her brother's marriage was solemnised and it was at his wedding that day she met Moosa.

She was eager to start working once again and Moosa sensed her urgency. He spoke to her at length about his home and how he wanted it to be decorated.

"I have simple habits, Aditi," he began, "I love very functional things and don't like the jazzy unliveable homes that most design magazines seem to be filled with these days."

"In fact, I love traditional designs, I love earthy colours, and I love our handicrafts, the rugs that we have here in India and the awesome repertoire of brass, clay and other stuff that our artisans produce," he explained.

She did not take notes, just listened intently to the man. She would spend a few hours with him for the next few days, getting to know his taste and see his home when he was there. Then she would begin work on her design.

Aditi did not feel any nervousness at the prospect of starting something without any experience. She was confident that she would do her best.

She went with Moosa to visit his house. She was stunned at the meticulously kept house. It was so clean, that she thought for a moment that there was a woman living in the house.

Seeing her surprise, Moosa asked her, "Anything wrong?"

"No, nothing, I was just surprised at how clean the place is kept."

"I love cleanliness, Aditi. I used to live in a shanty *kholi* in Dharawi and cleanliness was the last thing that you think of when you are living there. I guess, it's just one of those things," she loved the way he mentioned his past so honestly without colouring it, and without any excuses.

"Was that a long time ago?" she asked gently almost afraid of prying into his private life.

"Now that you ask me, yes, it was a long time ago," he said smiling at her, his eyes clouding, some distant picture cropping up in his mind.

"If you don't mind, you must tell me about it sometime. I have never met anyone who has lived in Dharawi and I am sure that it must have had a tremendous impact on your mind, isn't it?" she asked.

"Well, it would be my pleasure, Aditi. I didn't know that anyone would be interested in knowing about life in Dharawi," Moosa said looking at her.

"One does here so many stories of Dharawi and sometimes one does tend to forget that it's human beings who live there," she said.

"Yes, you are right. People do tend to forget that Dharawi is full of human beings like you and I, with some people who are far better human beings than so many other rich people that I know of," Moosa said, once more his eyes clouding again as if he was talking of someone he knew particularly well.

"Instead of telling me the whole story in one sitting, why don't you tell me pieces of it. That way, every time we meet I get to hear a new chapter and by the time this house is done up, I probably would have heard the whole story. Don't you think that would be a good idea?" she asked rather enthusiastically.

Moosa smiled at her almost child-like innocence and her curiosity. "If you have the time, we'll begin tomorrow. Come over to my office in the morning, if that suits you?" he asked her, willing her to say yes.

He knew that he was attracted to Aditi faster than the proverbial moth was to the flame. He did not know if this was love; he had never fallen in love before. Sure, he had his fair share of women. Women who were just like him – single, willing and able. There were no sentiments, no emotions, and importantly no connections beyond the night.

With Aditi, he knew that this was not some primeval sexual urge that he was dying to satisfy. He cared about this woman who seemed to have so much of pain in her eyes. He would ask her, one day, what had caused her the wound that kept cropping up within her.

"I will ask Murali to drop you home, okay? If you want, please tell him what time you'd like to be picked up and he will come back to your place tomorrow morning to fetch you," he offered.

"No, don't worry. I will get a taxi," she said, rather embarrassed by his offer.

"I thought you said we were friends?" Moosa asked her in mock hurt.

"Did I? Funny, but I don't ever remember making such a statement," she laughed at him.

"Yes, you did. When you shook hands with me for the first time? That's when you said it," he said seriously.

Glancing up at his tall frame quizzically, she quickly changed the subject and said, "Okay, you may drop me but I will find my own way back tomorrow morning to your office."

"Listen, Murali is not going to carry the car and you on his head. He is just going to drive you. There is no problem. I will ask him to pick you up tomorrow and for God's sake, let's not argue about such trivial things. I am elder than you are, and you need to listen to me," he said, raising a finger at her silencing her protests.

Relaxing in the back seat of his car, she thought of the man and wondered how it would have felt to grow up in Dharawi.

49

Moosa and Aditi

The next morning she was at his office, looking dapper in a beautiful hand-embroidered *kameez* and *churidaar*. She had on *kolhapuri chappals.*

Moosa almost whistled at her when she stepped into his office.

Seeing his appreciation, she asked him, "Do you like this outfit?"

"It's very beautiful and the colours do suit you well," He said.

The camaraderie between them was spontaneous and natural, and immediately they were conscious of it, falling silent wondering what made them behave in such a manner, almost as if they were two old friends who had known each other for all their lives.

Clearing his throat, Moosa asked her, "Would you like some coffee?"

"No thanks, I just had breakfast at home. Haven't you had breakfast?" she enquired.

"I normally don't eat breakfast. My favourite meal is in the afternoon and then I eat very sparingly at night. I am not a big eater as you would have noticed from my frame," Moosa explained.

"Carry on, you have coffee," she said picking up a magazine from his coffee table, relaxing back on the leather-upholstered sofa.

Carrying his cigarette case, he moved away from his massive desk and joined her on the opposite sofa.

"So, shall we begin my story? I will tell you my story on one condition. That you will tell me yours, just as I am about to, without holding anything back, okay?" Moosa said, leaning forward, looking at her as he spoke.

And so he began. He did not omit anything. He spoke of the agony of growing up under a cruel and sadistic father, he spoke of the beatings that he got and all that had happened to him as a young boy.

He saw her cringe when he described in detail about how he had killed his father when he tried to rape his own daughter, his sister.

He spoke of the times when he went hungry, looking into restaurants where people ate their hearts out without even a second glance at the young urchin who stood so obviously hungry outside.

Without any change in his tone, he told her of his graduation from one petty crime to another more serious offence, till the time he had become a hired killer, a dreaded gangster in the making and how he had expanded his operations to almost all of Bombay.

He saw a single tear welling up in her eyes, when he told her about losing Raashid and the tender smile that she wore when he told her about finding him back in Nagpur.

She got to know about Abubacker, how the two met had met at the Beach Hotel and she heard in silence about the man that Abubacker had now become, thanks to the man who was unravelling his past in front of her.

He spoke fondly of Bhaskaran who was in America working for one of the largest software companies there. He talked of the day, long ago, when they had met when he tried to fight with Bhaskaran's friend for a kite. He smiled when he told her of that rainy day when Bhaskaran had come drenched and cold to see him in the police station, overcoming his own fear and making those crucial phone calls to get him out of Police custody.

He told her about his current businesses and how he ran his entire empire. He confided in her and told her that her brother did head one of the businesses that he owned.

He had never spoken about all these things, so openly and so honestly to any single person. And he felt no qualms about talking to this woman, whom he hardly knew but with whom he was very comfortable with.

They hardly realised that it was almost three in the afternoon. Time had silently slipped by when he was baring his soul to Aditi, and in the silence of their thoughts, they wondered why destiny had brought them together.

Stirring out his reverie, Moosa looked at his watch and exclaimed, "Oh my God, how stupid of me, you must be very hungry."

"Actually, you must be much more hungrier than I would be. You have not had breakfast, remember?" she said, smiling at the way his mind worked, thinking of her before he thought of himself.

Standing up, he stretched and told her, "Come, I will take you to a nice place that I know and I will buy you lunch. After lunch, we are coming back here and I want you to tell me your story. That is how we are going to spend the rest of the afternoon."

"Give me your hand, I am stuck here," she said waving her hand up at him as if she was sinking.

He held her hand and wished that she would give herself to him for good. He wanted to hold her, tell her that he was there for her and that he would love her, and treasure her.

She pulled herself up and was ready to go for lunch.

"That's a nice thought, but don't you have work?" she asked him.

"What?" he asked, surprised for a moment at the question, almost afraid she'd heard his thought.

"I meant spending the rest of the afternoon listening to my story," she said.

Relieved, he said, "Oh, that! I just decided to grant myself a holiday today. I have instructed both the telephone operator and my secretary that I am not to be disturbed today. Come on *yaar*, I must have a holiday. I have hardly spent a day like this with anyone. Trust me," Moosa said very earnestly to her.

He asked Murali to drive them to the Oberoi. At the coffee shop, he asked her if she would mind if he ordered. She did not mind it one bit and actually liked the way he was pampering her. He seemed to know the menu and the steward well. She was amazed at this man who had just told her his entire life story and seeing him sitting there at this wonderful hotel, totally reassured of himself and smoking yet another of his cigarettes.

She felt herself drawn to this man, almost hypnotically. There was the rational woman in her who screamed at her to be careful, that she could not afford to break her heart once again. But the other part of her wanted to surrender her heart to this man who seemed to have suffered so much in his life and in comparison, she knew she had not seen half as much pain as he had in his entire life.

This, she told herself, was no Sanjay Bhatnagar. This man was a true gem whom circumstance had bastardised. Although he seemed to show not the least bitterness back at the world and seemed to display no visible effects of the trauma that his eyes had seen and which he had lived through.

Seeing her lost in her own world and poking at the food on her plate, Moosa's voice brought her back, "Don't you like the food, Aditi?"

"No, no, I love this. I was just thinking," She said, putting a forkful of food into her mouth.

"Thinking of what I just told you?" he asked her.

"Yeah!"

"Does that make you feel repulsive? Does that make you wonder if this monster in me is still alive and will it ever come out and strike you when you least expect it?" he said almost as if he had read her mind.

"No, I don't feel repulsive and I don't hate you at all for what you did," she said quite surprised at how quickly he had gauged her thoughts.

"Then?" he continued looking at her.

"I used to feel sorry for myself. I thought that I was perhaps the most abused person in the whole wide world. Today, I realise that there are people here on this earth, who have seen, felt and who have been hurt, far more than I ever was. I felt ashamed. Of myself. Of the way I was feeling sorry for what seemed like a scratch in comparison to the wounds that you have suffered."

"Don't think of it that way, Aditi. I just had to go through those things. I used to feel that way too, but not any longer. Today when I think back, I guess if those things had not happened, I would not be the man that I now have become. The Arabs sum up such things brilliantly; they say 'Mektoub' which means 'It is thus written'. I suppose that it was indeed written that my life had to be this way," he said.

She smiled at him.

When he called for the cheque, she was waiting to get back to the comfort of his office and the sofa. She wanted to lean back, to tell him all that had happened to her, and for the last time exorcise the demons that had haunted her, tortured her and which finally broke her.

After this day, Aditi wanted to be become a new woman. She wanted to live, for herself and this man before her.

It was dark outside and it was almost eight o'clock. The front of her dress was wet with the tears that seemed to pour as if they would never stop. She told him everything, how she felt cheated, dirty and used by a monster in the guise of human being. She told him how he had broken her down until she was a mere vestige of the once confident woman that she once was.

When he gave her his handkerchief, she nodded, refusing it, "Let them pour today, these tears of mine. They have been held back for far too long. I wanted to bury them inside me; I had promised that I would never talk to anyone of what I had undergone. And here I am today, telling you everything, without an iota of shame or regret that I did revisit the past one last time. I know that I already feel better, knowing that I have in you, a great friend, and a companion for life. I know that I must live, must continue to live, and that I should finally bury all that happened to me in the past, never to be re-opened again."

She smiled at him hoping that he would understand what she meant.

"I am glad that I came to your brother's marriage and met you. I promise you only one thing – for as long as I live, you will never ever feel this way. I will not lift a finger to hurt you, I will never abuse you, I will never break you. I will be happy to see you bloom, see you smile for the sheer joy that life is, and I promise you, nothing will give me greater pleasure or make me feel richer," Moosa said, holding her hands, kneeling in front of her.

"I will speak to your brother tomorrow and if he has no objection, I would like to speak to your parents. If they too have no objection to me marrying you and of course, provided you too don't have any objections, I would like you to be my wife," Moosa said clutching her hands to his chest.

More tears fell from her eyes and he held her close, wanting to comfort her and tell her that the nightmare was over. She knew that Moosa would die before anything came close to hurting her.

When Murali opened the car door for her and saw her bleary eyed, he wondered if his boss had said something to her to make her cry.

"Moosa Bhai never speaks badly to women. I wonder what happened to her," he thought silently.

50

Till Death Do Us Part...

When Samir Sharma, Aditi's brother took the call from Moosa he instinctively looked at his desk calendar. Moosa normally called him only during the board meetings that were held once in a quarter. No, this was not for the board meeting. He was feeling good about working for Moosa. He never interfered, gave Samir a free hand, and never ever spoke to anyone else but Samir in the organisation. He admired Moosa for that.

Samir was doing extremely well in his job as Managing Director. His company was a Logistics Company, which showed tremendous growth after he took over the reins. Most sceptics had predicted that with a young, inexperienced person like Samir the company would soon have to wind up. Samir not only proved them wrong, but also managed to turn a profit in the very first year.

Since then, he had come a long way. Moosa supported his every initiative and gave him all the encouragement that he needed. *Business Today* had featured Samir on its cover and praised the way he managed his company. In a comparative study, the article read, he was one of the most highly paid managing directors, in any industry in Bombay city. He showed the article to Moosa, who only smiled back at him.

"Remember what I told you. If you do well, you reap the benefits. That is all. Continue to do better and you will earn better benefits. Good show, Samir," he would say patting him on his back, "Keep it up."

The only things that Moosa insisted was that Samir adopt the same policies that his other companies had towards its people. Looking back, Samir knew that not only had it paid handsome dividends, but also that it had also ensured a level of productivity, which other companies in his line of work rarely saw.

All this was pushed to the back of his mind, the moment he heard Moosa on the other end.

"Yes, Moosa Bhai, what can I do for you?" Samir asked.

"Samir, I would like to come over to your office. I need some time with you," Moosa said.

"Of course, Moosa Bhai, you are always welcome. You know that you don't need an appointment from me."

"No *yaar*, I don't want to walk into your office. After all, you are the managing director of a company; you have your schedule, and your appointments, isn't it?" Moosa asked.

"Moosa Bhai, would you like to come in just now?" Samir asked.

"Fine, I will be there in about fifteen minutes," Moosa said hanging up.

Moosa landed at Samir's office in exactly fifteen minutes.

Without wasting too much time, he got straight to the point.

"Aditi has been spending some time with me. She has told me that she wants to start designing homes and I thought that since I wanted to re-decorate my house, she could begin there," Moosa said, looking in his usual style, directly at the person whom he was talking to.

"Yeah, Moosa Bhai. She told me what you had said. I told her to go ahead and that she has nothing to worry about."

"Samir, I want to ask you something. And I want you to be honest with me," Moosa said.

"Of course, Moosa Bhai, you can ask me anything. You know that."

"If you permit me to, I would like to marry your sister," Moosa said. Looking straight into Samir's eyes, he wanted to see any signs that would immediately tell him what Samir thought. Instead, all he saw was a relief, lit up by a smile that seemed to engulf the younger man's entire visage.

"Arrey Moosa Bhai, you had me worried there for a while," Samir said, blowing through his mouth in an exaggerated gasp.

"Do you know everything about her past?" Samir asked him, once again becoming serious.

"Everything. Likewise, she knows everything about me."

"In that case, I have no problems. I will speak to my parents, they are not fussy people, and as you know, they just want Aditi to have a good life and marry someone who will care for her. It's not them that I am worried about, I wonder what Aditi will have to say to this," Samir wondered aloud, pursing his lips.

"I have asked her and I have told her that I will marry her on the condition that you and your parents accept me. If you have any doubts in your mind, then I will not marry her," Moosa told Samir.

"Moosa Bhai, there is nothing to worry about. If Aditi has consented, you can go ahead and choose a date," Samir said, extending his hand to Moosa.

Taking Moosa's hand in both of his own, he stood up and told him, "Moosa Bhai, I don't know how to thank you. I was so upset when she lost her job and almost her own sense of balance, and now when I know that she is going to be happy, I cannot find the words to thank you."

"*Arrey Raja*, I must thank you. I do not have a single thing that I would say makes me a rich man than the thought of Aditi becoming my wife."

"And I want to promise you – a promise which you must repeat to your parents – that as long as I live, Aditi will never shed a tear of sadness, never will have to compromise on her self-esteem. I will treat her like the princess that she is," Moosa said, still holding onto Samir's hand.

Samir hugged Moosa in an embrace, a choked shudder and a muffled thank you expressed all that he wanted to say.

51

Moosa Weds Aditi

The next morning Samir called him informing him that his parents wanted to see him at their home. Moosa asked Samir if it was okay if he came over at around eleven in the morning.

At eleven, Murali pulled up in front of the apartment in which Aditi lived with her parents. Since his marriage, Samir had moved into another apartment along with his wife. He was there to welcome Moosa when he rang the doorbell.

Moosa Bhai followed Samir into the surprisingly large living room. He liked the clean flat. There was no furniture. There were mattresses on the floor, which was covered with colourful mats and rugs thrown in careful disarray. On the mattresses were a whole lot of pillows also covered in a riot of colours.

At the door of the living room, Moosa stopped and took off his shoes. Padding onto the mat in his socks, he chose a corner for himself and sat down, crossing his legs.

In a minute, Aditi's parents came into the room, smiling at the man sitting on the floor.

He rose, folding his hands in a respectful *Namaste* to both of them.

Aditi's father came to him, his arm outstretched, gripping Moosa's in a solid grip.

"I am glad that you could come. Sit down. Aditi will be here in minute."

"Samir briefed me about your conversation. We have no objection, not even to the fact that you are obviously a Muslim and we are devout Hindus. My wife was concerned that you might want Aditi to convert to Islam before you married her, what do you have to say to that, Moosa?" the senior Sharma asked him.

"Well sir, I am not too much of a religious man in the true sense of the word. I believe that God is within a man and does not live in the rituals and laws that man has created for various religions," Moosa said.

"I have nothing against any religion in general or in particular. It is my sincere belief that when someone is born, he or she is born without a religion and it's only later, that he or she is told of a religion," he continued.

"I have seen people killing each other in the name of religion. I have seen terrible acts of sheer atrocity in the name of God. I do not believe that any religion in its truest form said that taking a life in the name of God and religion is acceptable. So for me sir, Aditi can remain whatever she chooses to be. It's not her ideology and her beliefs that I expect to see change if she marries me. I want to see her happy, I want her to have children whom she can raise to become good human beings and not good Hindus or good Muslims. It does not matter to me what religion a man or woman is if he or she cannot practise being a good, decent human being. Goodness is a characteristic feature that lies in all of us, it's only that we have to reach inside ourselves and touch it, live it and show it to the world. For me that one quality is more important than the religious trademarks that people like to wear – the holy ash and *kumkum* that most Hindus sport, the Cross of Christ that many Christians wear and the Muslims who like to make a statement with their dress," Moosa said, speaking to Aditi's parents of something that was close to his heart.

"Despite all this, what is the point if we do not have kindness in our hearts? What is the point of being religious if one cannot treat another human being with dignity and honour? What is the point of having tons of money if we cannot practice the religion of giving to those that are less fortunate than oneself?"

"No Sir, I believe that God is not up there somewhere in that infinity that we call space, I truly believe that God is right here, now with us. I cannot believe that we have a separate God for the Hindus, a separate one for the Muslims, yet another one for the Christians. I believe in the oneness of God," Moosa said quite passionately, "So, answering your question, ma'am, I would like to assure you that Aditi would not have to give up believing whatever she has been taught to believe in just for the sake of marrying me."

Just then, Aditi came in wearing a sari and looking to Moosa's eye, a typical Indian bride. She was carrying a tray with several cups. She bent low in front of him and not looking at him, she said, "Please have some tea."

Mr Sharma spoke to Moosa and told him of how much he had heard of him from his son. He also told him what he had heard from others of his reputation as an underworld don and the head of an evil empire. He said he did not care about those things that people said. He just wanted to meet him and speak to him, he had done that, and he was happy.

"You know Moosa, when we give our daughters away in marriage, we perform a ritual called the *kanyadaan*. This literally means, giving away of the bride by the father of the bride. After that, the father or anyone else in the bride's family has literally no right over the bride. From that moment on, she has only one master – her husband. As the Christians say, 'Till death does them part', similarly, I am only interested in knowing that my daughter is happy with you. I know now that she will be."

He gave his hand once more to Moosa and shook his hand, "Welcome to our family. We are not as rich as you are, but you will receive such love from us and I am sure that you will have nothing to complain about."

"I am sure of that too, sir." Moosa said.

"Now that we have formalised the relationship, please stop calling me sir. My children call me Baba, you can call me Baba too or if you prefer, you can call me Sharmaji," the senior Sharma told Moosa.

"I will call you Baba too."

Moosa touched Aditi's parent's feet with the fingertips of his right hand and raised them to his head, seeking their blessings.

"God Bless you," they said in unison, placing their hands on his head.

Aditi and Moosa were married in a private function. There was no ostentatious wedding and no fanfare. That same day, she moved into his house, which she decided she would do up now, slowly over the years.

Exactly six days later, three men stopped a car in the basement of the building that housed PML Solutions, asking the driver of the car, Sanjay Bhatnagar, to step outside.

By the time they left in less than ten minutes, they had administered a beating that left Sanjay Bhatnagar dazed, hurt and bleeding. One of the gents crushed Sanjay's crotch with that massive fist of his and squeezed it so hard that Sanjay Bhatnagar could only yelp in deep agonising pain. Just before he slipped into black unconsciousness, he heard their final message.

"Never ever treat a woman badly, if you want to live," the man with that particularly huge fist said, before ramming it with a force that took out Sanjay Bhatnagar's two pearly front teeth.

52

Raashid Grows

Jeddah is a beautiful city. It has a rich cultural heritage and a population that is cosmopolitan.

Raashid found a small office in the heart of Jeddah, and quickly began working from there.

The whole web of money laundering that Moosa had personally managed now came under Raashid.

He ran it efficiently and smoothly, and within a few months, the operation had snowballed so big, that he had to bring in a few more trusted people from within Moosa's organisation to handle the business.

The bulk of the transactions involved huge amounts of money sourced from India and which needed to be converted to US Dollars and which needed to be delivered outside India.

He witnessed a steady growth in the remittances that salaried Indians were entrusting his company with and by the time he had completed one year, he was not just servicing the Indian population of Jeddah, but the entire Gulf region.

Within a short time he had established offices in Dubai, Sharjah, Abudhabi, Muscat, Doha, Bahrain, Riyadh and Dammam. Each with one or in some cases like Dubai, two men – who had grown up in the organisation and whom Moosa trusted.

If clockwork was a word to describe a smooth running operation, then this was a Swiss clock. There was no confusion, no delays, no problems – money was collected and delivered. There seemed to be nothing that could go wrong here.

Moosa was happy to see his brother's growth and made several trips to the Middle East.

Raashid seemed to be making up for the lost time and he was growing from strength to strength.

His web of businesses were intricately linked into each other and just like Moosa, he hired the best minds that money could buy to run many of those acquired businesses that he had bought.

53

The New Face of Madras

The city was growing and growing very fast. Nothing seemed to be the same and change was evident everywhere. A city which hardly had a handful of apartments blocks and high-rise offices, was now hell-bent on changing the skyline.

Once quiet, tree-lined avenues were becoming sub-arterial roads, with dust, heat and an ever-growing vehicle population that seemed to be growing faster than the human population of this town.

Conservative, they used to say, once of Madras. Television, cinema and the glitz that was once alien to this city, was now becoming the buzzword.

Political parties came and went with each contributing to the state and indeed the city in one way or the other. The city, with its English history had many of its roads named after English names. They now became a target for change. Old English names were replaced with the names of Tamil freedom fighters, writers, politicians, and even actors.

Business too had undergone a tremendous change. From a city that was essentially known for its traders, it evolved into manufacturing, and now the new mantra was Information Technology and software development.

It seemed that the bug bit almost everyone, that even parents now no longer drove their children to become doctors. Engineering and software was the mantra that their children chanted – and the distant shores of America seemed even closer with an engineering degree and the title of software developer.

This once sleepy town was changing day by day. It also seemed that there was a new breed of people here. Driven to ambition they seemed to be possessed with a level of energy that was almost foreign to this city.

Growth also became the initiative of the government. They were aggressive in their quest to attract talent into the state creating new ministries headed by technocrats, who were very different from their counterparts of yesteryears.

It was to such a changed, charged and very ambitious atmosphere that Bhaskaran came back to.

He had graduated in the top three of his class at MIT and immediately picked up by a leading software company. He spent seven years with them, improving his own knowledge and developing his management skills.

Believing that he now could venture out on his own, he spent time networking with his friends who had graduated from MIT and who were in good positions with other companies. Some of them even offered financial backing, while others promised lucrative projects.

Armed with this, he decided to wind up his sojourn in the US and set up shop in Chennai.

He decided to stay with his parents who were so refreshingly different that there was very little here to remind him of the past.

His brother, fuelled by the game that had brought him so much of fame, worked for a good company who had transferred him to Delhi, where he now lived.

Veena was married to a doctor and they were happily married and lived in another house.

His father had now more or less become the single entity of authority at Iced Cream's and the business now faced a whole array of competition from both local and multinational companies.

Ram Mohan had passed away suddenly after a massive heart attack and it was to Bala Govind that he left the company to. Instead of becoming aggressive and taking on the competition he had decided to remain a small but successful company and that is how Iced Cream was run now, focusing on their quality and retaining their clientele.

The house that Ram Mohan had bought for Bala Govind and his family was now quiet with only the two staying there and it was here that Bhaskaran decided to move into, at least for the time being.

54

Gilmax Technologies

Bhaskaran created Gilmax Technologies and went about looking for some of the best minds to become a part of an organisation that existed only in his mind.

He was keen on creating a truly world class organisation and an environment in which the people that formed this organisation could excel.

He would go slow and make sure that he got the best. He did not want to rush anything, he told himself.

The first people that he hired were not technologists. They were his Human Resource Managers. It was his belief that if they did not understand his vision, if they did not understand the quality of the people that he was looking for, they might land up sourcing talent that was brilliant technically but who were not great human beings. He wanted them to understand that and that is how he began his search.

When he was introduced to Albert Gonzalves, he liked the man immediately. There was an air of authority, an aura about the man that appealed to Bhaskaran. He knew without a doubt that this man would be capable of representing his new organisation at any forum and make the organisation proud. Albert spoke very well, and during their first meeting over lunch, Bhaskaran spoke of everything under the sun, except employment.

By the time the two were done with lunch, a friendship had developed. Bhaskaran wanted to spend some more time with this man and make him an offer, so they decided to meet the following weekend for dinner.

He discovered then, that there was a quality in Albert, which made him one of the best-loved people managers that were available in the market. The two companies that he had worked for in the past still had people who spoke very highly of him. From security guards, janitorial staff to project managers – there was nothing bad they had to say about the man. They loved him for the excellent human quality that he preached and practised.

Albert showed him a people's policy that he had created and which he said he would love to implement.

"I need the support and the climate to implement this," Albert smiled at Bhaskaran seeing that the other man was pleased at the contents.

"You know, it's like growing a rose in your garden which you'd liked at the Ooty flower show and brought it back. When you saw this rose, you thought how beautiful and huge it was, a piece of natural artistry. So, you buy this young plant and bring it back with you and when it flowers in your garden, you are disappointed that the plant did not bring forth the kind of award-winning rose that you had seen in Ooty. Instead, what has now appeared is an excuse for a rose and a poor shadow of the magnificence that you had originally seen."

He paused to have a sip of water and continued, "You make it a point to speak to someone senior in the Ooty Botanical Gardens, the next time you are there. You do remember your anger and your disappointment the next time you visit Ooty and do meet with someone there who listens to your complaint very patiently. He then asks you the methods that you had employed in your garden. You tell him that you have a gardener who waters it daily and weeds the pot, adds fertiliser and does all that is required. The man from the Botanical Garden smiles at you – and introduces you to another man who had nurtured the rose that you had been attracted to and which did win an award that year."

"This man speaks to the plant every day, sits up some times all night long, with an umbrella to shade the plant from the dew that could easily ruin the bud and in the morning wipes all the leaves clean with his fingertips. You are amazed, ashamed, being the gentleman that you are thank that man for an education, you apologise, and leave," Albert told Bhaskaran, as if narrating from his own experience.

"Similarly, in an organisation you might get the best human talent, but you have to nurture it, if you don't, you have no one to blame but yourself."

"Yes, I agree with you, Albert," Bhaskaran said, "I also want to instil a culture of values in this organisation. I want to see people working not simply towards the profitability of this organisation. I would like them to work towards their life goals. I would like to instil a value-based culture, Albert."

He'd learnt well from someone who'd graduated from the slums of Dharawi. A man who'd never been to school, but had become a master at steering through life. He had taught the educated Bhaskaran that although he knew about technology, management and the modern world, if he forgets that it's people who run businesses, he'd fail. If not now, then surely in the future.

He heard Moosa's voice, "One man who succeeds can foster a hundred more families to success."

"Yes Albert, we must foster an environment of values, where accountability is high, where delivery to a commitment is religion, where dreaming is encouraged, where innovation is supreme and where living one's dream is the penultimate success," Bhaskaran said remembering Moosa's words.

Finally, Bhaskaran knew that he had found the right man and offered a package to Albert. The man read through and seeing the figure, said "Bhaskaran, I have to tell you that you are offering me something that I have not been paid at all. Are you sure you are not making a mistake?"

"No Al, I am not making a mistake. I want you and I want every one who joins this company to know that I intend to make them proud of what they do here. I want you to know that you are a very important asset for me and for the organisation. I would like to make it known to anyone who wants to work here that we are a company that looks after our people; I want good minds to knock at our doors understanding that we have a culture that nurtures human talent and indeed the human spirit. I want you to build this organisation into the best employee destination and once our clients realise the quality of our people they will believe in the quality of the work that we produce and once that happens, we have no competition," Bhaskaran said.

Albert knew that the younger man was earnest and shook his hands in acceptance.

It was just a matter of time before Gilmax Technologies was moving into its own swanky Development Centre and it was time, he thought, to pay a visit to his old friend, Moosa Bhai.

55

The King in Exile

Sometimes in life, the best intentions and the best-laid plans go awry. All the good that one does simply does not seem to be enough and one act of madness seemingly dwarfs the best acts of love, charity and creates an image of one in the minds of people of a demon.

On a day that would perhaps be remembered and recorded in history for posterity to come, India watched in horror as hordes of driven men tore down an ancient structure called the Babri Masjid. In retaliation, Bombay went up in flames as an orgy of violence gripped this city, engulfing its population and disrupting lives. Lives were lost, as Muslims and Hindus battled it out, as if the very existence of the other threatened each other. Blood flowed, old enmities surfaced and when the carnage was brought to an end – it seemed as if some monster had satiated itself on the spilt blood and the sights that were effectively caught on television of mobs burning victims alive with tyres around their head, haunted Bombay like nothing before had.

Political parties blamed each other; the law blamed the underworld for taking an opportunity to decimate each other. The people of this city stood back taking stock of the damage that had been wrought, the living counting their dead and the wounded.

Just as the city was limping back to some normalcy and just when the media, the law, the government had identified certain people as the masterminds behind the riots, Bombay shook from the combined blasts of explosion that the authorities claimed were triggered by agents of a neighbouring state to destabilise the financial hub of a nation emerging as a powerhouse of economic growth.

It seemed that everyone was suspect and one of the first to feel the heat from the various agencies was Moosa. The many friends that he had developed and cultivated during the past seemed to evaporate and knowing that he would not be spared, he made emergency plans to leave the country.

Travelling incognito on a doctored passport, he left Bombay along with his small family for Jeddah and now lived there. Not having an extradition treaty with India, he felt it was safe to live there and it was here that he operated his empire out of.

Bombay, which had been his only home, became a destination that would seem like a distant dream for Moosa. He did not believe that he would ever see this beautiful city in his lifetime.

When Bhaskaran arrived in Jeddah to visit Moosa, he was saddened at the change in the man. He was thinner and had become very quiet and thoughtful.

He spent most of his time in his office and it was very rarely that he would spend any time at home with his family.

They spoke and Bhaskaran told him of the plans that were under way in Madras, now Chennai, and Moosa looked at this young man to whom he had given so much.

"I am so happy to hear all this. You say I have changed; you have too, my dear friend. You have become someone that I can be proud to say is a man who is now a name to be reckoned with – and that too – not with the notoriety that I am now infamous for," Moosa smiled at Bhaskaran.

They talked of their lives in the past, how they had met, and how their friendship had grown. Bhaskaran had never met Raashid and was happy to see the young man who now controlled almost all of Moosa's operations.

"Go to Kozhikode sometime, you should meet with Abubacker. He runs the entire area for me. He is doing a splendid job. He will ensure that you have a good time when you visit."

"I don't think that I will be going now, but if I do I will certainly call Abubacker," Bhaskaran told Moosa.

He had stayed at Moosa's fabulous villa and met with Aditi. She was the perfect hostess and Bhaskaran was surprised at her resilience, adjusting to living here in Jeddah and living with a man who had transformed so much. Life is funny. Just when you begin to think that you are blessed in abundance with all that your heart desires, it throws something at you, which questions exactly that premise.

Bhaskaran left for Chennai on a direct flight and would never meet Moosa again. It seemed to him that the relationship that he had cherished with him had ended. In the end, Moosa had won. He had wanted Bhaskaran to make something out of his life, to become someone that would be the exact opposite of what he had become. While one became a force that was hunted and wanted by several law agencies, the other was on his way to a respectability that the other man had never seen.

Isn't that what this whole rat race is all about? Bhaskaran thought. Money is a necessity but that is not the end of the story. Money alone is not enough if you did not have respectability, without it, money was not valuable.

Bombay had changed a great deal. Mumbai would never see Moosa Bhai as the representative face of the world that he had controlled for so long. Be that the underworld of which he was undisputed leader or the several legitimate businesses that he had started and which were all flourishing now, whose employees worshipped the man for his generosity and his desire to give them all a sense of belonging and a sense of being cared for.

The king had gone into exile and the sun had set on his kingdom.

56

Kozhikode

No one had seen a Muthalali as powerful and as connected as Abubacker was. He brought in a new meaning to business in these parts, helping even those who did not see eye to eye with him with countless opportunities.

The man was ruthless in his perseverance when it came to getting something done be that legal or illegal. He was faultless when it came to compassion and magnanimity.

He had indeed become the Muthalali of Muthalalis, and he realised that in the journey that he had made, there was no end, that life was a continuous journey which birth and death acting only as intermediaries to another path, another journey.

The three thousand people who were working for him in several of the organisations that formed his group were the only such group in all of Kerala that did not have a union, no union leader and while several attempts were made, overtly and covertly, they all had failed.

Abubacker asked his people why they should contribute out of their hard-earned salaries to support the existence of a group of people who did nothing except to supposedly 'fight' for their members' rights. He encouraged every person in his organisations to communicate with their supervisors all their needs, desires, and wants – anything under the sun. Despite such attempts if they did not get what they thought they deserved they could contact him. All his employees were given his personal numbers, both at home and at work, and a mobile phone number, which could be used in any emergency.

This was a legacy that Moosa had given not just to Abubacker, but also to Bhaskaran and this was something that these men practised very devoutly. They had both seen their own ambitions come to fruition because of one man and they realised that, just like them, these other people who worked for them, did have hopes and cherished ambitions to realise.

Both of them knew, accepted and believed that hadn't it been for Moosa they would probably not be at this juncture in their own lives. Therefore, both did everything that was humanly possible to ensure that the people who worked for them enjoyed a status and a confidence deep within themselves that they were in the capable and trustworthy hands of a management who cared about them and their welfare.

It was in these organisations that Abubacker controlled that there were the maximum number of home owners, where employees' children had gone on to study abroad, and the loved ones were treated with the best medical facilities that money could get and it was without any doubt that they unanimously called the man behind it God in the disguise of a man.

For Abubacker, such heady comparisons were quite embarrassing. He did not do these things for recognition, he would tell people who praised him. He made a distinctive effort to avoid such people, almost afraid that these would get to his head and perhaps change his very outlook on life and bring in an arrogance of thought and deed, which was the last thing he wanted.

Moosa would be proud of what this man had become and what people thought of him. Abubacker was someone for whom religion was not something that you wore to distinguish yourself from someone else – it was what you did.

The crowning moment in Abubacker's life that demonstrated once and for all the love and recognition that he enjoyed from the people of Kozhikode was when they urged him to offer himself as a candidate in the Parliamentary elections.

It was no surprise that when the results were declared, he was elected as their representative to the Indian Parliament as a Member.

57

Gilmax Technologies Reaches New Heights

In the three years since its inception, Gilmax Technologies had become one of the best software companies that existed now in India.

They had a list of customers that read like a list of 'Who's Who' and the envy of its competitors. Gilmax was the only company in the world that boasted of a zero attrition rate that many of its competitors thought was a fabricated statement.

The truth was that here was a company that would proudly boast of its sheer assets in human capital and treasured it perhaps as valuably as it did its financial assets.

Gilmax had one of the best facilities that one could find in the world of IT, the People Management Policy that Albert Gonzalves had written was now a widely-copied policy that other companies tried to adopt as their own, only to realise that to have a policy is one thing and practising it is a totally different ball game.

And then even if they did manage to pull it off, they needed a CEO like Bhaskaran. He believed that even Moosa… a man like Moosa who had engineered Bhaskaran's own career path had a vision. It was Bhaskaran's vision to create when he first created Gilmax, an organisation that would enhance and mould future leaders in business and technology and not be filled with nameless, faceless people who came in to do a chore and left in the evening. Here, at Gilmax, the fraternity that it had grown into was a powerful force. People married into each other's families not based on caste, creed, and religion but only on the belief that they would become part of a larger family than Gilmax already was.

Initiative was encouraged and Gilmax became the only company in India in its sphere of business that filed for more than two hundred patents and trademarks, it had become a powerhouse for new inventions. Gilmax received accolades for these inventions that they developed for more than happy clients and growth became a natural and a positive reaction of such confidence.

Investors, banks and the people of India made their maiden public offering a roaring success and thereafter any company that had a successful public offering was known to have done a Gilmax.

Moosa heard of these developments in Jeddah and smiled at the memory of a wet boy who had smuggled himself into a police station to visit his friend.

How time flies, he thought. People come into your life and leave an indelible impression in your heart and then fly away, leaving only faint memories and nostalgia, like moth-eaten faded photographs.

58

The Angel of God

On a warm day in July, Bhaskaran married Aarathi Rajendran, a protégé of Albert's, one of the few people in Albert's group who was a qualified Engineer and a good programmer, but chose to work with Albert, simply because she thought that she would do well in Albert's team.

She was right and had risen fast, and during her last promotion to a managerial position, she had been introduced to Bhaskaran. It was not love at first sight, but they liked each other and when they realised that they had many interests in common and were passionate about life and their jobs, they decided to become closer friends.

Three months later, they decided to marry. They chose an Arya Samaj wedding, only a few close friends, and no one from either family. They did have a reception where there was the entire Gilmax family and their own relatives, but the wedding itself was a quiet affair.

It seemed to Bhaskaran that he was lucky. Life had this strange habit of not giving him everything at birth but blessed him with a friend like Moosa and now a woman like Aarathi. She was everything that he could ask for in a wife and quickly became his best friend, confidant, and someone whom he loved with every breath of his life.

Aarathi too seemed to bloom with Bhaskaran's love and even her parents noticed the change in her entire being.

Six months after they were married, Bhaskaran was told that he was going to be a father and it thrilled him no end.

When Prarthana was born, it was as if the Angel of God that he always believed was around him, all the time, everywhere, had manifested itself into this tiny bundle that a nurse just put into his arms.

He peered at her and tracing an imaginary line around her round face said, "Thank you for coming into my life, I am very grateful to you and I will always be there for you."

Prarthana cheered loudly as if she had understood every single word that came out of this man.

As the nurse took the baby back to the nursery, he heard his father clear his throat, in the manner that he was so used to.

The soft smile still on his face, he turned around to face him.

"So, you have your temple complete, isn't it, Bhaskaran?" his father asked.

"I don't understand."

"You have Aarathi, your wife, whose name means a lamp and then you have a wonderful child called Prarthana whose name means a prayer. Aren't those the two most important things in a temple?" Bala Govind asked.

Bhaskaran looked up at the darkening sky and whispered, "Thank you."

It was always his dream of someday buying his parents, especially his mother, a home that would remind her of Parappuram and now he could do that with the kind of successes that he had with Gilmax.

Identifying a plot of land that was not as large as the plot of land on which Parappuram stood, he liked the proximity to the ocean and bought it.

"You have to get a good vaasthu consultant so that nothing untoward happens in your new house," his mother told him.

"Vaasthu?" Bhaskaran enquired. He was not a sceptic but preferred not to be too superstitious.

"Vaasthu is a science, which if you implement well, will cause you to live in peace and harmony with Nature. Vaasthu is the manner in which you manage the five elements of nature, and it's an ancient science. Even Parappuram was built as per Vaasthu recommendations. You might recall that there is always a sense of quiet and peace in all the old houses in Kerala including Parappuram, isn't it, Bhaskaran?" his mother continued.

"When the Gilmax complex was coming up, your mother and I had several meetings with the architects first and then with the builders. Even your office is situated as per Vaasthu recommendations. I have not bothered to tell you all this, but don't shoot down your mother's suggestions," His father advised him.

Bhaskaran did recall consenting to his father's suggestion that he would look after the construction at Gilmax, but was not aware of these revelations that he now heard from his parents.

He met with Jayavelu, one of Chennai's leading Vaasthu consultants who sat down with Aarathi, Bhaskaran, and his parents to discuss their requirements and had another sitting with the architects and they drew up a plan.

It was almost identical to Parappuram except that Parappuram never had a swimming pool and never had attached toilets and the modern facilities that Bhaskaran's new home would.

On the day that the earth breaking ceremony was scheduled, Bhaskaran met another personality. He was the Chief Priest of the Sri Pratyangira Devi Temple at Sholinganallur, close to the plot of land on which the house would come up. He was a close friend of Aarathi's family and they had invited him to be present and conduct the *puja* for the day.

Blessing the couple and their respective families, he blessed the new project in the name of the deity that he had dedicated his entire life to and whose temple was fast becoming a destination for those broken-hearted and problem-filled people that flocked there.

Wanting to know more, Bhaskaran asked the Swamigal more about the temple and its presiding deity.

"She is very powerful, Bhaskaran, you must come one day and seek her blessings. She is half Narasimha and half Devi; she has blessed many people miraculously. Come and seek her blessings," He repeated.

A few days later, Bhaskaran not only did visit the temple, but also spent considerable time with the Swamigal and promised a substantial donation to the temple fund to aid the various projects that the temple was undertaking.

"You don't have to give me anything Bhaskaran." The Swamigal smiled at Bhaskaran when he asked him how much he should give.

"If you feel that you do want to donate, please donate to the temple, not to me." The Swamigal once again reiterated.

Something about the man and his smile, something about this temple and its atmosphere left an impression in Bhaskaran's mind, which Aarathi also shared. They both felt that God was showing them new friends, associations and places, almost like a journey revealing newer secrets.

59

A New Home

Almost two years later, when Bhaskaran's new home was completed, it was indeed as if history had repeated itself. Several years ago, when Parappuram was built and when the Zamorin had inaugurated that house, people had said that there was never a house in the region quite like it.

Today, five years short of four hundred years, people said the same thing about this work of art.

Inside the drawing room, a large wall painted in stark white housed a painting that was both a portrait and a secret. Two powerful spotlights picked up the colours and below on a plaque was the name of this beautiful piece, 'Angel of God'.

It was a painting of some saint in armour, with a spear in one hand, and a shield of metal on the other, holding a sword, crowned in a halo with long braided hair. The colours that the artist used were brilliant and the intensity in the eyes of the figure on the wall, stopped people in their tracks. It seemed to have a life, almost willing people to look up.

Bhaskaran knew that Moosa had stopped calling him and almost all communication between the two was cut because Moosa did not want Bhaskaran to face any problems from the law. This was the second time in their lives that this had happened and Bhaskaran fervently hoped that it would not be the last.

For Bhaskaran, Moosa would only live in his mind and he could never display the love, respect, and admiration that he had for him as long as Moosa's current situation remained the way it was right now.

There were times even at work that he wished that he could have displayed a few photographs of Moosa's, for people to see, but he knew he could never do that.

This painting, then, was his way of remembering Moosa, every day, in the privacy of his home.

If there were others who had seen Moosa, they would tell you that the likeness in the images was startling.

That same month Bhaskaran was listed as one of the richest Indians on planet earth and his company, Gilmax Technologies, became a Nasdaq listed company.

The people that made up this company had become very rich, the shares that they had in their possession, making some of them millionaires themselves.

The boy from Kozhikode and Mahim, whose life was transformed by an Angel of God, was now King of all that he surveyed.

As he held his young daughter's little hands in his own, he thought of a very important lesson that Moosa had taught him when he asked him one day, a long time ago what made him give so much to people, as if he did not care about his own welfare, as if tomorrow did not exist.

"This is something that someone taught me a long time ago, from the *Bhagavad Gita*, which you Hindus consider a sacred book. What have you brought into this world that you are so afraid of losing?"

Life, Bhaskaran had learnt, was for giving. Give, another Angel of God had once taught, give and it shall be given back to you, pressed down and shaken together, three times over.

Glossary

Muezzin	–	Arabic. Man who calls out, five times a day announcing prayer times in a mosque.
Sura	–	Arabic. A verse from the Holy Quran.
Kuffiyeh	–	Arabic. Arab Headdress
Mathi	–	Malayalam. Salmon
Ayla	–	Malayalam. Mackerel
Muthalali	–	Malayalam. Boss.
Varunu	–	Malayalam. Answering a call to say, "I am coming."
Bhai	–	Hindi. Brother.